The Time Traveler's

Apprentice

By
Kelly C

1

Dedicated to the real Simon and Bryn, who have always been and always will be my heroes.

Thanks to Jeff Petersen who found me a bibliothecarius.

Cover design by Bryn M. Carr
Cover illustration by Gail Park

Copyright 2010

To the Reader,

I regret to say that this book is full of historic facts and events. Because of that, you will likely learn quite a bit about life in the Middle Ages. I apologize, but there is nothing to be done about it. I have tried to make up for it by inserting a significant amount of imagination and fiction however. King Henry II and his Queen, Eleanor, certainly did live in 12th century England. Their troubled marriage is well documented. Thomas Becket was murdered quite brutally in Canterbury Cathedral and Hildegard of Bingen really was given as a tithe payment to the church. Much of what you will read about daily life in the Middle Ages is accurate, but quite a lot is also imaginative. You will have to listen carefully in your history class to figure out fact from fiction, which while tiresome, will at least give you the satisfaction of making your history teacher wonder what you are up to.

The Author

"What, then, is time? If no one ask of me, I know; if I wish to explain to him who asks, I know not."
St. Augustine

Chapter One

"Do you think he's dead?" Baldwin asked in a quavering whisper.

"He smells dead." Roger's voice sounded nasal as he tried to answer without breathing through his nose. In a show of bravado he poked at the body on the ground with the toe of his boot.

"Who is he?"

"How do I know? Can't see his face, can I?"

"Maybe we should turn him over?" Baldwin had taken a step back as he offered this advice.

"If you're so interested, YOU can turn him over," Roger snarled.

"Let's just get out of here, Roger. Jasper will whip us good if he finds we're gone." Baldwin turned and started to trot off back toward the path. Roger, finding no audience to admire his audacity, followed with one glance back at the body of the boy who lay face down among the damp and decaying leaves on the forest floor.

Chapter Two

The body lay unmoving until the sounds of the boys' footsteps faded into silence. Then it lay for just a few minutes more, for good measure. Finally, it slowly raised its head and turned to look in the direction Roger and Baldwin had gone. All clear. The boy, his face covered with mud and bits of decaying leaves, carefully lifted himself from the ground. He moved as if unsure of the condition of his body, for indeed was he unsure of it. He came to a squatting position, rotating his head slowly, checking that it was still securely attached to his shoulders. He lifted one shoulder then the other, then stretched his arms above his head. Satisfied that all was in working order, he got to his feet and brushed off what he could of the dirt and debris on his clothing. The boy, Simon by name, took a deep breath and slowly let it out.

"Ugh! I DO smell like I'm dead." While the smell had worked to his advantage in convincing Roger and Baldwin that the body on the ground was dead, it was rather less welcome on a living body.

"What in heaven's name...?" Simon started to search his clothing, patting pockets and emptying out the small leather sack that hung from his belt. From his jacket pocket he pulled out a very dead and decaying fish.

"At least it's you that smells, not me." He tossed the fish into the leaves.

"Well, this was rather unexpected." The sound of his voice seemed loud in the quiet of the sun-dappled woods. He slowly turned full circle, taking in his surroundings. A forest, early spring, bits of sun coming through small, new, green leaves. Very quiet. A distant bird song and the sounds of small rodents in the underbrush. The smell of wet earth and new growth. Perhaps 300 feet to his left was an outcropping of shale with what looked like an eroded area several feet above ground level. That would do for now. He would see if it was big enough to provide some cover and shelter for the night. The sun was already low in the sky. He would soon need somewhere to rest and think. Simon looked down to make sure he had left nothing behind him, then walked to the shelter of rock taking care to keep to grassy tufts, leaving no trail behind him.

The hollow in the outcropping of shale was indeed just barely large enough to accommodate him. He was rather tall and thin but if he bent his legs he could maneuver himself to a comfortable position in the shallow cave. He sat down and leaned back against the cold stone.

"Let's try to determine where and when we are." He ticked off the facts he could gather on his fingers.

"Nothing to indicate modern society that I can see. No planes overhead, no traffic noises, no light or telephone poles."

He thought for a moment, stretching out on the floor of the shallow shelter. It was now dark, and he had risked starting a small fire. Despite its cramped size, Simon thought it quite cozy, at least compared to what he had put up with in the past.

"Now, the two boys. Couldn't risk looking at them, but their voices were young, accents maybe British. And they were off by themselves in the middle of the day and in some fear of 'Jasper' whoever he might be."

Simon thought for a moment, looking into the flames of the fire. While this was not his first journey, the others were carefully planned and controlled. This time he was suddenly and

7

violently flung here, not knowing where or when "here" was. It had shaken him more than he cared to admit.

"Well, I don't have much to go on, but I would say I've landed in pre-industrial Britain. Not a very precise guess, but the best I can do for now."

Satisfied that he had done all he could with the little information he had Simon lay down by the meager fire, his arm under his head for a pillow, and slept

He was awake just as the horizon began to lighten. Simon got up from the cold ground that had been his bed. The fire had gone out but he couldn't risk rekindling it now. His side ached where a rock had nudged him all night. His stomach was empty and grumbling. But these were minor concerns. Simon didn't know if the boys would return, perhaps bringing someone with them this time. He couldn't risk staying too close to this place. Running his fingers through his dark hair to dislodge the twigs and leaves still tangled there, he took one look at the rising sun and set off in an easterly direction.

Simon guessed he had been walking for about an hour, but time didn't really matter. While he had learned to appreciate and even enjoy the feeling of freedom his travels gave him, he also found it a bit disorienting.

"So, why head east?" he asked the empty forest around him. Hearing a voice, even his own, helped to dispel the feeling of disconnect that his travels often brought.

"I always choose east when I don't have anything else to guide me," he said to no one. "East is the sacred direction of many cultures. The Navajo, for instance, always face the doors of their hogans east. Many Jewish and Greek temples are built facing east. The sun rises in the east…"

"And it happens to be the only direction that is downhill from here."

"Well, yes, there is that…" Simon stopped abruptly. While he was used to carrying on conversations with himself, this voice was not his own. He jerked around quickly but saw nothing. Turning full circle, slowly surveying the forest around him, he found himself alone. This was somewhat worrisome. His habit of conversing with himself had sometimes made others think he was a bit mad. Now he was beginning to wonder if perhaps they were right.

"Let's not jump to conclusions," he said hesitantly to himself. "If I am not crazy then there must be someone else here." The thought was a bit disturbing. He could see no one as he looked around him.

"Well, you were a bit quick to eliminate the possibility that you are crazy if you ask me." A girl stepped out from behind a large oak tree. "I think you might reconsider that idea."

Simon stood still and quiet, observing the girl. He did not like to make contact with natives until he had time to observe and gather information. He preferred to make himself known when he was ready. And he was not ready.

"For someone who has been talking nonstop for the last five furlongs you seem speechless right now." The girl, dressed in a white chemise under a dark green tunic with a gold embroidered hem, slowly circled Simon, carefully looking him over as one might inspect a cow or horse before making an offer to buy.

"Well, your clothes are a bit worse for wear and are not of any cut I recognize. Your conversation shows you are educated, but your circumstances indicate you are fleeing something or someone. Hmm, if a nobleman's son, you would have little to fear, no reason to run. You could be an oblate, or perhaps a novice fleeing life as a monk?" Simon was becoming more uncomfortable as the girl continued to slowly circle round him. She didn't seem at all concerned that he did not reply to her observations.

"But your clothing and hair do not support that assumption. So, I would venture that you are a runaway. Perhaps your master found it useful to educate you so that you could work as a scribe or secretary to him? If so you have shown great ingratitude by running away. Perhaps you think you can survive for a year and a day, when you will be legally free?" She had stopped directly in front of Simon looking confidently into his eyes. Suddenly her face changed, her nose wrinkled and her hand came up to cover her mouth.

"What IS that smell? You smell like Gladys the fishmonger."

During this one-sided conversation, Simon had had time to pull himself together.

"Well, that at least is an accurate observation," he said, regaining some of his confidence. "As it happens, I did have a fish in my pocket that I parted with some time ago. I apologize that the smell has not parted with me."

"A fish. In your pocket." She had taken two steps back to distance herself from him. "And whose decision was it to part ways – yours or the fish's?"

Simon began a retort when the ridiculousness of the situation hit him. He laughed. The girl smiled and then she too began to laugh.

"You look hungry and tired, and you smell horrific. Come, I know someone who can offer you some food and shelter and won't ask too many questions. But first, a bath."

Chapter Three

Professor Moira Ananke stared at the dust motes in the broad shaft of sunlight that filtered through the very dirty windows of her museum basement office. In moments when she wasn't focused on a piece of ancient manuscript or medieval textile, she would often stare at the ever present whirls and eddies of dust that floated between her and those nearly opaque windows. Unlike other museum personnel whose thoughts might tend toward cursing the slothfulness of the cleaning staff, Moira Ananke, when allowing her mind to wander, wondered where that dust in the air, where that dirt on the windows had been before taking up residence in her office.

"Because this earth is a closed ecological system," she had once told Simon, "every drop of water and every particle of dust has been around as long as the earth has existed. It's all eternal, at least in our limited perspective."

"So this dust," Simon had countered as he swiped at the air and made the sun-enhanced dust particles dance, "could have once been on the chariot of Ramses II, or the top hat of Abraham Lincoln."

"Yes, I suppose so. Kind of gives it some dignity, doesn't it?"

"I wish my uncle felt that way. He takes the unreasonable position that the quantities of dust on my bedroom dresser and under my bed need to be removed," Simon said in as serious a voice as he could manage.

"I'll never understand some people," the professor absentmindedly answered, and somehow Simon felt she was quite sincere.

Now, as Professor Ananke stared mesmerized at the quantities of swirling dust particles she felt a sense of unease. Simon had come to her office as usual after school. She was working on a palimpsest from 12th century England. He was eager to help and pulled up a three-legged stool to the large, cluttered worktable where the manuscript was laid out.

"Where did this come from?' he inquired.

"It was sent to me by a colleague at the University of Durham in England," Professor Ananke told him. "Many early manuscripts were written on parchment, often sheepskin that was scraped, stretched and dried. It is much more durable than paper."

"Why is this one so difficult to read?" Simon asked. "It looks like it has several layers of writing on it."

"This is a palimpsest. Both paper and parchment were valuable and not always easy to come by in the early Middle Ages. Scribes would sometimes scrape off the original writing from a piece of parchment and re-use it. Hence the word *palimpsest* that comes from the Greek and Latin meaning '*again*' and '*I scrape*.'"

"Hmm, pretty literal folks weren't they?" Simon said with a smile.

"The problem with this one is," Professor Ananke continued, seeming not to notice Simon's sarcasm, "not only has it been scraped and re-written – the author has crossed out and written over even the second text. But it appears to be a pattern. The endings of the words have been changed. Look here." She pointed with a latex-covered finger at a line of words.

"Notice how two different hands have written here. The first wrote the original sentence. The second, in slightly different handwriting, has changed the endings of the words by writing above each one."

12

"But what does that mean? Why would anyone do that?" Simon asked, more to show he was paying attention than out of real interest.

"I don't have enough of the manuscript to make an educated guess at this point. But something about this is familiar to me. If I could just remember where I have seen this kind of thing before."

Simon was fiddling with objects on the cluttered table while Professor Ananke spoke. He picked up a fossil fish she used as a paperweight and was tracing the stone scales with his fingertip when there was a loud noise in the hallway. Simon instinctively dropped the paperweight into his pocket. While Professor Ananke enjoyed his company and appreciated his eagerness to learn, other staff members did not like the idea of allowing non-museum personnel into the private areas of the museum, especially someone as young as Simon. He knew she had often been scolded by administrators for allowing him such freedom of access to the back rooms of the museum. Professor Ananke on the other hand, had a great appreciation for Simon's intellect and natural aptitude. She not only enjoyed his company, but also gained inspiration from his questions and fresh perspective regarding historical conundrums.

At the noise in the hall the professor looked quickly at Simon as if to warn him to be quiet and got up to look out of her door into the hallway. At first she saw nothing, but then down the dim hallway, at the end where it turned sharply to the right, she saw a mop handle and bucket on the floor. She took a few steps into the hall for a clearer view but saw no one.

"False alarm," she said, coming back into her office. She turned to smile at Simon but found the office empty.

"Simon?" she said quietly. She slowly scanned the large, cluttered office. Between piles of books, stacks of leaning boxes, various sized tables cluttered with artifacts and instruments, and several storage closets, she knew Simon could be investigating something that caught his eye. He was likely down on his hands

13

and knees pulling at a piece of fabric or dislodging a dusty book from the bottom of a tower of dusty books.

"Simon?" she said a little louder as she circumambulated her office. No, he was gone. She was alone in the office, the silence thick and unfriendly. She sat down at the table and thought, staring absently at the palimpsest in front of her.

"I wonder what could have prompted this?" she asked herself softly. She found herself automatically tracing the Latin text of the manuscript. Looking at it more closely she said to herself, "Hmm, I wonder... well, he's a clever boy, and it's not his first journey. I am sure he'll be fine." But still she felt a small knot of anxiety lodged in her stomach.

Chapter Four

"I'm Bryn, by the way. Bryn Berengar," the girl said as they walked together through the sun-dappled wood. "And yes, I know it's a boy's name. Blame my father. He wanted a boy and since my mother was Welsh she wanted a Welsh name, so they compromised. I got a Welsh boy's name."

"I'm Simon." There was an awkward silence as Bryn waited for more information. When none was forthcoming, she continued.

"My horse is tethered over there," she pointed to a lovely white palfrey comfortably clipping new grass in a sunny glade just ahead.

"I suggest we both walk and lead the horse. Until you're cleaned up, I'd prefer not to have to share a saddle with you." Bryn laughed but Simon knew she meant it.

"Right. I understand. Really, I don't mind walking beside you if you want to ride."

"No. We're only a few furlongs from my home. It's a pleasant walk, and maybe it will give us time to decide what we are going to say to everyone about you?" She glanced sideways at Simon, raising an eyebrow in question.

"I'm sorry, really. It's just that I kind of suddenly find myself in a rather difficult circumstance, and I don't want to get you involved in something maybe you shouldn't be involved in."

Bryn said nothing but waited for him to continue.

"You know best what I am walking into. What would you suggest we say? I mean, until I can get all this straightened out."

15

She had stopped walking and turned to look at him for a moment without speaking. Once again Simon felt her uncomfortable and penetrating gaze. He noticed for the first time that she was actually quite lovely. Her blond hair hung in a thick braid down her back, and her light blue eyes were clear and confident. "Likely some Saxon blood there," he thought to himself as he squirmed under her gaze.

"OK, we'll do it your way until you feel you can trust me enough to give me the truth." She blunted the criticism with a smile.

"I have a friend that lives on the manor. She owes me a favor. We'll go there and get you cleaned up and fed. You can stay with her. We'll say you are a visiting relative. Don't worry, she'll be fine with it. Trust me." This last part was spoken with some sarcasm.

They gathered the palfrey's reins and in a short time came out of the woods to the edge of a newly ploughed field. Bryn stopped for a moment and the horse immediately started to graze on the short grasses bordering the field. Ahead of them lay manor lands: common pastures, two areas of ploughed field and a third parcel of land left fallow. Simon saw a mill on the river that flowed in a gentle bend through the manor lands. He could see a small village had grown up along both sides of the river. Between the village and larger manor house was a road where a simple church of crude stone stood.

"This is one of Lord Montbury's manors," she said, and she looked to see if Simon recognized the name. At his blank expression she laughed. "Sir Robert Montbury? Lord and Lady Montbury are the biggest landowners in Yorkshire. You must have heard of them."

Simon shook his head. Bryn stared at him in wonder. "Perhaps you have fallen from the sky? Are you one of the green children of Wulpet?" she teased.

"Green children?" Simon asked confused but intrigued.

"Oh come! Surely, even if you come from a far-flung manor, you would know of the green children of Wulpet? It was the most exciting thing to happen in most people's lifetime. William of Newburge even wrote about them." Seeing Simon's astonished look, she shook her head in exasperation. "Well, perhaps you will be an even bigger mystery," she said and clicked her tongue for the horse to follow, moving toward the village.

Bryn pointed to a small, thatched roof cottage on the outskirts of the village.

"There. That is where Agnes lives. You will stay with her until I decide what to do with you."

Simon would have taken offense at the implication that she could somehow order him about, but he was so tired, dirty and hungry by now that he was starting to feel weak. The thought of a bath, food and a place to lie down made him hold his tongue.

"Agnes is a cook at the manor house. She had a son who was born simple-minded and crippled. I am sure even you would know what can happen to a child born thus. I convinced Sir Robert to let her keep him and care for him as best she could. He did not live long. But Agnes never forgot my support and will do anything for me now."

They were nearing the small yard of the cottage. It had a tiny garden in back where Simon could see some newly sprouting plants pushing up through the soil. A neat wattle fence surrounded the yard where two chickens scratched and pecked at the earth. The doorway was low with the thatch from the roof hanging over it like a bushy eyebrow. As he looked, the door opened and a short, round woman with very red cheeks and grizzled gray hair appeared. She wiped her flour-covered hands on a white apron.

"Oh! My dear!" she cried when she saw Bryn and trotted out to the road to meet her.

"Hello, Aggie!" returned Bryn. "May we come in? I have a favor to ask of you."

Agnes looked from Bryn to Simon, sharply nodded her head and waved them in.

It took some time for Simon's eyes to adjust to the darkness of the cottage. The floor was dirt, and there were no windows. He could see a hearth in the center of the floor, unlit in the spring weather, but no chimney. The blackened walls and roof rafters indicating that when the fire was lit, smoke circled through the room until it found its way out a hole in the roof. In the corner, a mattress stuffed with straw lay on the floor. Against a wall was a large trestle table, now covered with wooden bowls and dusted with flour. Two, three-legged stools stood near the table.

"How long it has been since you've come to see me here," Agnes gently scolded Bryn.

"Oh, Agnes!" Bryn laughed. "I came by on Maundy Thursday, bringing you some nuts from the manor stores. Surely you remember."

"Was it just that long ago?" Agnes shook her head. "I seem to be forgetting things so easily lately, but tell me, what brings you to me today?"

"Agnes, this is my friend, Simon. He is in a bit of trouble —nothing bad you understand—but he could use a washing up, some food and a place to stay until we figure out what to do. We were hoping…"

"Of course, my dear! You know I would do anything for you. And he is a handsome young man, isn't he?" Agnes winked at Bryn, who blushed and sharply retorted.

"I'm not sure how you can tell under all that dirt and smell. But thank you, Agnes. We thought you might say he was a nephew perhaps, stopping by on his way to Durham to live with relatives?"

"Oh yes, of course my dear. I do hope I can remember all that, but people don't seem to really pay any mind to what I say anyway so I imagine it won't matter. Now, you just leave him to me, and I will get him cleaned up and fed." Simon was rather alarmed at the way Agnes was looking at him. He was beginning to think these two women saw him as a curious new possession.

But he felt nearly ready to collapse and so gave himself up to plans over which he felt he had no control.

Chapter Five

As Bryn rode into the courtyard of the manor house, she saw three boys near the stable door. From their tense stance, she guessed a fight was about to break out.

"Hey there!" Bryn called out, hoping to diffuse the situation. She saw now that it was Baldwin, the cooper's son, Roger, the son of one of Sir Robert's vassals, and an older boy she couldn't quite place the name of, perhaps from the village mill.

The three immediately stepped back, the older one hiding something behind his back.

"What do you have there?" Bryn asked the boy. He hesitated and then held out the remains of a dead fish.

"I have had enough of dead fish for today, thank you. To what purpose were you hiding this offal?"

The older boy glanced sideways at Roger and Baldwin but said nothing.

"He was teasing us," Baldwin said indignantly. "Yesterday Roger and I found a dead body in the woods. We came back and told Jasper about it, and this morning we took him back to the place were we found it. But there was nothing there."

"Except a dead fish!" laughed the older boy, dangling the fish remains in front of their faces. Bryn remembered his name now. Yes, he was from the mill. Fordwin was his name if she remembered correctly.

"A dead body?" asked Bryn thoughtfully. "Where did you find this body?"

"In the woods, near the shale outcropping."

"You didn't recognize the body? How did you know it was dead?

Roger, who had been silent until now, joined in.

"It was lying face down in the leaves, we couldn't see its face. We know it was dead because nothing alive could smell that bad."

"Nothing could smell that bad," Bryn said almost to herself, then she laughed and the boys stepped back in alarm. "Well, perhaps you were dreaming, or perhaps," she leaned down from her saddle so her face was near to the boys. They instinctively leaned in toward her. "Perhaps you were bewitched? Perhaps it was a demon you saw? How else could it just— disappear? Or perhaps," she said, looking at Fordwin still holding the fish carcass, "it changed itself into a dead fish so it wouldn't be found."

The boys, their faces registering alarm, took several steps back from her. Fordwin looked at the fish in his hand and threw it down with a yelp. Bryn straightened up in her saddle, clicked her tongue and the horse walked into the stable, ready for a brush down and a bucket of oats.

Agnes in fact already had a large, fire-blackened cauldron of water heating on a peat fire in the yard in back of her cottage.

"Today's cooking day, isn't it?" she said, as she led Simon out from the cottage. "It's fortunate for you that I always keep water warming on cooking day. Otherwise it would be another week afore you'd have warm water to wash with." She took a wooden ladle and a rough piece of cloth, none too clean itself, and handed them to Simon.

"There you go now. I'll leave you to it. When you're done, come back in and I'll have some nice bread and cider for you. Might even find a piece of cheese if we're lucky."

Simon lay on a pallet of fresh smelling straw in the far corner of the cottage as the sky darkened for the second time since he had begun his journey. He never felt so exhausted but his bath had refreshed him, and the simple food filled his hollow stomach. He had made himself useful around the cottage while Agnes cooked. She usually worked in the large manor house kitchen, but when she had extra stores of flour at home, she made loaves of bread to be exchanged in the village for things she needed. Agnes took him out to her garden while the bread rose inside. She pointed out tiny new plants pushing through the soil.

"That's chamomile. It's good for fever and snake bites, but especially to ease the pains of child birth." Simon made no comment. He knew nothing, and preferred to know nothing, about childbirth. "And over there is sage. You know the saying, 'how can a man die when sage is growing in his garden?'"

The only use Simon knew for sage was to cook the Thanksgiving turkey. The saying certainly didn't apply to turkeys, however protective of humans sage might be.

"Just outside the fence is my comfrey. So useful for skin irritations and for broken bones, but it does spread and take over the garden if I am not careful."

Simon dredged his memory. "Confera is Latin for 'knit together.' This plant works to knit broken bones together?"

"Aren't you clever!" Agnes patted Simon on the shoulder. "Well, I don't know Latin, but people come to me for help when they have a sick child or a sore bone or a troublesome stomach. I learned from my mother to use God's gifts from the earth." She stopped suddenly and looked at Simon intently. "I stay away from the devil's work, you know. You won't find any Monk's Hood in my garden."

Simon was familiar with the dangers of being accused of witchcraft, especially for an older, single woman. Having Monk's Hood, an herb that witches supposedly used in their potions, could be a death sentence.

Agnes was careful not to question him about his sudden appearance at her door, but he caught her looking at him frequently during their meal together. Once she smiled, touched his hand, and said, "I once had a beautiful boy."

As the sun lowered in the sky, Simon thanked her for her kindness and asked if he might retire early. His exhaustion was evident and Agnes quickly brought in fresh straw to make a pallet for him on the floor. He would have liked to use this time when he was finally alone and all was quiet to gather his thoughts and make some plans, but within minutes he was sound asleep.

Chapter Six

The polite knock on the door was quickly followed by creaking as it opened. Moira looked up to see Dave's head poking in through the opening.

"Thought you'd still be here, ma'am. Sorry, but I've got to lock up for the night."

"Oh yes, of course." Professor Ananke stood up, gathering an armful of documents to stuff into her battered leather satchel. "I'll be just a minute Dave, if you don't mind. You go ahead with what you need to do. I'll just tidy up here and let myself out."

"That'd be fine." Dave bobbed his head. "Just didn't want you locked in for the night." He bobbed his head again and closed the door behind him as he left.

For a moment Professor Ananke looked blankly at the table in front of her. Frankly, she found it rather inconvenient that she had to leave her work each evening. She would be perfectly fine working through the night in her museum office. She had a battered and broken reclining chair that she had inherited from whomever had inhabited this office before her. It was permanently stuck in the reclining position but was still quite a comfortable place to take a catnap when her mind needed refreshing.

Museum policy did not allow her to take artifacts out of the museum so she had to make copious notes and drawings and lug home heavy books if she wanted to continue her studies at home. Until she had met Simon, it had never occurred to her that she could use a camera to photograph whatever she was studying from many different angles, using the pictures to continue her work at home. Simon had brought her a digital camera that his uncle had discarded after buying a newer model. Simon showed her how to use it and often spent his time with her after school photographing whatever she was working on and uploading the pictures to the computer. The computer was her other nemesis. Professor Ananke was, as Simon had once said, "old school." Her work had always been recorded by hand in black leather journals. She had dozens of these journals on the sagging shelves of her office. They were covered with cryptic numbers and letters of a filing code that only she knew how to access. When her relationship with Simon developed, she'd allowed him to take the journals down and browse through them. Her handwriting was spidery but precise and clear. The pages were covered with beautifully drawn sketches of objects or maps or ancient inscriptions. Each journal documented a different archaeological excavation or research project she had pursued.

It was through these journals that Simon had discovered her secret. Perhaps that was not the best way to put it. She knew that by allowing Simon access to her journals he would eventually figure out her secret. Perhaps she just could think of no other way to tell him and in some ways, it was a final test. If he really was bright and intuitive, he would figure it out himself. If not, the secret remained with her. But Simon lived up to her expectations. She remembered the afternoon with clarity.

Simon sat cross-legged on the floor in a shaft of sunlight quietly reading through one of the journals. He had other journals stacked on the floor near him. It had taken several months for him to get this far. She only allowed him to start with the most recent journal and then work backwards when she was satisfied that he had read and understood each one. The most recent one recorded her work with Kent Weeks and the rediscovery of KV5, the tomb of the princes of Ramses II in 1995. He thought then that her comments comparing this excavation to the discovery of

King Tut's tomb in 1922 had been purely academic. Then he read about her excavations with the University of Wisconsin in Harappa, Pakistan in 1986. Simon asked intelligent and thoughtful questions about the Indus Valley people, about methods of excavation and the beautiful inscriptions she had found. As he slowly worked back from there, they read and discussed her work in 1979 with the Institute of Holy Land Studies and the discovery of the only object with the Hebrew letters, YHWH, or God, that exists outside of biblical texts. He seemed interested in each project, often getting up to find a book or ask a question to help him better understand her notes. In this way too, he learned from her smatterings of Greek, Latin, Hebrew, even the ancient Cuneiform language. Once she had taken a large scrap of parchment and made him translate "Mary Had a Little Lamb" in Latin to practice his calligraphy. Jokingly, she hung it up on her wall.

"Let some archaeologist find that someday!" she laughed. "I'd like to hear their explanations for it."

Simon picked up an especially battered and dusty journal that afternoon. First, brushing the dust off the spine he saw the date—1922. He looked up at her with a quizzical expression. She said nothing, just continued to watch him. At the time it occurred to Simon that he had no idea how old Professor Ananke was. Her hair had some gray, her skin some wrinkles, but her eyes were very young. He looked down at the book again and opened it. As he expected, it was a detailed description of the discovery by Howard Carter of the Tomb of Tutankhamen. Not research or commentary on the discovery, but an eyewitness account of her own participation.

Simon looked up again at her. He put the journal down and turned to look at the remaining journals on the shelf. He tentatively lifted a hand to take the next journal, but paused and moved to choose one much further down the row. He slowly took out the book and blew the dust from the cover. *The Discovery of Troy. My Work with Heinrich Schliemann, 1871.*

He put the book down and took another one, further down the shelf. *Travels to Petra with Johannes Burckhardt, 1812.* Simon wasn't sure what to say. "Gee, for someone going on 200 years old, you're in pretty good shape" somehow didn't seem appropriate. Fortunately, Professor Ananke broke the silence.

"He was a very difficult man to work with. Schliemann I mean, not Burckhardt."

"I don't understand," Simon said simply.

"Well, he was pig-headed and had some questionable techniques." She smiled then, knowing he wasn't talking about Schliemann.

"I think you do understand actually. At least the main idea, if not the supporting details."

"How old are you and how..."

"Simon, I would think you would know it's not polite to ask a woman her age. But I can answer you frankly that I don't know, or more accurately, I don't remember. In terms of eternity, time has no relevance. I don't really have an age."

"How did... how does... how do you..."

"It's not something I can explain, or you can understand, in a short time. If you really want to know, I can begin to teach you. But I must warn you, Simon. With this information comes a great responsibility. This is not something you can commit to and then walk away from. Do you understand?"

Simon did not take his eyes from her face. He was not at all sure that he wanted to know more, and he was fairly sure he didn't like the sound of what she was saying now. But he did feel that somehow this was supposed to happen. His meeting her, developing a closeness to her, had seemed the most natural and right thing in his life.

"I don't understand – not yet. But I want to."

And so it had begun. They would meet everyday as usual, after Simon got out of school. Little by little she taught him about the nature of time and time travel. At first Simon seemed to almost fight her, expressing incredulity and skepticism, but as he opened up his mind and stretched the boundaries of what he could believe, he began not only to accept, but to ask more and more sophisticated questions.

"I've read many books and seen a few movies about time travel."

"Ridiculous." Professor Ananke was indignant. "They nearly all involve some huge mechanical machine that spins and spits out sparks. It fits perfectly with industrial man's need to control his environment with some machine or contraption."

"Then how is it done?" Simon finally found the courage to ask. He was afraid she would say this was a secret she couldn't share, and that would be then end of their discussions. He was also not at all sure he wanted to know. What would he do with this knowledge if he had it? What would he be allowed to do with it?

"People have a very linear perception of time," she patiently began. "We mark off days of the week and month, rip off a calendar page and throw it away when it is passed. It is human nature to think of things always progressing, always going forward, discarding the past as gone like smoke." While she was speaking, she pushed clutter around in the drawers of her desk, looking for something. "Ah, here." She held up a dingy, graying deck of playing cards.

"Imagine each one of these cards is a moment in time. Our conventional view is that only the moment we live in right now is reality – the top card if you will. Both the past and future exist only in our imagination or in our memory." She picked up the deck of cards and holding one edge tightly, she moved her thumb quickly down the other edge of pack, riffling the cards with a quick motion.

"In reality, each moment continues to exist once we have passed through it, like layers of cards in a deck. We pass through each moment only living in one moment at a time, like passing through this deck of cards, only cognizant of the card we are on at the moment."

"I once saw something called a flip-book, I think. It was a series of pictures of someone walking. When you flipped quickly through the book, it looked like the person was really moving, like a motion picture." Simon was trying to visualize what she was saying.

"Yes, that is very similar to what I am trying to explain. Except each page in the book is a moment in time. If you flipped through it, your life would play out like a movie. But we imagine that we can only move forward, on to the next new page, making a new image in the book. What if you could turn around and walk backward through that book? Those pages don't go up in smoke once you have 'lived' them. They are still there, still in motion, as part of your past."

"But the book you are talking about is the history of the world. I could not only move backward through my own life – I could move through the history of the world." Simon was beginning to get excited about this idea. He loved to read, especially about history. He often imagined himself as a character in the stories he read. Thinking of walking backward through living pages of time was not so unbelievable.

"Yes, but don't imagine this is some kind of game. Time is a living, organic and rather fearful creature. Being able to travel through time does not in any way mean controlling time. In fact, in some ways it means allowing time to control you. I have many, many years of experience with time travel and there is still much more that I don't know than I do know about it."

"You still haven't told me how you do it," Simon said softly.

"Well, I am not sure I can tell you." Simon's heart sank at her words. This must have shown on his face because she laughed when she looked at him.

"I don't mean it's a secret. Well, I suppose it is, but what I mean is, it is different for each person. I had to learn how to make it work for myself just as you will also have to learn your own individual method."

"But how did you learn? Who taught you and when?"

Moira had looked searchingly at Simon for what seemed like a very long time before answering.

"I am not sure that is for you to know. I am not sure that is my story to tell. " She paused. "Perhaps one day."

They spent the next several months expanding their discussions of time and time travel. To Simon, their progress seemed glacially slow. He wanted to experiment, to try out what he had learned, but Professor Ananke continually cautioned patience.

"It is dangerous to play around with things you know little about. You must take your time to fully understand something before making an attempt to use it." Her face took on distant look. "I clearly remember trying to explain gunpowder to Muhammad Sa'im al-Dahr. Must have been around 1378 AD if I remember correctly," she added for Simon's benefit.

"He was a delightful man, if a bit uncompromising in his religious views. He was outraged when he saw peasants in Egypt making offerings to the Sphinx. He nearly injured himself trying to destroy the mammoth structure. In order to distract him, I began a long discourse on the inventions of gunpowder and dynamite and how in the future such things would be done. It didn't occur to me that he would try to create his own explosives to destroy the Sphinx."

She laughed a little self-consciously. Simon listened with fascination as she spoke.

"Well, he wasn't completely successful, but—"

"The nose!" Simon jumped up. "The nose on the Sphinx! People have wondered for centuries how it was destroyed!"

Professor Ananke looked chagrined. "Yes. Well. Let's keep this information just between us shall we? Anyway, my point is, a little knowledge can be dangerous."

Simon laughed with delight. "I don't suppose you gave the captain of the Titanic driving lessons did you?"

"No, I did not," Moira Ananke said indignantly. "Although I did offer some advice about the nature of helium gasses to Dr. Ludwig Durr." The name meant nothing to Simon. Dr. Ananke explained.

"He was the designer of the Hindenburg. And no, he did not choose to take my advice with rather disastrous consequences as you likely know."

This was another reason for the slow pace of their time travel lessons. Dr. Ananke had so many tales from so many different times that the point of the lesson was often forgotten as the two became diverted over the telling of one of her adventures. But they did progress. Simon slowly began to understand the nature of time and how to access it.

"Have you ever heard a sound, or smelled an aroma, and suddenly it takes you back to some event that happened long ago?" Dr. Ananke asked Simon one afternoon. "For some people, hearing a piece of music immediately brings back vivid memories of their youth. For others, it might be the sound of an ice cream truck coming down the road. "

"Sound of an ice cream truck?" Simon asked puzzled.

"Oh, never mind, before your time I guess," she smiled.

"No, I understand what you mean. This might seem really strange, but even though I have no real memories of my parents, in the spring, when I hear the call of chickadees, for some reason, I have—not a memory—but more a feeling of being with them."

Simon saw a fleeting look of sorrow and compassion in Dr. Ananke's eyes. They had never spoken about his life in any detail. She knew he lived with his uncle, who took a very casual approach to parenting. As long as he heard from Simon at semi-regular intervals he assumed all was well. She had decided to let Simon talk about his personal life in his own time and on his own conditions.

"Yes. That is exactly what I mean." Professor Ananke quickly moved the conversation forward.

"That is what you must find in order to be able to cross time periods. You need to find your own sort of talisman, or sight, or sound or smell, or mental condition, that allows you to escape from the moment that holds you. At first, this might change each time, but eventually, as you gain more control, you will be able to use the same---prompt shall we say?--- to jump from one time to another."

The rattle of a cleaning cart brought Professor Ananke's thoughts back to the present. A present that Simon suddenly disappeared from. She picked up the digital camera from the table and stuffed it into her leather satchel, took one last look around the room and closed the door behind her.

Chapter Seven

Bryn rolled over and pulled the heavy blanket down enough to expose her eyes and nose. The light through the window was pink and yellow, telling her the sun was just coming up. The air in her room had a fresh, clean smell of spring but with it a chill that required the warm wool blanket on her bed. She realized how lucky she was to have such luxuries. Few girls her age would be given the freedom of movement she had, a room of her own, and most especially, access to an education.

Bryn's father had been one of Sir Robert Montbury's most loyal vassals. He'd fought by Lord Montbury's side and had once saved him from an enemy's arrow. Her mother died giving birth to Bryn and her twin brother shortly after her father's death. Bryn was raised in the Montbury household while her brother, John, was sent off to the d'Ambray household, distant cousins of Lord Montbury's. Bryn rarely saw her brother except on certain holy days when many of the extended family visited for celebrations. As a ward of Sir Robert, she was well cared for and looked upon almost as one of the family. But Sir Robert and his wife were rarely at his Yorkshire manor, leaving Bryn on her own for most of the time.

This suited her well. Sir Robert had been impressed by her maturity and ability to learn. So much so that he felt comfortable being away for some lengths of time, leaving this manor to be run by his steward, Jasper but with the unspoken understanding that Bryn was the "de facto" representative of the Montbury family when they were not in Yorkshire. Despite her youth, Bryn's education, her ability to read and write Latin, French and English and her reputation for having good common sense balanced out any lack of faith in her abilities because of her age and sex.

Sir Robert was a very religious man. He sponsored the building of many abbeys and monasteries in Yorkshire, built the beautiful stone church of St. Mary in the village and commissioned an illustrated psaltery to be made by the monks of the Bridlethorpe monastery. When he realized Bryn far outshone even his own sons in her ability to read and write, he requested that she begin to write the Montbury family history. Bryn gladly acquiesced, partly because she felt the need to repay Sir Robert for his kindness, but even more so because it gave her access to the libraries of Bridlethorpe, much to dismay of the monks there. Of course her access was limited and always chaperoned. She was not allowed in the libraries or the scriptorium at any time the monks themselves were there. However her unusual position in the Montbury household, and her commission to write the Montbury history, did gain her grudging and brief access to these wonderful places when the monks were in prayer in the chapel.

She had in fact arranged with the abbot to visit the monastery today and she wondered how she might fit Simon into those plans. Much about him was still a mystery, a rather intriguing mystery. His education and obvious intelligence led her to believe he might be a useful asset to have on this trip. She was searching for a particular manuscript that outlined the Battle of the Standard between King Stephen and the Empress Maud, where Sir Robert's grandfather had fought valiantly. The manuscript had up to now eluded her, but perhaps with Simon's help...

The door of her chamber opened and her chambermaid, Gunnora, entered bringing in a bowl of water and a bone comb to help Bryn prepare for the day.

Chapter Eight

When Simon finally awoke, his half-opened eyes took in the thatch roof above his head, the wattle and daub walls and the dirt floor. His sleep-muddled brain took several minutes to process what he was seeing, finally alighting on the memory of yesterday and his sudden jump from Professor Ananke's office to the medieval wood. He sat up as quickly as his sore muscles would allow and saw that Agnes had laid out some clothing for him. A pair of thick, brown hose and a russet tunic tied together with a fraying cord lay in a neat pile by his pallet. While he did not relish the thought of wearing these rough, woolen garments, Simon realized he could hardly walk around in his modern clothing. Agnes had insisted he take them off before he lay down to sleep the night before so that she could wash and mend them.

He rolled to his side to reach for the clothes, hoping to pull them under the moulting fur cover that Agnes had given him as a blanket and dress in relative warmth under the covers. The movement brought a sharp pain to his back that of course came from sleeping the night on a thin straw pallet on a dirt floor. He had grim satisfaction in remembering his repeated refusals to accompany his neighbor's son on scouting camp outs. If this is what waking up in a sleeping bag on the ground felt like, he couldn't imagine anyone actually choosing to do this for fun. Suddenly he heard Bryn's voice in the next room.

"Agnes?" she called out as she came into the cottage.

Simon quickly got up, grimacing in the chill morning air and at the aches all over his body. He pulled on the rough wool

35

hose and drew the tunic over his head. It smelled dusty, but also had a slightly pleasant smell, like hand lotion.

"Lanolin," he thought, "from the sheep's wool."

He grabbed the cord and tied it around his waist. The clothes were too large for him, but except for bagging around the knees and ankles, they were quite wearable. He walked into the front room to find Bryn sitting at the table with a large slice of dark brown bread in her hand.

"Well, good morning," she said with a smile as she ripped off a chunk of the bread and popped it into her mouth. "I must have just missed Agnes heading for the manor kitchens to put her bread dough in the ovens. "

She tore a large piece of coarse brown bread off and offered it to him. He took a stool from the corner and sat at the table, taking the bread. It was nutty and smelled like molasses. Bryn cut slices of cheese that she speared with a knife and offered to Simon.

"I am off to Bridlethorpe monastery. I have an appointment with the bibliothecarius to look at some manuscripts."

"Sounds like a dinosaur," Simon said through a mouthful of bread.

"A what?" Bryn looked oddly at him.

"A...never mind. What is a bibliothecarius?" he asked, cutting another slice of cheese.

"He is the monk in charge of the library. The library and scriptorium of Bridlethorpe monastery are famous. Sir Robert has commissioned an illustrated psaltery from them. He likes me to stop by once in a while to check on their progress with the psaltery, but my real motive in going is to try to find a manuscript that documents Sir Robert's grandfather's role in the Battle of the Standard." Bryn wiped crumbs from her dress and brushed her hands together sending more crumbs flying.

"Anyway, I'd like you to come with me." She got up and Simon quickly stuffed the last of the bread into his mouth and followed her out the door.

Bryn walked on ahead as she continued talking. Simon found it somewhat irritating that she assumed he would follow, but then what choice did he have?

"The monks, especially the bibliothecarius, are not pleased about having a female on the premises. They are especially loathe to let one near a book. Afraid we'll taint it or maybe our feeble minds will explode being near all that knowledge." The irritation in Bryn's voice was evident and perhaps she realized that, for she stopped and turned, waiting for Simon to catch up, and then smiled and shrugged her shoulders. "Really, I shouldn't complain. But it is only because I am a favorite of Sir Robert, and he has endowed nearly 30 monastic houses, that they swallow their indignation at my being amongst them, however briefly."

"Agnes was telling me last night about the Montbury family history you are writing." In fact, Simon remembered, Agnes had not been able to stop telling him about how wonderful, intelligent, brave and beautiful Bryn was. He'd found the more she talked, the more he doubted the objectivity of her opinion regarding Bryn. Not that he would tell either Agnes or Bryn that.

"Is that why you are looking for this manuscript?" he asked.

"Yes." She started walking again, this time with Simon at her side. "Well, that and something else."

Simon said nothing, knowing she would tell him whether he asked or not.

"Let's get the horses from the stables and I'll explain as we ride." She stopped short and faced him. "You do ride, right?"

"Of course I ride," Simon said scornfully. No doubt Agnes would tell him what an excellent horsewoman Bryn was when he returned tonight. In fact, he had never ridden a day in his life, but how hard could it be?

Chapter Nine

Moira Ananke juggled her satchel and two books, holding the stack of mail she had just gotten from her mailbox in her mouth, while she opened her apartment door with the key. The door opened with its usual squeak onto a spotless living room. She leaned back against the door to shut it and then dumped her armfuls of materials onto the living room coffee table. She dropped her coat across a chair, threw the mail on the end table, kicked off her worn shoes and walked into the spotless kitchen.

"Looks like no one lives here," she thought as she pulled open a cabinet and took down a mug from the shelf. "But I suppose that's better than looking like I live here." This, at least, brought a chagrined smile. Moira knew that housekeeping was not her strength. Her office at the museum bore witness to that. She hired a housekeeper to come in twice a week and tidy her apartment. Tidy might not be the right word actually. Dig out might be better. In the few days between the housekeeper's visits, Moira managed to do what she termed "uncreation."

"You know, the bible says God created order out of chaos?" she once explained to Simon. "Well, I create chaos out of order, sort of a uncreation if you get my meaning. I like to think of myself as the personification of entropy," she laughed.

When she was busy again with a manuscript she was restoring, Simon got down the dictionary to look up entropy. "A measure of the disorder of a system." He didn't quite understand but at least got the general idea that Professor Ananke seemed to create a mess wherever she went.

She lit her gas stove, put the battered blue sponge ware kettle on to boil and took from the shelf over the stove a chipped crock with a cork stopper. Lifting the stopper out she dipped a spoon into the cocoa powder and put two heaping spoonfuls into her mug. The kettle was starting to whistle as the steam pushed through the spout. Moira poured the steaming liquid into her mug and stirred the cocoa. She could never complete this process without thinking of an argument she'd had with the great Aztec leader, Moctezuma, around 1500 AD it must have been, about the proper way to prepare xocolātl—the Nhuatl word for chocolate.

He insisted on a set formula for adding the native chocolate, spices and vanilla, and beating it to froth so that it melted in one's mouth. Moira's haphazard cooking habits drove him mad. Moira finally gave in and followed his instructions. It was true that this was a drink from heaven. While tea was always her drink of choice, ever since being introduced to this rich cocoa mixture, it became her favorite comfort food at the end of a hectic day. It was also a favorite in Moctezuma's court and he himself was said to drink up to 50 cups of it a day. Moira knew that one day, not 20 years into his future, he would offer this favorite drink in a golden goblet to the Spanish Conquistador, Hernando Cortez. The thought of what would follow that fateful meeting took the joy out of their visit that day. But Moira knew better than to interfere in his fate.

Bringing her mind back to the present, she took a cautious sip, and then opened her small refrigerator to drop a splash of milk into the mug. That done, she took a loaf of uncut white bread from a 1940s style breadbox. The breadbox was what she thought of as "landlord green" in color and had a curved cover that rolled up into the top. She cut herself as thick a slice as her toaster would allow and popped it into the one side of the toaster that worked. The wires inside glowed red and there was a wisp of smoke. Moira never knew if that came from the bread or from the wiring in the toaster, but as long as it kept working, she didn't think it worth the effort to find out. While the toast was warming and the cocoa was cooling, she opened another cupboard and took down a jar of peanut butter. Peanut butter toast and hot chocolate were her favorite comfort foods. The mature, rational part of her brain told her this was not a nutritious supper. And while Moira prided herself on her mature, rational brain, sometimes she ignored it.

"People who always eat nutritious food, and exercise regularly will someday find themselves in a hospital bed dying of nothing. At least I know I will be dying from too much chocolate and peanut butter, with a smile on my face," she thought with some satisfaction as she took a butter knife out of the drawer to help remove the too-toasted bread that was apparently stuck in the toaster.

"I don't mind dying of chocolate overdose," she said as she yanked the toaster plug from the wall first, "but I do know enough not to electrocute myself."

She dug at the toast now firmly stuck and smoking in the toaster. She tried turning it upside down and shaking it over the sink. A cupful of questionable crumbs ("what did I toast that is green?") fell out followed by the rather battered piece of toast.

"Perfect!" Moira grabbed it from the sink, up-righted the toaster, plugged it back into the wall and slathered peanut butter thickly onto the toast. Then she scooped up her mug of hot chocolate and walked into her study to sit at the computer desk. That the study was off-limits to the cleaning lady was obvious. Stacks of books leaned precariously on the floor. Piles of papers and folders covered the desk, window sills, and shelves. Strange objects of varying sizes, shapes and colors, but obvious antiquity, randomly occupied any available space. With hands full of toast, cocoa and the digital camera that she had retrieved from her satchel, Moira used her elbow to slide over a stack of papers on the desk, making room for the food. She sat down and punched the silver button that started up her computer. Just above the computer, tacked crookedly to her wall, was one of the nursery rhymes she had made Simon translate into Latin. He'd really gotten quite good at medieval calligraphy. The computer chime called her attention back to her work.

The museum had purchased new computers for its staff but Moira left hers in the box in her office, hesitant to invest the time and effort it would take to learn how to use it. Simon found the box, dusty and covered with newspapers, in the corner of her office.

"Oh cool!" he pushed off the papers and blew away the dust. "You haven't even opened this?"

She ignored him, being too absorbed in a brass rubbing she was trying to finish.

"Can I open it?" he asked eagerly.

"Hmmmph" she had replied, a charcoal pencil in her mouth.

"Great!"

For the next hour Simon created a storm of cardboard, Styrofoam and plastic as he unpacked the computer, various cords, keyboard and monitor. By the end of the day he'd gotten it all set up, configured the wireless network and was already setting up her email account.

"Look!" he said proudly. She turned, charcoal smudges on her nose and cheek. "You can check your email now."

"Simon," she said severely, "I have absolutely no intention of checking my email. Do you have any idea what kind of time I will have to spend sorting, reading, deleting and responding to email if I start doing that? Right now the museum administration knows I do not ever look at email. If they want me badly enough, they stick a note on my door."

"But this is so much more efficient and quick," Simon began.

"Exactly. Email allows everyone to shoot off communications in seconds. No need to make sure it is literate, thoughtful or even necessary. You end up with dozens of messages that are frankly the rambling gibberish of someone who has nothing better to do than send emails out all day. If they know they have to pick up a pencil and paper and actually write me a message, walk all the way down here and tape it to my door, you can bet they will make sure it is worth the effort first. I might get three notes a week stuck on my door. And even those I mostly just throw away. If it is known that I will be checking my email, I will be inundated with messages about "casual Friday," and "bringing in donuts to share on Tuesday," and "so-and-so's baby shower reminder for Wednesday." I told Ray Tomlinson it was a mistake over 30 years ago." She turned back to the rubbing.

Simon quickly typed *Ray Tomlinson* into Google and found he was the inventor of email back in 1971.

So the computer became Simon's. He frequently did research for her, finding journal articles and photographs she needed. She had to admit he'd convinced her that the internet did have its uses. But she was especially excited to see how he could upload all the digital photos he had taken of the artifacts she was working on so that she could access them at home.

"Of course you realize to access them at home you are going to need a computer there too," he had said with a smile.

She stared at him but could think of no argument. So they spent one afternoon online purchasing a computer to be delivered to her home. She ordered pizza for supper on the evening it came, while he unboxed and set up the new computer in her study. The next several evenings were spent with Simon giving her tutorials in the basics of computer use.

Now as she sat at the computer she took the digital camera, popped out the secure digital memory card and stuck it into the small slot on the side of her computer. She felt some pride at being able to download the pictures on the disk and watched as they quickly flashed across the screen. Sipping the cocoa and taking a messy bite of the peanut butter toast ("Lean back if you're going to eat at the computer, for heaven's sake!" Simon had scolded her. "Don't you know what crumbs can do to your keyboard?") She clicked on the folder to look through the most recent photographs.

A few days before, Simon had photographed a Sumerian cuneiform tablet for her. The first six pictures showed the broken tablet from several angles. Moira clicked on the arrow to see the next picture, and stopped with the cocoa mug partway to her lips. On the screen in front of her was a blurry picture of the palimpsest she had just showed Simon that day. He must have started to photograph it when she had gone out into the hall to see what had caused the noise. The photo had a jagged, bright, white line diagonally across it—a flash or streak of light cutting the photo in half. The top left of the photo showed the stained, yellowed, faded palimpsest just as she knew it looked on her desk in the museum right now. But the bottom right of the photo showed the same palimpsest with dark, elegant letters and beautiful bright, clear painting. In fact, it showed the palimpsest as it must have looked when it was first created.

Moira caught herself just as the mug was tipping, sending drops of hot cocoa into her lap. She set the mug down and leaned in closer to look at the photo. So this was what had happened. Simon had started to take a photo of the palimpsest and that had triggered a crack in time. He had photographed the exact moment when, somehow, the manuscript itself had pulled him back. She closed her eyes to recall the details of the manuscript. It had been created at Bridlethorpe monastery around 1170 AD. At least now she knew when, and where he was. She just didn't know why.

Chapter Ten

Simon rode sullenly and silently a few feet behind Bryn's white palfrey. The horse he was on was a barrel-chested affrus, or draft horse. Its coat was still thick and long from the winter cold. Its legs had white feathering around the hooves, the same color as the mane and tail. But the coat was a beautiful golden caramel color.

"This is Alizay," Bryn had told him as she led the horse out of the stable for Simon to mount. "He needs a bit of a brush down but that will have to wait I'm afraid."

Simon said nothing as his heart was in his throat. The creature looked tremendous. Its legs looked like tree trunks and its neck arched with bulging muscles. Simon's knees felt weak as he slowly approached the beast.

"He's a sweetie, if a bit stubborn sometimes. I'm afraid he's used to working in the fields. It will do him good to go for a ride today." Bryn waited for Simon to take the reins she held but he seemed rooted to the ground. He finally forced himself to step closer and reached out to take them from her. Standing next to the horse he could hear its breath coming in short and irregular snorts from its nostrils. Alizay's flanks would twitch to rid himself of flies. At each twitch Simon would jump, sure the horse was about to rear up or run off dragging him with it. He had not a clue what to do next and decided to watch Bryn and follow her lead.

Bryn returned to the stable yard leading her own smaller white horse.

"You've met Eleanor already. I've named her after the queen. She is as lively and beautiful as the queen, don't you think?" Bryn reached up and grabbed onto the saddle's pommel. She put her left foot into the dangling stirrup and then swung up onto the horse's back.

Simon slowly turned and did his best to mimic her movements, although it took him three hops to get his leg up and over the wide back of Alizay. He sat stiffly in the saddle, his legs feeling uncomfortably stretched over the expanse of Alizay's back, his hands, wet with perspiration, holding so tightly to the reins that his fingers felt numb. Bryn was silently watching from her mount. Simon tried to relax but somehow the horse had grown several feet higher since he had gotten into the saddle. The ground looked very far away. Bryn clicked her tongue and Eleanor started off. Alizay immediately began to follow, the sudden movement taking Simon by surprise. He jerked backward but quickly righted himself just as Bryn turned around.

"The monastery is through the wood, on the other side of the rock outcropping. We should be there before midday."

They rode silently for some time, Alizay plodding along behind the graceful step of Bryn's palfrey. At first they rode single file but then the path widened and Bryn slowed to let Simon come along side. His back ached from the strain of keeping himself upright in the saddle with the swaying of the horse. The muscles in his legs burned from hugging its flanks tightly.

"Let's stop here for a rest," Bryn suggested. "There's a stream just there," she pointed. "The horses can drink."

As much as he wanted to get off this creature and rest, he feared even more trying to get back up on it. His face must have showed his dismay. Bryn looked at him and said, "You've never ridden a horse before have you." It was not a question.

"Of course I have," Simon began angrily but realized how obvious his inexperience was. "No, I haven't," he said quietly.

"You could have said so you know. Not many people can afford a stable, it's nothing to be ashamed of."

"I'm not ashamed!" Simon began. "I just…" Actually, he had no idea why he'd lied about his lack of experience with horses. He still felt vulnerable and lost in this new place. She was overly confident and even arrogant, he thought. She didn't need one more thing to feel superior about.

"You really are doing very well. If you relax a bit, move with the horse instead of against it, you'll be more comfortable. Come on. Let's rest the horses for a bit. " Despite her gown, she gracefully swung one leg over and slid off her horse. She reached up for Simon's hand. He swallowed his pride, grabbed her hand and with rather less grace, came off the horse in a controlled fall. They led the horses to a small stream and sat down on a sun-warmed rock while the horses drank.

"Did you know this place is enchanted?" she asked casually, her face serious.

Simon looked at her.

"Roger and Baldwin met a demon here. In fact, it was the same day you appeared out of this very wood. You see, just over there where the shale outcropping is? They found a body lying on the ground. When they returned, it had turned into a dead fish." Bryn slowly turned and looked directly at Simon.

"A really smelly, dead fish."

"Does this kind of thing happen frequently?" Simon asked with interest.

"No, not frequently. But dead bodies and smelly fish are more frequent occurrences than strangers who show up in strange clothing out of nowhere."

Just then Alizay shied and pulled against his tether as a rabbit ran across the path.

"We'd better get moving if we are going to make your appointment on time," Simon said, quickly getting up. As much as he dreaded getting back on that horse, he much preferred it to this conversation.

Chapter Eleven

Bryn pulled her palfrey to a stop. Alizay stepped up beside Eleanor and the two horses nuzzled each other, soft nose to soft nose. Simon was grateful that Alizay seemed to have cruise control. He had done nothing but let the horse have its head during the whole journey. Alizay simply followed the palfrey's lead, stopping when she stopped, or trotting along side her in open fields or through wooded glades. Now they had reached Bridlethorpe and the two horses stood waiting at the large wooden door.

Bryn edged her horse up to a smaller door set into the larger gate. She pulled at a rope on the side. A little, square window slid open in the center of the door and a hooded face peered out.

"Good day, Porter," Bryn said with a smile. "We are here on an errand for Sir Robert Montbury. We have an appointment with Brother Felix."

The window slid closed. The sounds of something heavy being slid across the door, and the clinking of metal could be heard. The door swung open and Bryn and Simon, ducking their heads, rode through.

"The brothers are attending prayers in the chapel," the porter informed Bryn. "Brother Felix is expecting you, I will stable your mounts and he will meet you in the scriptorium"

Bryn and Simon dismounted, Simon with a bit more grace than previously. His legs felt wobbly from two hours on horseback. It reminded him of the first time he had gone roller skating at his neighbor's birthday party. He'd finally felt comfortable on the skates by the end of the event, but after taking them off, couldn't seem to get his feet to work right in his regular shoes. Now he forced his legs to move forward even though they felt like half cooked strands of pasta. Bryn obviously had been here before. She moved quickly and with confidence across the courtyard toward a stone tower.

"The brothers are in the church for noon prayers. It's the only time the prior allows me to come so they won't have to see me." She turned to grin at Simon. "Although I'll bet there are quite a few who wouldn't mind seeing a woman once in a while."

They had reached the tower and Bryn opened a thick wooden door with iron strapping and a large lock. Inside were steep stairs that followed the wall of the tower up. As they climbed, Simon stopped at each tiny slit of a window to look out. The monastery lay spread out beneath him. A large church, stables, refectory where the monks ate, the cloisters, infirmary and far off what looked like a blacksmith shed. Beyond that, cultivated fields and a mill on the river that flowed past the monastery. At the top of the stair was another wood and iron door. Bryn had to push with her shoulder to open it. It made a loud creaking and scraping noise as it resisted.

Simon stopped in awe at what lay before him. The room was spacious with carved pillars at intervals looking like great stone trees. Large windows filled two of the walls letting in clear, bright sunlight. Perpendicular to each of the windows were long benches with tables where there were acutely slanted work surfaces. Each work area had large sheets of parchment in different stages of completion. Bryn pointed to an area in the corner.

"That is where the monks in charge of preparing the parchments work. They smooth and chalk the surface. It then goes to that area," she indicated one of the rows of slanted worktables, "where one group of monks is responsible for marking the manuscript with lines and copying the text. Over there the younger monks, those still learning the art, are in charge

48

of keeping supplies ready. They cut goose feathers for quills. The monks that copy the text need their quills sharpened 50 or 60 times a day. They also must prepare the inks. They mix charcoal or oak galls to get the black inks. Finally, the illuminators get it. They are the ones who add the artwork. They even have thin sheets of gold that they apply to the parchment."

They walked over toward this area. Simon looked in wonder at the incredibly beautiful pieces of art in front of him. The manuscripts were large and covered with Latin text. The letters were perfectly formed, art in themselves. But the first letter took up fully a quarter of the page. Simon bent to look carefully at one parchment. The first initial on the page was a large "S" painted in a rich blue. He saw it began the Latin word "Sanctus" or sacred. Green vines twined around the letter and purple and yellow flowers sprouted from the leaves of the vines. In each curve of the "S" was a miniature landscape. The top was a tiny portrait of a man at a desk very much like the ones in the scriptorium. He, too, was studying a tiny book. Simon got as close as he dared to read the letters on the tiny book.

"*Eusebius Sophronius Hieronymus,*" he read.

"St. Jerome," Bryn explained. "A favorite of the monks who work in the scriptorium because he was such a scholar."

Simon moved on to the next table.

"*In principio creavit Deus cælum et terram,*" he read. "In the beginning God created the heavens and the earth."

Bryn turned quickly to look at him.

"You read Latin?" she asked in surprise.

"Some," he answered.

"Another clue to the mystery," she said mockingly.

The noise of a door opening at the other end of the room made them both jump.

"Brother Felix," Bryn turned toward a very thin, very bent, very old monk. Simon wondered if he'd been ill. His robe fell from his shoulders in great sweeping folds as if he had once been a much larger man than he now was. His back and neck seemed permanently bent so that he had to look up from under

49

bushy eyebrows to see what was in front of him. An involuntary shiver ran down Simon's spine. Between the overhanging eyebrows, the glaring eyes and the great sweeping brown robe, the monk reminded him of a large vulture.

"Simon, this is Brother Felix, the bibliothecarius of Bridlethorpe monastery."

Brother Felix slowly turned his gaze from Bryn to Simon. Simon involuntarily took a step backward.

"Bonus Meridianus,[1]" Brother Felix bowed his head.

"Quod vobis quoque," Simon answered.

Brother Felix looked quickly up at Simon and then to Bryn.

"You are here to access the library?"

"Yes, if you please," Bryn said. "Simon is here to help me. Sir Robert thought I might make quicker progress if he helped." Simon shot Bryn a startled glance but said nothing. Brother Felix looked again at Simon and he felt sure he was about to be expelled from the monastery. Bryn was confident as always, looking Brother Felix squarely in the eyes. He gave one quick nod of his head and began to move toward a door at the far end of the scriptorium.

Bryn grabbed Simon by the sleeve and pulled him along behind the monk. They came to a door with a large iron lock. The lock was of very curious workmanship. It was finely carved with many decorative vines and flowers. Simon could see not one, but two apertures in which to insert two obviously different keys. But even stranger than this were two thin channels that ran at a 45 degree angle from the side of the lock face to each hole. Brother Felix stood directly in front of the lock so that Bryn and Simon could not see him unlocking the door. After some time and what seemed to Simon to be considerable fumbling, Brother Felix pushed open the heavy door. It swung open smoothly and silently, unlike every other door they had thus far encountered in the building. The walked through, into a much smaller room than the one they had just left. It was warm and stuffy with a smell of dust and age. There were four single lecterns in a square in the

---

[1] Good Afternoon   And to you also.

50

middle of room. High up the walls were windows that let in streams of dusty light that reminded Simon of Professor Ananke's office. The windows were too high up to see out, or for someone to see into. They were too small to climb through but were many in number so that considerable light came into the room.

All around the room were armaria, chests used for storing books, of every size and design. Each was locked and some were even encircled with chains. With a sweep of his hand, Brother Felix indicated that Bryn and Simon should take a seat at the lecterns in the center of the room. Once they were seated, he moved to one of the chests and unlocked it. Simon leaned to one side to see around the lectern. He saw the monk moving his finger along the inside of the lid of the trunk. There was writing covering the inner lid that seemed to be a kind of catalog for what was in the trunk. It reminded Simon very much of the box of chocolates he had once gotten for his uncle on Valentine's Day. When you lifted the lid, there was a grid on the inside that noted what kind of chocolate was in each of the crinkly brown paper nests in the lower part of the box. Brother Felix seemed to find what he wanted for he lifted out a large codex with a wood cover. Simon noticed the book had a metal ring affixed to it from which hung a chain. The monk took a ring of keys from inside his robe, chose a small key and unlocked the other end of the chain, freeing the book from the chest. He carried the book over to the lectern where they sat, used his ring of keys again to unlock a metal rod that ran on the underside of the slanted desk. Then he inserted the end ring of the chain attached to the book over the rod and locked the rod back into position. The book was now resting on the slanted surface of the lectern, but was safely chained to the lectern by the rod that ran under the desk.

"I must join the others at prayers," Brother Felix said. "I will return afterward to replace the book."

"Thank you, Brother Felix," Bryn said graciously. "We will be most careful with the book."

51

With a doubtful nod, Brother Felix left the room. He shut the door and to Simon's great dismay, he heard the monk turning the two keys in the lock.

"He's locked us in!" he said in a panicked whisper to Bryn.

"Don't worry, he'll be back. You're not afraid of books are you?" she said with a laugh. "He is very protective of his library. Come on, we have little time to search while he is gone."

Chapter Twelve

Professor Ananke was in her office even earlier than usual the next morning. She grabbed armfuls of clutter from her large work table, dumping it all into an empty box she had found in the copy room. She needed space and for once she wanted an uncluttered work area to study the palimpsest. Now, with only the manuscript on the table in front of her, she sat down in the chair and took a deep breath.

"Quis, quid, quomodo, ubi, quando, cur---Who, what, how, where, when, why? My good friend Cicero believed these questions could solve any problem. So, we have some of the answers already I believe." She took a sip of the steaming cup of herbal tea she had purchased at the museum café on her way down to her office. It wasn't open at this time of the morning but Jenny, who ran the café, was accustomed to her odd hours and always ready to accommodate her.

"The Quis—who—appears to be the monks who created the manuscript. Or instead the who is Sir Robert Montbury, who commissioned many manuscripts—perhaps this one too? Or maybe the who is the person or persons he had it made for?" Moira sighed and took another sip of tea. This was going to be more difficult than she thought.

"Let's move on. How. Well, it was Simon's focus on the manuscript with the camera and the fact that he is now more sensitive to passing through time. The manuscript was waiting for someone with the ability, the willingness and the concentration. Simon was just the right person at the right time in the right place. This thing has probably been sitting in a dusty storage box in a cathedral archive for a thousand years waiting for the right person to free it. The where must be Bridlethrope monastery, or at least…" Moira stopped to get up and quickly scan her bookshelf. She found what she wanted—a book on medieval monasticism in England.

"Yes, Bridlethorpe was located in Yorkshire. So if not exactly the monastery, we know it must have ended up somewhere in Yorkshire. But then again, we are not sure where the manuscript was sent when it was finished. Maybe the "where" is someplace outside of Yorkshire?" Moira made a note in the black journal she was using to record information about the palimpsest. She would try to get more information on where this manuscript ended up.

"The when must be around the time the manuscript was created. The date we have is 1170 AD. If I remember from my last visit there, England was ruled by Henry II and his Queen, Eleanor of Aquitaine. Although heaven knows what a mess that marriage was."

Moira stared blankly at the wall in front of her, sipping her tea. She recalled the weeks she had spent with Henry and Eleanor, trying to get them to agree to talk to each other civilly. Their son, Richard, had been Eleanor's favorite while John was Henry's favorite. This was one of many points of contention between them.

"Of course back then," Moira said to herself, "being dad's favorite meant inheriting a kingdom—or not, as the case may be."

She brought herself back to the present. She put the tea down and walked over to the large window to open it. Years of experience told her that this window was going to fight her efforts. Damp wood swelled the frame and built-up layers of paint meant getting it to open even a few inches required determination. After a few minutes she managed to pry the window open enough to let some fresh spring air into the office.

"Maybe that will clear the cobwebs out of my brain," she thought and then looked down at her hands. They were covered with dust and grime from the window.

"Oh, for heaven's sake," she muttered angrily and headed out the door, down the hall, to the women's rest room to wash her hands. The hall was still dim, with only the night lighting on. She knew that shortly the custodian would be by to turn on the bright, if ugly, industrial lighting that glared during the day. She passed the custodian's closet, the drinking fountain that hadn't worked in years, and came to the women's restroom.

Now what?" she thought angrily. There was a long piece of yellow and black tape across the door and a hand lettered sign taped to it. *OUT OF ORDER PLEASE USE OTHER RESTROOM*

With a snort of impatience, Moira walked to the next door down the hall. It had a plastic nameplate on the door reading MEN. Someone had taken a black marker and written in a *WO* in front of the sign to indicate that, temporarily at least, this would be the WOMEN's and not the MEN's bathroom.

"Well, let's hope people actually stop to read that or we might have some interesting…" Moira stopped mid-sentence with the door only partway open. She quickly turned around, letting the door slam behind her. Forgetting her dirty hands, she ran back to her office.

"The Hunterian Psalter," she said out loud as she pulled books from the bookshelf, rifled through piles of folders and finally remembered what she wanted was in one of her black journals. She quickly ran her fingers along the lines of journals until she came to the year 1807.

"Yes, here it is. William Hunter, physician to Queen Charlotte, bequeathed his entire collection of books and manuscripts to his nephew, who then gave them to the University of Glasgow, Scotland in 1807." She pulled out the journal and blew the dust off the cover, bringing it back to her desk. She carefully but quickly flipped through pages that were yellowing at the edges.

"I remember I was in Oxford at the time. The university asked me to come up and help them catalog over 650 manuscripts. Well, that was over 200 years ago wasn't it? You surely can't expect me to remember every one of the manuscripts," she said to her empty office. "Yes, here it is! The Hunterian Psalter. That's where I remember seeing it. Folio 208r." She pulled her long-necked desk lamp closer to the journal page. The handwriting was beginning to fade. She read her own words of 200 years before.

These prayers were originally written in Latin for a female supplicant. Note how the Latin female endings have been altered to be male endings. Likely the manuscript was originally written for an Abbess of a convent but, for whatever reason, ended up in a male community or monastery. The endings were changed to be correct when read by a male instead of a female.

The sign on the restroom door, changing Men to Women had jogged her memory of this manuscript. Moira pushed the book away and moved the light to shine on the faded palimpsest. She had pointed out to Simon that someone had crossed out endings of words and written in above them different endings. Most of the words were too faded or written over to decipher. But there were a few that she might be able to figure out. Yes, she could see now that many of the masculine Latin word endings had been changed to female endings. But that was not all that had been changed.

"Here the original is *caedere*. To kill, or murder or slaughter. It is crossed out and changed to *necare.*" Moira sat back and picked up her now cold tea. "Well, *necare* can also mean to kill so really what would be the purpose of marking up a perfectly good manuscript just to change one word for another word that means the same thing?" She ran a finger, now covered with a latex glove, along the manuscript. "And here, *clades* meaning pest or bane. It has been crossed out and above it written *inimicus*. Again, it really means nearly the same thing as far as I can remember." She sat up in disgust. "This is getting me nowhere. Time for more tea."

Moira headed out into the now well-lit hallway and up the stairs to the main floors of the museum. School groups were already lining up in the lobby and echoing young voices were bouncing off marble columns and domed ceilings. Young voices. Moira felt a stab of worry for Simon.

Chapter Thirteen

Simon was impressed with how carefully, even reverently Bryn handled the codex. He knew from his studies with Professor Ananke that the codex was the first form of the book to replace the traditional scroll. They were usually made of pages of parchment bound together with a wooden cover. This library was under heavy lock and key, the books were locked in armaria and chained to the desks. He watched again to see how carefully Bryn now opened this book. It gave him a pang of guilt to think of the school library books that moldered under his bed, pages folded over to mark a place. Or his textbooks with scribbled pictures in the margins that he'd drawn to keep himself awake during Mr. Forte's endless lectures in biology class. It was strange to realize that there was a time when books were more valuable than gold, when they were kept under lock and key like precious jewels. Of course now books were not only printed in mass numbers from machines that produced with lightening speed, more and more books were sent across the ether to appear on someone's laptop or Kindle or Blackberry. He looked at the page Bryn had opened to in the book. Each letter was meticulously hand copied onto parchment, arduously created from animal skin. The beautiful illuminated letters were made by hand also, with miniature pictures drawn using inks made from plants and minerals. Simon realized he would never look at a book in quite the same way again.

"Here it is, look at this." Bryn pulled at Simon's sleeve, drawing him closer to the page. He leaned over, careful not to touch the book. He saw a page filled with tightly spaced Latin text. Much of it was in a script too difficult for him to read.

"See here, down in the bottom left corner. The text here is separate from the rest and in a different hand," she whispered, pointing to the square of text. He could read this more clearly. He murmured the Latin under his breath, translating in choppy segments as he struggled to remember his Latin vocabulary. If he stumbled, she would offer a suggestion or an alternate meaning.

An enemy ended my life, deprived me of my physical strength; then he put me in water and drew me out again, and tied me in the sun where my skin hardened and my hair was lost. After that, the knife's sharp edge bit into me and my rough skin was scraped away; the bird's feather moved over my brown skin, making meaningful marks;... leaving black tracks. Then a man bound me, covering me in a leather shroud, decorated with gold;...wound about with shining metal...

Simon looked over at Bryn with a perplexed expression.

"What is this?" he whispered.

"That's why I wanted to bring you. I'm not sure," she whispered back excitedly.

"Bryn."

"Yes?"

"Why are we whispering?"

She looked at him for several seconds, then straightened up and cleared her throat. She looked around at the empty, quiet room.

"I don't know actually," she said with an embarrassed grin. "There's just something about this place, this book, that makes me feel like I am somewhere I shouldn't be."

"Really?" Simon couldn't resist the jab. "You're not afraid of books are you?"

"Funny." Bryn brought his attention back to the book. "I found this when I was researching Sir Robert's genealogy. It caught my attention because it was so obviously not a part of the original manuscript. Not only is it sort of crammed into the margin of the page here…"

59

"It's also in a different hand," Simon added thoughtfully.

"Yes. And it's a bit, I don't know, gruesome, don't you think?" Bryn shivered. "What do you think it means?"

They both looked in silence at the page again.

"It does sound like someone being tortured and murdered. And then some of it sounds like gibberish too," Simon thought out loud.

"Well, I think it's important but I don't know why. Here." She brought out a quill, a small vial of ink and a scrap of parchment from the cloth satchel that hung from her shoulder. "I brought these from the manor. Sir Robert supplies me with what I need to write his history. Let's copy this down so we can study it when we get back."

For the next few minutes Bryn and Simon worked, one dictating while the other scratched the words onto the parchment.

"We need just a few minutes for that to dry. Simon, I don't think anyone's looked at this book for decades. It was written just after the Battle of the Standard in 1138. That was nearly forty years ago. We might be the first ones to read this since it was written. I have to know what it means. You see…"

Just then they heard the scratch of the key in the door. Bryn quickly closed the book, stuffed the scrap of manuscript into her satchel and stood up. Brother Felix had returned.

Chapter Fourteen

Brother Felix escorted them both back down the tower stairs, through the courtyard and out the gate. Bryn thanked him for his help. As they mounted their horses he raised his hand to Simon in a blessing saying, "*Bene ambula et redambula.*[2]"

Simon opened his mouth to answer when Bryn replied, "*Te valere jubeo.*" Brother Felix frowned and quickly turned back through the gateway door, shutting it behind him.

Bryn, with a satisfied smile on her face, apologized to Simon. "It bothers him so much that a female should know Latin. You saw his surprise when you replied to his "good afternoon" when we first arrived. I think he was hoping I had given up and brought you with me to save me from embarrassing myself."

In fact, Simon hadn't really noticed that Brother Felix had been speaking only to him. He was very distracted since his conversation with Bryn in the tower library. She mentioned the codex they were looking at had been made in 1138, "nearly forty years ago." This was the first indication Simon had of a time or date since he had arrived.

"We must be somewhere between 1170 and 1180 then, " he thought to himself, trying desperately to remember what he knew about England during that time. He brought his thoughts back to their present conversation.

---

[2] May you return safely. I bid you farewell.

"It's bit ironic isn't it, I mean him being 'Brother Felix?' Felix means happiness, right? He is one of the most morose looking people I have ever met," Simon said.

Bryn laughed. "Yes, he is. But then, it is true that he has very onerous duties. He is in charge of the scriptorium and the library. It's a huge responsibility that he takes very seriously." She was thoughtful for a moment. "You know it is odd though."

"What?" Simon asked.

"Well, there are almost always two brothers in charge of the library. Did you notice the two key holes in the door and the same in the locks on the armaria?"

"Yes, I wondered about that."

"It's really for security," Bryn explained. "In most monastery libraries, access to the library itself, and to the armaria or other book storage always requires two separate keys that are held by two different people. It keeps people honest if you know what I mean."

"I'm not sure that I do," Simon replied.

"Well, two different people, with their separate keys, are required to get access to the books. If one of them was tempted to steal a book for any reason, he would have to have the collusion of the other one too. And if anyone outside the library wanted to steal a book, he would have to convince both key holders to agree, or overcome both men to get the keys. You see? It just makes it a lot more difficult if any access requires two people in cooperation, not just one."

"Then why did Brother Felix have all the keys to the library and the armaria himself?" Simon asked.

"Brother Barnabas shared the duties of librarian with Brother Felix. He was here the first time Sir Robert brought me to the monastery. But I haven't seen him since then. Brother Felix has been around so long, maybe everyone knows he can be trusted to handle the job himself."

"Oh, that reminds me. What were those two channels that run diagonally down the lock to each key hole?"

Bryn laughed. "Well, I have seen those used in the manor house but likely not for the same reason. They are made to guide the key into the slot when it is too dark to see, but also when the master of the manor is too drunk to steady his hand. They are quite effective and it keeps the master from having to wake a servant, or worse yet, his wife, to open the door for him."

"I suppose it is unlikely Brother Felix would be too drunk to insert a key in the lock, but I can imagine he might need it if it were dark in the tower."

"Yes. Especially because they keep the use of torches to a minimum so that the risk of fire in the library is lower. And if you noticed, Brother Felix's eyesight is not so great anymore. He does a lot more seeing with his hands than his eyes." Bryn opened her mouth to add something, but stopped, studying Simon for a moment.

"Yes?" Simon encouraged her.

"Oh, never mind. Maybe I'll tell you later. I can have secrets too you know." She smiled slyly and kicked her horse to a canter. Simon had no choice but to hold on while Alizay took off after her.

It was nearly dark by the time they returned to the manor. Simon felt battered and bruised from the long ride back, although he also felt he was starting to master some of the finer points of staying on a horse. A stable boy took the horses to brush and feed them. Bryn invited Simon into the manor kitchen for an evening meal and to discuss what they had found in the library.

The kitchen was spacious and warm. Two large trestle tables stood in the center of the stone floor. Two fireplaces, big enough for Simon to walk into, were along one wall. Each had iron racks with large blackened cauldrons hanging from hooks over the fire.

"Agnes will have already served supper to what little household is here right now," Bryn explained. "When Sir Robert and his family are not here, we don't make too much ceremony

63

of meals." She walked over to one of the large black pots and dipped in a wooden ladle. Filling two wooden bowls, she placed them on the table and signaled Simon to join her.

"Oh, grab that bread, and some cheese from the cupboard would you?" she asked Simon.

Soon they were feasting on dark bread, hard cheese and vegetable barley soup. Simon realized he was starving. It was several minutes before either of them spoke.

"What were you going to say when Brother Felix interrupted us in the library," Simon finally said.

Bryn looked blankly at him.

"Just as we were looking at the puzzle," he reminded her. "You said, 'I have to know what it means, you see…' and then we heard Brother Felix at the door. What were you going to say?"

"Oh. Yes." Bryn took another mouthful of soup. "I'll make a deal with you." She looked sideways at Simon while reaching for another slice of bread. "I'll trade you secret for secret. You tell me something about yourself and I will tell you part of my secret."

Simon stared at his hands for a full minute before replying. "I don't know if I can do that—not yet anyway. You see, I am not sure why I am here, what I am supposed to be doing."

Bryn replied with some anger. "Haven't I proven myself to you yet? Haven't I shown you can trust me? And I have no reason to trust you at all."

Simon made up his mind. "OK, but, well, you are going to have to be very--open minded I guess is the right phrase."

Bryn pushed her food away, turned to face him, folded her arms across her chest and said, "I'm ready."

Simon smiled. "I doubt that actually."

Chapter Fifteen

Professor Ananke forced herself to spend several hours on the research she was doing for the new museum exhibit on Sumerian tablets and signature seals. While she normally would have relished working with the fragments of clay tablets and the beautifully carved seals, she was so anxious to return to her study of the palimpsest that she rushed through the task in a way very uncharacteristic of her usual meticulous study. In the last two hours of the day, she finally had time to return to the manuscript. She put in an overseas call to Dr. Thomas Carr at the University of Durham. He sent her the manuscript several weeks ago, on loan for the museum's exhibit on early writing. She looked at the notes she had scribbled down from the phone conversation.

Dr. Carr explained that this piece of manuscript had in fact been found amongst the pages of a much larger codex that he was working on. Because of that, they were unsure if it was actually part of the codex, or was a torn fragment from some other manuscript.

"We have analyzed the parchment itself using terahertz spectroscopy," Dr. Carr told her. She had to admit that here her notes devolved into doodles of stick figures fighting each other with laser beams as Dr. Carr had explained how, "terahertz time-domain spectroscopy, THz-TDS is a technique where short pulses of terahertz radiation are used as a non-invasive means of determining the component parts of materials." Moira's stick figures began to cut each other up into 'component parts.' She dragged her mind back to what Dr. Carr was saying. She wanted the results, not some incomprehensible explanation of how they got the results.

"…so in the final analysis…" Dr. Carr summed up over a crackling and hollow sounding phone line. Moira wondered why, in this modern age, a simple phone call to England sounded like people yelling at each other from a toilet bowl. "…in the final analysis, we determined that while the manuscript does appear to have been created between 1160 and 1200 AD, the ink and the parchment itself indicate that it was not in fact part of the codex that it was found in. It was likely torn from some completely separate work."

So. Moira was unsure what this meant, or how it helped Simon. She got up and stretched her cramped legs and rotated her neck. She often got so engrossed in her work, bending over some object with a magnifying glass, that body parts went numb. She sighed and walked to her bookshelf. She found two books she wanted to take home tonight to study; a book on the reign of Henry II and a biography of Eleanor of Aquitaine.

"You two, " she said, stuffing the books into her satchel, "will have to keep me company tonight instead of Simon. She opened up the satchel and looked down into it, thinking of her time spent with the two hot-headed monarchs.

"And no arguing down there, we have work to do." She flicked off the lights and locked the door.

Chapter Sixteen

Simon had some difficulty convincing Bryn he was too tired to continue their conversation that night. She reluctantly agreed to meet the next morning. Together they had concocted a story that Simon, as a relative of Agnes, had been sent for to help Bryn compile the Montbury history. This would explain his presence in the village and his frequenting the manor house to work with Bryn. Simon set off for Agnes' cottage and Bryn to do final duties as acting chatelaine of the manor. She walked through the manor house, making mental notes of things that the servants needed to tend to the following day. She looked into the buttery and the pantry to check on food stores. This time of year they were very low; new crops just planted and the last harvest so many months before. Sir Robert was a good, if often absent, master. He made sure that Jasper was aware of the needs of his tenants, that food was available and that widows like Agnes had what they needed to survive the winter. Not all tenants were so lucky. Bryn felt responsible to continue that stewardship in his absence. She reminded herself to check with Agnes the next day and be sure her grain bin was full.

After securing the house, Bryn made the rounds of the courtyard and stables. Satisfied all was quiet, she returned to her own room where her servant, Gunnora, had laid out her nightclothes and pulled back the blankets. As she settled into bed, her body was ready for sleep, but her mind was spinning with thoughts of what she and Simon might discover tomorrow, both about the puzzle they had found in the library, and about each other.

Agnes had insisted on feeding Simon even though he protested that he had already supped at the manor house. To please her, he ate some dried fish she had ready and drank a mug of something Agnes called hydromel. She explained it was a mix of honey and water. Once she was satisfied he was filled, she allowed him to go to his pallet and sleep. Simon never thought a pile of straw would feel so good to his aching body. He lay down, pulling the patched fur covering over him. He too wondered what tomorrow would bring. No matter how he went over it in his mind, he couldn't find a way to make anything he could say to Bryn sound believable. His anxiety over her reaction to the truth of his being here kept him from sleep for a long time. Eventually, despite his worries, he rational thoughts mixed with dreams and he slept.

Simon was awakened in the dim morning light by a soft plop on his bed covers. He sat up, eyes still blurred with sleep, to see a small creature scurry off the fur cover and into the dark recesses of the corner. Some small rodent, having made its home in the thatch of the roof, had fallen onto his blanket while he slept. The thought made Simon quickly lift the covers and jump up, kicking at the pallet with his foot to make sure he wasn't sharing a bed with anything else. The air this morning seemed less chilled than yesterday and he took his time getting dressed.

"There are some advantages to having one set of clothes," he thought wryly, "less time picking out what I will wear every day anyway. Although, if I am honest about it, I pretty much wear whatever isn't shoved under my bed or in the clothes hamper at home anyway." Simon's uncle rarely if ever paid attention to those kinds of things. He counted on Simon to tell him when he had grown out of his clothes and needed more, and Simon did know how to use the washing machine, even if he put the task off as long as possible.

Agnes was out in the garden but had left food on the table for him. He found a bowl still warm of some kind of porridge made, he guessed from the smell and nutty taste, from a grain like barley. It was very filling and that, with a mug of warm hydromel was sufficient. As he finished eating Agnes came in from the garden.

"Good morning!" she said with a smile. The apron she always wore over her loose kirtle was covered with dirt and grass stains. She was wiping her hands on it as she greeted him.

"Weeds seem to grow so much faster than my herbs. I've already pulled a whole basket full of them out of the chamomile. My! Just look at my hands!" She laughed and held up two very green-stained hands.

A sudden memory jolted Simon.

"Agnes," he said, "do you know about the Green Children of...I can't remember where they were from."

"Wulpet? The Green Children of Wulpet? Of course I do! Who wouldn't know of them?" she said with some surprise.

"Tell me about them, please. I didn't hear much about it where...where I come from."

"Oh dear, it was the biggest event in my lifetime anyway." She pulled up one of the stools and sat at the table across from Simon. "Wulpet is named such because of the many wolfpittes dug there to trap wolves. One day, villagers found two young children who had fallen into one of the great holes. They say they were terrified and crying piteously. The villagers of course brought them into the village and cared for them. The poor dears were cold and so thin you'd think they hadn't eaten for a fortnight. No one could understand their language, their clothes were not like any the villagers had seen before but, " here Agnes leaned in close to Simon and said in a whisper, "the strangest thing about them is they were green!" She sat back with a look of satisfaction as if she had just completed a conjuring trick.

"Green?" Simon asked in astonishment, "What do you mean, the children were green?"

"Just that. A boy and a girl and they were both as green as the weeds I've been pulling. But that's not all. They were brought to Sir Richard de Calne to be cared for. They were washed and clothed but even though they were starving, they wouldn't eat anything set before them!" Simon saw that this, to Agnes, was even more unbelievable than the fact that the children were green. "Imagine that! Finally a servant brought some green beans to them and the children ate them all down, stalks and all. For weeks that's all they would eat."

Agnes was fully enjoying Simon's rapt attention to her story. It was so rare she was paid any mind at all. Simon listened intently to this strange tale.

"Well, after some time they started to eat regular food and adjust to life in Wulpet. Even their skin eventually started to lose its green hue. Unfortunately, the poor little boy died. His sister continued on in Sir Richard's household and over the years lost her green coloring, becoming just like the other children in the village. She eventually married a man from King's Lynn."

"But, did they ever find out who these children were, where they came from?" Simon asked.

"When the girl learned to speak English, she told a strange story. She said they were from a village called St. Martin. One day she and her brother were tending her father's sheep when they heard church bells ringing. They followed the sound and found themselves lost and in a cave. As they wandered, looking for the way out, they eventually came out into the bottom of the wolfpitte where the villagers found them. That's all she could remember."

Simon sat thinking about this strange tale. It was fascinating and unbelievable. Unbelievable, yet it actually happened. Suddenly he saw a way to explain his situation to Bryn. He thanked Agnes and started out the door and up the dirt road that led past the peasant cottages and tilled fields to the manor house.

He saw Bryn in the manor courtyard near the well. She had a young boy by the ear and was scolding him with some fervor.

"…besides being dangerous, it could ruin the well. You do understand that don't you?"

The boy nodded as best he could with his ear being tightly and painfully grasped.

"Then don't ever let it happen again, Baldwin." She let him go and he scurried off, one hand covering a very red and bruised ear.

Bryn watched him go with her hands on her hips and a shake of her head. As she turned, she caught sight of Simon leaning against the wood shed. When he'd heard her call the boy Baldwin, Simon knew he must be one of the boys who had found him in the woods. Simon was sure neither boy had seen his face, but didn't want to take any chances. He'd quietly moved toward the shelter of the wood shed until Baldwin had escaped.

Bryn smiled when she saw him and wished him a good morning.

"The day has just started and already we have a crisis," she laughed. "Baldwin, who is kind-hearted but empty-headed, was trying to save a turtle from the cooking pot by hiding it in the well. When I came by he was nearly head first down the well trying to keep the turtle from falling out of the bucket."

They walked into the manor house, this time through the central entrance in the front rather then the back kitchen door as they had last night. Simon stopped in wonder at what he saw. Bryn was several steps ahead of him before she realized he had stopped. She turned to find him staring up at the high oak ceiling with its arching wooden beams. The room was large with a raised dais at one end. Upon the dais was a long, solid oak table. Two other tables ran perpendicular to the dais on the floor that was covered with a thick layer of straw. Low benches ran along the two longer walls of the hall. In the center of the floor, between the tables, were two iron braziers, cold now but with fires laid in them, at the ready for lighting.

"It's quite impressive isn't it?" Bryn said with some pride. "When Sir Robert is here, he of course brings his whole household and retinue. We sometimes have 100 men to feed and bed down in the hall. It does seem odd to have it quiet and empty." She looked around, following Simon's gaze, as if seeing it for the first time.

"It actually is a bit smaller than his manor in Suffolk though. This one was given to him by King Henry in reward for the Montbury family's support of Henry at the Treaty of Wallingford. This gave Henry the throne after Stephen died." Bryn shrugged her shoulders "As you can guess, this manor once belonged to a nobleman who didn't throw his support behind Henry."

She turned and strode toward the south end of the hall. Simon hurried after her toward a richly carved wooden door topped by a graceful arch. Bryn chose a large key from the ring of keys that hung from her belt. She unlocked the door and pushed it inward with her shoulder, waiting for Simon to enter the room before her.

"This is Sir Robert and Lady Montbury's solar. It is their private quarters and so is of course the most richly decorated set of rooms in the manor house." Bryn came in after Simon. "The servants wouldn't dare come in here, I thought it would be the safest place for us to talk without fear of being overheard." She walked over toward a group of chairs around an elaborately carved table of nearly black wood. They were arranged in front of a large window of tiny, diamond shaped leaded glass.

"Sir Roger is very proud of these windows. They are some of the first made from a process begun in Germany. He explained to me once that they create the glass from potash instead of the old fashioned use of soda ash. They blow a large glass sphere and then swing the still-molten sphere until it forms a cylinder. While it is still hot, the glass cylinder is flattened to make the panes."

Simon walked up to look more closely at the tall, graceful windows. Beyond being forced each spring to help his uncle take down storm windows and wash them before putting screens up, he'd never really thought about the windows in his house before. Sleeping in Agnes' dark, windowless cottage had made him realize how much he took for granted.

Bryn had pulled out two chairs for them, he sat in one while she took the piece of parchment they had copied from her satchel. The room was good size but much smaller than the great hall. The walls and floor were stone and both were covered with deeply hued tapestries. Pictures of flowers, animals, hunting scenes and even a unicorn were woven into the wall coverings. Simon realized these tapestries were not purely for decoration, their primary purpose would be to halt the cold from creeping into the room through the damp stone walls. The large windows faced south to get the most from the weak winter sun.

When he brought his attention back to the table he saw Bryn watching him.

"You do remember our agreement," she said. "You will tell me something about yourself, and I will share my secret with you. So—who goes first?"

Simon opened his mouth to speak but she held up a hand.

"Wait a minute," she said. "Let me first tell you what I have observed. I don't want you telling me something I've already guessed and thinking that will count as your part," she smiled and continued.

"First, you are obviously well educated. Certainly not a peasant. And yet you have no experience with horses. You surely would have if you were from a noble family. Also, your reaction to the great hall and this solar lead me to believe you have never been in a manor house before, that frankly would be strange whether you were a noble or a peasant. My best guess is my first guess on seeing you the first time, that you are a runaway oblate or novice, escaping from a monastery. That would explain your knowledge of Latin. Still, even that doesn't really fit." She sat back, arms folded across her chest. "So?"

Simon squirmed a bit to get more comfortable in the hard wooden chair. He took a deep breath and began.

"Do you remember when we first met, you said something about the green children of Wulpet?"

Bryn looked startled and then laughed.

"What in heaven's name does that have to do with anything? You aren't telling me you are one of them?"

"No. No, it's not that. It's just that I have been trying to figure out how I could explain things to you—how I could make you possibly believe me—and it occurred to me that maybe the story of the green children would at least be a starting point."

Bryn looked even more confused but said nothing.

"I mean, no one has been able to explain where they came from, or who they were, or why their language and clothes were so different, right? Even today no one can understand that, yet you know they were real, it really happened."

"So?"

"So my point is, there are things in this world that we sometimes have to accept as possible even though we can't explain them, or even if our minds tell us what we are seeing or hearing is impossible."

Bryn smiled slyly at Simon. "For instance, how does a dead body turn into a fish?"

"How do you know…" Simon began, astonished.

"Baldwin and Roger both told me about finding a dead body, a boy they said, though they didn't see his face, lying in the wood by the stone outcropping. They told me when they went back the next day, the body was gone but a rotten fish was in its place. It doesn't take much to put that together with the fact that only a few hours later I met you, very disheveled and covered with debris and smelling like dead fish. So while I might have some idea of what happened, I don't know why or how."

"I'm not sure I know why or how either," Simon said, more to himself than to Bryn.

"Yes, that was me that Baldwin and Roger saw. That's why I tried to stay out of his way this morning, just in case he recognized me, although I very much doubt he would."

Bryn said nothing, waiting for more.

74

"Sometimes, when I travel it is, well I guess 'rough' would be the best word. I mean you can get kind of battered and come down rather roughly. This time was particularly bad. I think it was because I wasn't at all prepared for the journey, it took me by surprise. In fact, when Roger and Baldwin found me, I was still very dazed and unable to move."

"When you travel? Where were you coming from?" Bryn asked.

"Time," he answered. "I was coming from Time."

"As in, Stokely-on-Tyme?" Bryn said with some sarcasm.

"No, as in future time," he replied.

There was silence as the two looked at each other. Bryn looking for some indication that Simon was mocking or teasing her, Simon looking for some indication that she was willing to believe him.

"Go on," she said quietly.

"I'm not from here, as is obvious. I live in…in a place that you don't even know about yet and doesn't even exist yet. I live in a place over 900 years in the future."

Bryn still said nothing. Her face showed nothing, not disbelief, not anger, not shock. Simon did not know what she was thinking or feeling.

"I have a friend. She works in a musuem. Her name is Professor Moira Ananke. She is a time traveler, although I didn't know that for a long time." Simon had leaned forward eagerly and was talking quickly in his rush to tell her everything.

"When I finally did find out, she started to teach me about time and how to travel through it. I have only just begun to learn. I have taken two other journeys but they were carefully planned and I was prepared. I knew where and when I was going. This time…well, I don't know what happened. One minute I was in her office taking a picture of a palimpsest and the next minute I was flat on my face in the woods in 12th century England." He sat back, unsure of what else to say.

Bryn still said nothing. She looked at him for what seemed a very long time and then slowly turned her head to look out the window, her chin on her fist. They sat this way for several minutes. Simon felt a trickle of sweat run down his back under his thick woolen tunic. The breakfast he had eaten an hour before sat like lead in his stomach.

"You are right," Bryn said at last.

"Huh?" he was startled by her sudden speech.

"There are many things in this world that we can't explain, yet they are true, we can't deny them."

Simon took a deep breath and realized he'd been holding it for some time. Was it possible she believed him?

Bryn turned and looked directly at Simon. Her face serious.

"When I was very young, I had just come to live in the Montbury household, I remember one day there was such excitement and nervousness. The household was turned upside down. Someone finally explained to me that King Henry and his queen, Eleanor of Aquitaine, were coming to conference with Sir Robert about trouble on the Welsh border. Lady Montbury turned the whole house out to clean and prepare for their visit. I did my best to stay out of the way. When the royal entourage arrived it was so exciting! They stayed for several days and the house and outbuildings were full of royal servants, soldiers, ladies in waiting, horses, and of course all the animals brought in for many evenings of feasting." Bryn smiled at Simon with the memory of it all.

"I was young enough to have a nurse who looked after me most of the time, but old enough to sneak away from her as often as I could to spy on all the activity. I wanted more than anything to see the queen. I had heard so many stories about her. I remember one evening especially. The feasting had gone on until very late. Most of the men were drunken with too much ale to notice me. I had managed to find a box to sit on in the great hall, behind a stack of bedding that would be pulled out for men to sleep on later. Suddenly, a woman walked by and saw me sitting there. She was lovely and dressed in very fine linens. I knew it must be Eleanor."

"I hope you didn't tell her you named your horse after her," Simon said laughing.

Bryn gave him a disgusted look.

"I didn't even have the horse then. Actually, I think she would have liked that though, if I had told her. Anyway, I was certain she would send me off to my nursemaid but she didn't. She smiled and came over and sat next to me on the pallets. She asked me my name and what I was doing in Sir Robert's household. We spoke for a long time, about many things. She told me about all the places she'd been and the people she'd met. I was so entranced. I could never imagine a woman being able to do such things. I talked too, in my childish way. I told her how I was studying with Sir Robert's sons and I know I bragged about being a better student than they were. I talked about how I admired her, the fact that she had gone on a crusade, that she was ambitious and smart and courageous. She stopped me and laughed. She said she was not the queen, that she was a guest of King Henry's but she knew the queen and agreed with me. She listened to me even though I was just a child. Finally, she got up and said she had to go. She told me not to give up on my dreams, to continue to study hard, to be courageous. She told me she thought I might be a great woman one day, like Queen Eleanor. And then she asked me my name and I told her. She held out her hand and said to me, 'Very nice to meet you, Bryn. My name is Moira Ananke.'"

Chapter Seventeen

Moira Ananke sat once again in the cluttered study of her apartment. This time however, she was not in front of the computer but sat with her legs pulled underneath her, a very ugly quilt over them, in the wide green wingback chair that took up a corner of her study. The wingback chair was one of her favorites. She had once been told by a friend who sold antiques that it was very valuable, being an original American wingback chair from, he'd guessed, the mid-1700s. She could have told him the exact date it was made--1751--and who made it. It was on that date that Dr. Thomas Bond invited her to come to the opening of America's first hospital, Pennsylvania Hospital. Dr. Bond and Benjamin Franklin were instrumental in founding the institution. They were having some difficulty however in finding the right person to run it. Moira had suggested a friend of hers, a Quaker widow named Elizabeth Gardner. Bond and Franklin decided after meeting Mrs. Gardener to appoint her as head matron of the hospital. They were both so grateful to Moira for helping them fill the position they gave her the wingback chair as a token of their thanks. It was upholstered in a green, blue and gold fabric that looked like peacock feathers. She reached over to turn on the lamp next to the chair, pulled the two books she'd brought from work out of her satchel, and began to read.

"The problem is," she said to herself, "I was focusing purely on Henry and Eleanor's marital difficulties and not really paying attention to the politics of the time. I need to refresh my mind about what was going on in Henry's kingdom around

1170." For the next hour and a half Moira read intently, taking notes in her black journal.

"Yes, of course," she finally said. "The kingdom was in turmoil for years. There was certainly enough trouble at home, between their tumultuous marriage and their sons constant fighting with Henry and amongst themselves for power, but the bigger picture of course was Thomas Becket."

Moira stared into space for several minutes, chewing on the end of her pencil. She then put the books down, pushed the quilt to the floor and walked into the kitchen. Her stomach was reminding her that she had neglected to eat supper when she came home. She pulled down a book titled "*De re coquinari: Apicius*" from the shelf above the stove and opened it to a bookmarked page.

"You'd think I'd remember how to make this after so many years," she said to herself. She began to read the recipe and pull out ingredients. The recipe, and in fact every recipe in the book, was in Latin, *Apicius* having been written in the early 5th century as a cookbook. Although she was not much of a cook, she liked to try different recipes out as a way of clearing her mind from her studies. She flipped through the pages and found Minestra Maritata, better known as Italian Wedding Soup.

"Let's see, oil, broth, wine, leeks, mint," Moira crashed around the kitchen opening and closing cabinets, rummaging through the refrigerator, gathering ingredients. With her arms full of vegetables, a wooden spoon held in her teeth and a green pepper under her chin, she leaned over to read the rest of the recipe. "…small fish, small tidbits capon's kidneys and pork pancreas."

"Hmm, I may have to get creative here." She dumped her armload of ingredients on the counter and opened the pantry door once again. "Well, no fish or capon's kidneys or pancreas," she mumbled. Suddenly she dove into the far reaches of the closet. "Ah ha! Perfect!" She brought out a can of Spam. Looking back at the book she read, "crush pepper, lovage, green coriander, add a little honey, and of the liquor of the above morsels, wine and honey to taste; bring this to a boiling point skim, bind, stir well sprinkle with pepper and serve. Sounds easy enough," and ignoring all the instructions, she dumped everything into a large pot, put it on medium heat with a cover and went back to the study.

Once again settled in the chair she picked up her journal and began reviewing her notes. Thomas Becket--the history book had called him Thomas a Becket.

"Why they keep propagating that grammatical error for centuries is beyond me, the man was Thomas Becket, plain and simple," Moira muttered under her breath.

Henry had met Thomas through Theobold, Archbishop of Canterbury. They had become close friends. King Henry even sent his young son and heir, Henry the Young King, to live with Thomas and be educated in his household.

When Theobold died, Henry had Thomas put into the very powerful position of Archbishop of Canterbury, hoping he could use Thomas to take control away from the church and augment his own power. But things did not work out quite as he planned. Some said the new Archbishop grew to take his spiritual responsibilities seriously, others said he just wanted to increase his own power. Whatever the reason, Thomas refused to do Henry's bidding, frustrating the king's attempt to gain power over the church. The two men, once the closest friends, now were the bitterest enemies.

In 1164 Henry tried to force Thomas Becket to sign the Constitutions of Clarendon, giving King Henry many privileges and powers over the church. Becket refused to sign. For the next few years Becket and Henry fought, one trying to weaken the church's power, the other trying to turn the pope against Henry and consolidate his own power.

"Yes, I do remember now," Moira said to herself. "Henry was ill when he got word of the latest refusal of Thomas to cooperate with him. Supposedly he cried out, 'Will no rid me of this meddlesome priest?' or some such thing." She quickly flipped through several pages of the book in her lap. "Here. Here it is."

On December 29, 1170, four of Henry's knights, Reginald Fitzurse, Hugh de Moreville, William de Tracy, and Richard Brito burst into Canterbury Cathedral to confront Thomas. He refused to cooperate with them and they attacked him. Following is an account written by Edward Grim, companion to Thomas Becket and eye witness to the attack.

The wicked knight leapt suddenly upon him, cutting off the top of the crown (of his head) which the unction of sacred chrism had dedicated to God. Next he received a second blow on the head, but still he stood firm and immovable. At the third blow he fell on his knees and elbows, offering himself a living sacrifice, and saying in a low voice, 'For the name of Jesus and the protection of the Church, I am ready to embrace death.' But the third knight inflicted a terrible wound as he lay prostrate. By this stroke, the crown of his head was separated from the head in such a way that the blood white with the brain, and the brain no less red from the blood, dyed the floor of the cathedral. The same clerk who had entered with the knights placed his foot on the neck of the holy priest and precious martyr, and, horrible to relate, scattered the brains and blood about the pavements, crying to the others, 'Let us away, knights; this fellow will arise no more.

Moira shivered. "Gruesome stuff." She suddenly looked up from the book and sniffed the air. She jumped up from her chair and rushed into the kitchen. The pot on the stove was boiling rapidly, spitting soup over the counter tops and stove. Moira hurriedly grabbed a cloth, shut off the stove and started to wipe up the mess. When all was once again in order, she picked up the wooden spoon, dipped it into the pot of soup, blew on the steaming spoonful and sipped.

81

"Yes. Well." She looked at the spoon with a frown. Moira put the spoon down, put a cover on the pot of soup, and began to assemble the makings for hot chocolate and peanut butter toast.

Chapter Eighteen

Simon stared in disbelief at Bryn. He had come here this morning knowing he would be telling her a tale beyond belief. But she had turned the tables on him. He was the one looking at her with incredulity.

"That's not all," Bryn said, now enjoying Simon's reaction. "Before she left a few days later, she searched me out and gave me this." Bryn lifted her long, heavy braid and untied a thin black cord that ran around her neck. She pulled out from her laced bodice a necklace with a small silver figure and handed it to Simon. He took it and looked at it closely. It was a tiny figure of a woman dressed in long flowing robes with a veil over her head. She sat in a simple chair. In one hand she held a spindle from which a thread came down and passed through her other hand.

"Strange gift." Simon handed it back to Bryn.

"I asked her what it meant. She just smiled at me and said someone as clever as I was would be able to figure it out."

"Well, did you?" Simon asked.

"I guess it's time to start sharing some of my secrets." Bryn took him over to a large chest on the opposite wall of the solar. She chose yet another key from the ring that hung from her belt and inserted it into the lock on the lid of the chest. Simon peered over her shoulder to see what was inside. There were several lengths of what looked like very rich fabric, some silver plate and at the very bottom, wrapped in pieces of wool blanket, several books.

"These belonged to our tutor." Bryn lifted one of the heavy volumes out with some difficulty. "He was actually Greek and was brought back by Sir Robert when he returned from the Crusades. It caused quite a stir around here I can tell you." She sat on the floor, her back against the chest and the book on her lap. Simon sat down beside her. "He was a wonderful man really. Although Sir Robert's sons didn't appreciate him. They preferred to be outside practicing their swordmanship or hawking. Perhaps that was good for me, because they would often sneak off during lesson time and I would have the tutor to myself. Anyway, he was quite old when he came here and he died about six years later. Since he had no family, his books and writing implements were left with us. No one else in the family much cared about them, so Sir Robert let me have them." Bryn lovingly moved her hand across the carved cover of the book in her lap.

"This one contains the letters and writings of the Greek philosphers. It also has many Greek myths. Lady Montbury wouldn't let me keep it if she knew that---all that heathen nonsense she would say."

Bryn opened the cover of the book. It was large enough so that opened it lay flat across both their laps as they sat next to each other on the floor, backs against the open trunk. She opened the book up where a ribbon marked a page.

"One day, during lessons, Aescapulus, our tutor, saw my necklace. He brought this book over to me and had me translate this paragraph from the Greek." Bryn moved her finger along the text, reading it to out loud to Simon.

Ανάγκη (Ananke) represents fate, and destiny. She is often shown holding a spindle. She and her husband, Χρόνος (Chronos) are the creators of time. The other gods and mortals see her as a powerful controller of fate and inevitability. She is the mother of the Moirae, the three fates, whose father is Zeus.

It seemed too much for Simon to take in. Instead of finding answers, he seemed to be sinking deeper into mysteries that were beyond him. Bryn looked up at him.

"When Aescapulus showed me this, I didn't know what it meant, but I felt it was important somehow. That is why I have kept this necklace all these years, not showing anyone. I knew it was somehow important, that Moira Ananke was more than she appeared."

"I don't think I understand," Simon said. He wondered if he knew anything at all about the woman who had been his friend for the last year.

"Maybe we can't understand everything yet, but I know she was kind and good to me, and she believed in me, in my potential for becoming someone of value. I don't know about your world, Simon, but in my world, that is not something most women can hope for.

"Women are primarily property and child bearers. Our opinions are ignored, our lives are not our own." Bryn held the necklace tightly in her fist. "I have held onto this for a long time because it gave me some hope that there might be more for me." For the first time Simon saw that there was a vulnerable young woman behind the wall of confidence that Bryn had built.

"Maybe that's why I am here," he said thoughtfully. "I mean, I didn't come here by choice this time. I was pulled here by something. Maybe it was that necklace? Maybe it was you?"

"Well, if it was, it was without my knowing anything about it. But however you got here, there must be a reason why you are here." She lifted the book back into the bottom of the trunk and closed the lid. "Maybe, it has something to do with other secret I have."

"I don't know if I can take much more," Simon complained as they walked back to the sunlit table by the windows. Bryn ignored him, sitting down at the table where lay the riddle they had copied from the library.

"I think it's important that we figure this out. But before we do that, I want to show you what else I have found." She pulled out two more, smaller pieces of parchment from her leather satchel.

"Last harvest season I spent a lot of time at the monastery library. Sir Robert had just commissioned me to begin the Montbury family history. There are several weeks when the monks have to spend a lot of time in the fields and orchards, gathering the crops in before the first frost. This gave me more time to be in the library without intruding on them." She paused. "And frankly, it happened that Brother Felix was in the infirmary with pneumonia and I had much freer access to the library. I wanted to take advantage of that. The prior assigned me a young monk as a guide, and I am sure, to keep an eye on me. Fortunately, he was a sweet, gullible young man and within a couple visits I essentially had the whole library to myself."

For a brief moment Simon felt compassion for the poor young monk who had been manipulated by Bryn. He imagined she had him wound around her finger in a short space of time.

Simon," Bryn said sharply, "focus please, we have a lot to do."

"I'm listening. You had the whole library to yourself."

"I came across a book I was looking for that detailed the Montbury family's connections to lands in France. Toward the back of the book, written in the margin, in a different handwriting, was a short message." Bryn unfolded one of the small parchment pieces and showed it to Simon. He held it up to the light. As expected it was in Latin. The short message read.

"It is not me, although he will try to make it appear so. I am frightened. You must…"
Simon looked questioningly at Bryn.

"I couldn't imagine what it could be. My first reaction was anger that someone would deface a manuscript by writing in it. Of course I was intrigued but my time was limited there and I had no idea what it was or what to do with it. But I did copy it down, and also copied down the name of the book it was in and where it was from."

Simon looked again at the small piece of parchment. Do you remember if it was in the same handwriting as the riddle we just copied down today?"

"I thought of that but no, I don't think the script was the same." Bryn unfolded the third parchment on the table.

"A month later I was back again at the library. This time I found this, not written in the book itself, but just stuck loosely in between the pages of a large codex I was studying." She smoothed the wrinkled parchment out on the table. Simon pulled it closer and began to haltingly translate.

"It must be hidden so that no eyes but ours will see it. It cannot be destroyed, we might hope to use it against him some day."

"This one is the same handwriting as the first, I remember checking them." Bryn put the two older, smaller texts next to each other. "The person who feared for their life, also wrote this message, but did not write the puzzle."

"Maybe they are not even related to the puzzle then," Simon suggested.

"I can't believe that could be true," Bryn said dirisively. "Surely we don't have a gang of vandals breaking into libraries to write puzzles in the margins of manuscripts. You see how carefully guarded the books are. No, I think there must be some connection."

"Well, what do you suggest we do?" Simon asked.

"We figure out what this puzzle means, and we get back inside that library ."

Chapter Nineteen

Moira rubbed her eyes and leaned back against the oak headboard of her bed. It was late and she was tired. She had brought her books and journal to bed to continue her studies, but being underneath the warm down quilt only made it more difficult to keep her mind from shutting down.

She had read through both history books, reminding herself of the tumultuous relationships between Henry and Eleanor and their children. She had ordered the historical events in her journal, trying to recall what her own experiences had been during her brief time there.

"ArchbishopThomas Beckett is murdered in the Canterbury Cathedral, holding on to the altar. He is murdered by four of Henry's knights. Many people heard Henry's wish to be rid of the knight." Moira reviewed her notes with her eyes closed. She opened them to scan her journal again.

"Thomas quickly becomes a martyr. Stories of his piety and saintliness multiply. Even though heaven knows he'd made enough enemies when he was alive. Anger over Thomas's death grows and is focused against Henry. Henry gets nervous and blames his knights. He says he never meant for Becket to be killed, his guards misinterpreted his words said in a moment of frustration."

Moira's thoughts turned toward the kitchen and a cup of tea. She pushed the books off her lap, threw back the quilt and climbed out of bed, walking barefoot over the cold floor into the kitchen. As she ran water into the kettle and turned on the stove, she continued her narrative aloud to herself.

"But things get worse. Henry's sons, supported and encouraged by his wife, Eleanor, plan a revolt to overthrow him. Many people see this as a sign that God is angry with him. He decides to make a pilgrimage to Thomas Becket's tomb trying to win back public support. Henry manages to put down the rebellion."

Moira's thoughts were interrupted by the ringing of her phone.

"Blast!" She picked up her tea and walked into the study to answer the phone.

"Is this Dr. Ananke?" a masculine voice asked.

"Speaking."

"I'm terribly sorry to call so late, but it took me some time to find your name and number."

"Who is this please?" Moira asked impatiently.

"Oh, of course, I'm sorry. My name is David Grant. I think you know my nephew, Simon."

Moira's stomach turned a somersault. How could she have forgotten?

"I'm terribly worried about my nephew. He didn't come home last night. I assumed he was in bed because I got home very late, and then I thought perhaps I had just missed him this morning but he still isn't home and it looks like his bed hasn't been slept in."

Moira was furiously thinking while he spoke. She couldn't possibly tell him the truth. He wouldn't believe it if she did.

"Oh dear! I feel just terrible Mr. Grant. Simon is with me. We have been working on a project together at the musem and I am so technologically illiterate he has been doing all the computer work for me. I'm embarassed to say he'd asked me to phone you and let you know he would be here and I completely forgot."

"Well frankly, Dr. Ananke, Simon should have phoned himself. I am quite angry with him right now. May I speak with him please?" Moira froze. It would be one heck of a long distance call to enable him to speak with Simon right now.

"Actually Mr. Grant, I've sent him on a quick errand back to my office in the museum. Perhaps I can take a message?"

There was an angry 'hmmph' at the other end of the line.

"I am leaving in the morning on a business trip to Amsterdam. I will be gone for several days. With the school holiday coming up, Simon will be on his own for a while. Please tell him I have made arrangements for our housekeeper to check in frequently with him to be sure everything is OK while I am gone."

"I certainly will Mr. Grant. I wonder, it would work quite well if Simon stayed with me while you were gone. We could work on our project and I could keep an eye on him."

There was silence on the other end of the line for several seconds. Moira guessed he was torn between the convenience of having a place for Simon to stay, and wondering just how crazy this lady from the museum was. She hoped that Simon's relationship with her over the last year would win him over.

"I would appreciate that Dr. Ananke. Thank you."

"No problem at all, it will be my pleasure. I'll be sure to tell Simon you called."

Moira put the phone down and let out a long breath. Sometimes, the present was much more trouble than the past.

Chapter Twenty

As much as they would have liked to spend the day working on the manuscript, Bryn's responsibilities at the manor were many. Simon offered to help and so Bryn gave him a list of things to do. His first job was to deliver a sack of flour to Agnes. Bryn was concerned that Agnes' stores were getting low. Although the cottage was not terribly far from the manor house, the sack of flour seemed to grow heavier with each step. Simon finally managed to push open the gate to Agnes' front yard and deposit the sack on the table. She was pitifully grateful for it, and Simon was forced once more to listen to endless praises of the saintliness of Bryn.

"Always thinking of others she is," Agnes went on. "Such a dear."

"Yes, right. Well I'll be going now Agnes. Got a lot of work to do today."

"Oh, of course dear! How selfish of me to go on and on. It's just so few people come by to talk with me you know." She put down a woven reed basket full of flowers on the table. Simon suddenly felt very guilty. This woman had been kind to him. She fed him and gave him a place to sleep. All she wanted was some company.

"Those are beautiful flowers," he said looking at the basket she'd just brought in.

"Aren't they lovely!" Agnes was once again animated. "These are thornapples, sometimes called Devil's Weed." She picked up a few stalks of the pink and white flower and held them out to him.

"Just smell them. They have a unique scent." Simon bent over to smell the flowers. Their stalks were thin and prickly, the flowers small and bright pink and white. But the smell was strong and very distinct.

"I use them for calming the heart," she said. "Oh, I don't mean for someone who is love sick, I have other plants for that. I mean for when old Gilbert's heart starts to act up after too much work in the fields. It works a treat to calm it down. But they are also lovely, aren't they? I was just going to take some up to the manor house. Perhaps you can bring them for me?"

"Of course I will." Simon picked up the basket. "And I'll bring your compliments to Bryn."

"Thank you dear. Now, I'd better start my bread dough."

Simon thanked her and started back up the hill to the manor. He delivered the thornapple to a servant in the kitchen and then went out again, heading to the blacksmith's shop. Bryn had asked him to have Edwin, the smith, make a key for her.

Simon heard the blacksmith before he saw him. The rhythmic clang and ping of a heavy hammer on hot metal rang out across the long open yard between the house and the smithy. As Simon approached the shed, he saw a young man with knee length leggings covered by a heavy leather apron. In one hand he held a short-handled sledge hammer, in the other a pair of tongs that were buried in red hot coals. Simon watched while he waited for the blacksmith to acknowledge his presence. The smith, Edwin, glanced over and nodded at Simon but continued his work. He pulled the tongs out of the fire and Simon saw they held a glowing piece of metal. With practiced, economical strokes, the smith brought the hammer down again and again on the metal, twisting it with the tongs as he moved the hammer up and down the slowly cooling iron. Simon saw it begin to form itself into a graceful curve ending in an leaf shape. The smith dipped it into a wooden bucket of water at his feet. The iron hissed like an angry snake and steam rose up around the smith's shoulders. He took it out, looked carefully at the piece, nodded his satisfaction and laid it down on the battered and burn-marked table behind him. Then he brushed off his hands and apron and turned to Simon.

"What is that?" Simon asked. He was fascinated with the process.

"That?" The smith sniffed. "New hinge for the stable door. That's what most of my work is like when Sir Robert is gone. When he's here, I work on armor or weapons, that's when I can use my skill."

"Weapons? You mean, like swords?" Simon recalled reading Ivanhoe in English class. He wished he could talk about this "field trip" in class when he returned. But his interest was more than purely academic. His uncle had let him take fencing classes at the local youth bureau and he had faithfully gone every Wednesday night to class. He felt considerable pride in his abilities. His uncle even suggested that he might earn a scholarship to college someday on a collegiate fencing team.

Edwin smiled. He was not all that much older than Simon but he had obviously been working as a smith for some time. His upper body and arms showed strong muscles developed from years of swinging a hammer and working with iron.

"Yes, swords and shields and chain mail. That is the most time consuming." Edwin sat on a short, three-legged stool and wiped the sweat from his face with a dirty cloth. "But my guess is you have something less challenging for me today?"

"Oh. Right." Simon held out a piece of paper upon which Bryn had traced the outline of two keys. "Bryn asked me to give you this, and ask if you could reproduce it for her. She says they are keys that she would like a copy of, in case the originals are lost."

Edwin took the paper and looked at it.

"Well, it doesn't look too difficult. The problem is the size and thickness. We have to assume the key itself is slightly smaller than this outline, and I don't know how thick it might be. Why doesn't she just give me the original keys and I can much more easily make copies for her?"

"I don't know actually, she didn't say. Should I return and ask her for it?"

"Oh, never mind, just leave that with me and I'll see what I can do."

"Thanks." Simon put the paper on the table. "Do you mind if I look around a bit?"

Edwin looked at Simon oddly. "No, go right ahead."

"Great," Simon thought to himself. "I should have a camera and a Hawaiian shirt and name tag that reads 'Hi! My name is *tourist from 900 years in the future*.' What an idiot I am!" Still, it was hard not to be excited. He saw hanging neatly from pegs on the walls several broad swords, maces and shields. Edwin wasn't just bragging when he talked about using his skill. He obviously knew his job and did it well. Simon walked up and gingerly touched a broad, heavy sword that hung from two pegs, the cross-shaped handle holding it securely.

"Sir Robert was a Crusader," Edwin said behind him. "My father spent months preparing his armor and weapons. That's how I learned my trade. That one there was used in the siege of Damascus with King Louis VII."

Simon could hardly contain himself. "Can I…" He stopped. Of course he couldn't hold it. What was he thinking?

Edwin walked over and gently took the sword down from the wall. It was beautiful but obviously well-used. He handed it to Simon. Simon took the sword with his right hand, but quickly grabbed it with his left also, unprepared for its weight. He used a thin, flexible foil in his fencing class. This broad, flat sword was used more to hack and cleave than to stab or impale. This was nothing like what he was used to.

"Bryn tells me you are here to help write the Montbury family history?" Edwin asked.

"What?" Simon brought his mind back from his fantasy of using this sword on horseback. "Oh, yes, that's right. I, um, I have some training in reading and writing."

"Hmmm," Edwin nodded. This perhaps explained Simon's fascination with Edwin's work. "The poor kid has probably been raised in a monastery and never seen the real world." Edwin thought to himself.

"Edwin," Simon said tentatively.

"Yes?" Edwin put down the hammer he had just picked up again and turned back to Simon.

"Have you ever…I mean, do you think…"

Edwin raised an eyebrow in question.

"I heard a while ago about a new kind of sword." Simon wondered why he was doing this. "It's very different from this. It is very thin and flexible, very light."

"What good would that be? Swords are used for fighting men, not swatting at flies," Edwin said scornfully.

"Yes, but this sword is…I mean I've heard that it has many advantages over the broad sword. It is light and fast and easy to wield. It is meant to puncture and impale rather than to hack and cleave."

"For a monk, you've got some strange ideas," Edwin laughed. "Here, show me what this twig would look like." He pointed to the dirt floor. Simon quickly sketched a foil in the dirt with his finger. Edwin looked at the drawing thoughtfully for minute, hand on his chin. He asked Simon several questions about the foil. How long was it, what did it weigh, what shape was the blade? Was it stiff or flexible? Simon answered as best he could.

"Interesting," Edwin said. "Now, tell Mistress Berengar I'll have the keys for her tomorrow, but she might have to bring them back if they don't work until we can get the width exactly right."

Simon thanked Edwin, feeling he had made a friend, or at least not completely made a fool of himself and that was all he asked for right now.

The next several days were busy for both Bryn and Simon. Jasper supervised most of the agricultural workings of the manor, that were considerable, especially at this time of year when the fields were planted. But Bryn was in charge of the domestic household, the manor house and outbuildings and ironing out problems or concerns with Sir Robert's tenants. As they sat at supper after a particularly busy day, Bryn told Simon they were returning to the monastery the next day.

"Are we going back to the library?" Simon asked.

"I hope so, but first I need to obtain some more parchment for the Montbury history. I have made arrangements for us to meet with Brother Mark who is responsible for making all the parchment that is needed in the scriptorium. The scribes, once they have a finished piece of parchment, cut it to size for the book they are making. I have been fortunate to be able to get many of those scrap pieces to use for household needs, and my own small projects. But I am running out of the larger sheets that I use for Sir Robert's genealogy."

They left early the next morning. Simon had taken every opportunity to ride Alizay and was feeling much more confident, and much less sore, while riding. His newly developed horsemanship made the trip to the monastery faster. The porter monk, now familiar with Bryn and Simon, let them in without question and took their mounts to the stable. Bryn led Simon away from the central courtyard of the monastery to a shed built up against the thick stone walls that surrounded the compound. As they approached, Simon noticed a faint odor and felt his eyes start to sting. Bryn explained.

"Brother Mark makes parchment for the scriptorium here. It is a long process that requires the use of lime. In strong concentrations, it does have a smell and can burn your skin and eyes."

As they approached, Simon noticed several large, wooden barrels full of liquid. Surrounding the shed, like a fence, were many racks with animal skins stretched tightly over them

"Welcome!" Brother Mark called to them as he came out of the shed. His robes were girded up between his legs and his long sleeves pulled up above his arms. His hair had once been red, Simon guessed from the scant ring that encircled his head. He obviously enjoyed a very un-monk-like appetite given his size. His cheeks were as red as his hair, from exposure to wind and sun.

Bryn introduced Simon and explained that they needed some parchment for Sir Robert.

"Well, you picked a good time. The planting season is taking most of the monks away from their normal duties so work in the scriptorium has slowed." Brother Mark saw that Simon had wandered away to look into one of the barrels.

"Have you ever seen the process for making parchment?" he asked Simon.

"No, I haven't. What is in these barrels?"

Standing behind Brother Mark, Bryn heaved a sigh and sat down on an upturned barrel. She should have warned Simon that Brother Mark, often alone out here with animal skins and smelly chemicals, loved the opportunity to talk to someone about his art. She tilted back against the shed wall, closed her eyes in the warm sun and settled in for a long wait.

Brother Mark put his arm around Simon's shoulder and guided him toward the back of the shed. There Simon was struck by another unpleasant smell and an even more unpleasant sight. A dead sheep lay on the ground, obviously in the process of being skinned. The white fleece was stained red, and pink flesh showed where some of the skin had already been removed. Simon took a step backward and covered his mouth and nose with his hand.

"You get used to it eventually," Mark explained. "We don't slaughter healthy sheep. That would be a waste, but culled sheep, that will die soon anyway, are killed and brought to me."

They walked past the carcass and toward some more barrels holding fleeces in liquid.

"Making parchment is an art, you know," Brother Mark began. "Of course, the thing people see when they look at a book is the beautiful text and illustrations. It doesn't occur to them that none of that would be possible without a perfect sheet of parchment." He looked inquiringly at Simon.

"Have you ever read *Schedula diversarium atrium?*"
Simon shook his head. "It's a wonderful book written about fifty
years ago by a Benedictine monk named Theophilus Presbyter.
He very carefully explains all the steps in making parchment. I
used his instructions when I was first assigned this duty by the
abbot. I can tell you it took many months of practice until I got a
useable parchment, and even then the monks complained." He
smiled and led Simon closer to the barrels. "But they don't
complain anymore," he said proudly.

"The first step, you see, is to remove the skin from the
animal—sheep or goat is best—and soak it for two days in water.
You need to change the water several times until it remains
clear." Brother Mark stirred one of the barrels and Simon saw a
large fleece slowly revolve in a red-stained bath.

"Once it is clean, you then put it into another barrel with
lime and water." They moved several meters further along to a
line of four barrels. The fleece in these barrels floated in a cloudy
white liquid.

"Past days, people used urine instead of lime." Brother
Mark laughed and slapped Simon on the back. "Glad we don't do
that anymore!"

"What does the lime do?" Simon asked, leaning over one
of the barrels. He grabbed hold of a long wooden pole that stuck
out of the barrel and slowly stirred the contents. It took both
hands to be able to move the heavy, wet fleece in the liquid.

"It makes it easier to remove all the hair from the skins.
Don't get that on your hands now or you'll feel it!" Simon let go
of the pole and followed Brother Mark around to the far side of
the shed.

"The skins stay in the lime bath for eight days, of course I
have to stir them several times a day. If you leave them in too
long, they will fall apart. Now, these barrels here are to rinse the
skins off. Then we put them in for a second lime bath, another
eight days." Simon noticed Brother Mark's hands were reddened
and the skin was cracked. He thought of all the time his hands
must be exposed to that caustic liquid.

"Got to keep an eye on them of course," Brother Mark continued, walking to the next station. "If they stay in too long, they will be too weak to be stretched."

As they neared the front of the shed, where they had begun, Simon noticed the racks with skins stretched tightly over them.

"Once the skins are rinsed well with water, you need to remove all the hair from them." Brother Mark reached into the shed and brought out an evil-looking, curved knife.

"This tool is used to scrape off all the fleece or hair until the skin is smooth." Brother Mark pointed to the racks of stretched skins. "Then I lace them onto these racks and pull them tight. I let them dry for two days, then moisten them with water and use this." Brother Mark reached into a wooden bowl and brought out a handful of what looked like dark, grainy sand. "This is pumice stone. I rub the skin with this to smooth it out while it is drying. Finally, and this is what makes them ready for the scribes, I rub a mixture of flour, egg whites and milk into the skins. It polishes them to a beautiful sheen." Brother Mark finished.

"What an amazing amount of work!" Simon said in admiration. "And these finished parchments are beautiful! It almost seems a shame to cover them with writing."

"You know, I feel the same way myself. All those black chicken scratchings all over my beautiful smooth white parchment! If it weren't the word of God, I think I should keep those scribes, rubricators, and miniators away from my works of art!"

Bryn had come up behind them at this last remark.

"Rubricators and miniators add all the flourishes and artwork to the text already written by the scribes," she explained to Simon. "Well, Brother Mark, do you have anything for me?"

Brother Mark looked questioningly at Bryn and then remembered why they were there.

"Oh! Of course!" He walked back into the shed and brought out a roll of parchment wrapped and tied in a wool cloth. "Take care of that, now." he said, handing it over gently.

"We will, and thank you so much. Ummm, do you happen to know if Brother Felix is around? He was going to let us into the library to do some research."

"Was he now? He must have forgotten. The prior sent him to Durham to pick up a manuscript loaned to us. You'll have to come back later." Brother Mark bid them goodbye and turned back to his animal skins.

Bryn seemed quiet and thoughtful as they headed back across the courtyard. Simon thought she must have been very disappointed by Brother Felix's absence. They would have to come back another day to get into the library. Bryn stopped by the stables where their horses were waiting for them. She looked around.

"It's very quiet," she stated simply.

Simon stopped and listened. "Yes, I wonder where everyone is"

Bryn looked at him. "Everyone is in the fields. The next few weeks will take most of the monks away from their usual jobs to help plant the crops." Simon said nothing. Bryn seemed tense or perhaps excited.

"Simon. This is our chance." She grabbed Simon by his sleeve and pulled him quickly into the stables. Here she carefully tied the roll of parchment to the saddle and then turned to him and whispered. He was already worried about what "our chance" might be and was pretty sure it was not going to be good news.

"We need to get back into that library to see if there are any more puzzles or messages. Brother Felix never lets me look at the books on my own, and is very particular about what books I look at. He's not here! All the other monks will be in the fields until Vespers, we need to get in there now."

"How can we do that? The door is locked," he asked, fearing her answer.

Bryn slowly smiled and brought out two iron keys from inside her tunic.

"Where did you get those?" Simon had a hard time keeping his voice to a whisper.

"Do you remember I told you how the young monk had to help me in the library when Brother Felix had pneumonia?" Simon nodded. He should have guessed. "Well, the second time I came back, I brought him some wine to thank him for all his help. Between the fact that he doesn't get much wine as good as Sir Robert's, and, well, umm, the fact that Agnes helped me put some poppy juice in it, I managed to borrow the ring of keys while he snored in a chair in the corner and trace their outlines on a scrap of parchment."

"You didn't!" Simon was appalled. "That was what you had me give to Edwin the blacksmith to copy."

"Yes," she said smugly. "So now you are as guilty as I am and can't back out."

Simon thought this was rather faulty logic but wasn't about to let her go in there alone.

"We have to hurry, we don't have a lot of time."

They both walked casually across the courtyard, in case they were being observed, and then ducked into the tower door and climbed the stairs. When they got to the scriptorium, Bryn was about to push open the door when Simon stopped her.

"Wait," he said, reaching into the small fabric sack that hung from his belt. Agnes had given him this to carry his lunch. He pulled out a small piece of cheese and squished it in his fist. Bryn looked strangely at him.

"For heaven's sake, Simon. We can eat when we finish here."

Simon shot her a look and then opened his hand, now covered in a buttery oil. He rubbed the large hinges of the door with the palms of his hands, transferring the oil to the hinges. He slowly tried the door. It opened easily and silently.

Bryn's face broke into a large smile and pushed the door the rest of the way, first peeking around the edge to make sure the scriptorium was empty. They both walked into the cavernous room, their footsteps making a muffled echo off the stone walls. The sunlight streamed through the windows but there was no one in sight. They quickly moved to the door in the far wall that opened into the library.

Once there, Simon stood behind Bryn, his back to her while she bent over the locks to try the keys. He could hear the scraping of the keys in the locks and a rattle as she tried to turn them.

"God's bones!" Bryn muttered under her breath. "They won't turn. They seem stuck."

"I told you Edwin said he needed to know how thick to make them," Simon hissed. The sweat was beginning to trickle down his back and he wondered how Bryn had ever talked him into this.

"Wait! I think I've got it." Simon heard the door creak and he turned just as Bryn was squeezing through. "Come on, we're in!" she called to him in a whisper. He took one last look at the empty scriptorium and then turned and went through the library door.

Chapter Twenty One

Moira was back at her table in her museum office. She hadn't slept well the night before and her eyes felt gritty, her brain fuzzy. She had awakened several times during the night with her mind buzzing with thoughts about Simon and the palimpsest. This often happened when she was working on a puzzle or mystery. She had read somewhere that the brain worked best when asleep but she could never remember what it was she had figured out when she awoke. This led her to experiment once by leaving a pencil and notebook by her bed. She remembered she had been trying to work out a Hittite tablet that said something about the Battle of Kadesh. She was sure that if she wrote down what came to her in the middle of night, when her brain was unconsciously working on the puzzle, she would have the answer in the morning. So when she awoke with a stroke of brilliance at 3:00 in the morning, she forced herself to write down her thoughts. Then she fell back on her pillow, pleased that she had caught her inspiration on paper. The next morning she woke up and, rubbing her eyes, quickly grabbed the notebook to see what now-forgotten piece of inspiration had occurred to her during the night.

"*Peel the banana from the bottom,*" it read. So much for midnight inspiration.

She felt just as uninspired this morning. She pulled out her black journal now filled with notes about Henry and Eleanor and Thomas Becket.

"OK, let's review what we know." She pulled up a stool to the table and spread out her notes in front of her, her ever-present steaming cup of chamomile tea within arm's reach.

"Henry is accused of wanting Thomas dead. His sons and his wife have fomented a rebellion against him. The people are sympathetic to Thomas, who is soon made into a saint. Henry decides to make a pilgrimage to Thomas' tomb in hopes of gaining back the people's favor." She flipped through a few more pages of notes. "So then what happens? Well, Henry puts down his sons' rebellion and locks up Eleanor in Winchester Castle for the next 15 years. She essentially becomes a prisoner although she does sometimes move from one castle to another."

Moira took a drink of tea, and stared at the shafts of sunlight coming through the window. "So what?" She pushed her notes away and pulled the palimpsest towards her.

"Come on, Moira, this is not so difficult," she chided herself and stared at the palimpsest. "Don't think, just let everything you've read marinate in your brain for a bit." Still she stared at the palimpsest as if wishing it to tell her its secret.

It was frustrating to have so much of it be illegible. Suddenly she sat up with a quick intake of breath. "What a fool! What have I been thinking?" She grabbed her leather satchel from the floor and dumped it upside down on the table. A myriad of objects fell out and rolled across the table or slid to the floor but Moira found what she was looking for—the photograph Simon had taken of the palimpsest just before he disappeared.

It was as she remembered it, a jagged bright white line cutting the photograph in two. The top diagonal was an image of the faded palimpsest, but the bottom diagonal showed the image of the object as it was when it was first created. When she first saw the picture, she was only struck by its significance as the "prompt" that had pulled Simon into the past. She hadn't taken any time to look closely at it. Now, she saw the lower corner of the picture was filled with clearly written Latin text, as if newly inscribed, as indeed it was. The words that were now faded into illegibility by time were clear and readable in the photograph.

Moira pulled it close, drew the long-armed desk lamp down over the photo and took out a magnifying glass from the table drawer.

"*Mitte*—send, *Liber*—book, *missi errant*—they have been sent." Moira murmured to herself as she quickly wrote down her translation of the partial message in the photograph. She finally sat back and let out a long breath. She picked up her paper and read what she had written.

"*…send the book! I have returned the others, they have been sent to… put them in a…only way to communicate…get message to…*" Moira found one more readable word, or at least part of a word, in the very corner of the manuscript. "*Aliénor.*" Was it possible? Alienor, Countess of Poitou, Duchess of Gascony and Aquitaine, in fact, Queen Eleanor.

A knock on the door startled her.

"Come in," she called, hiding her irritation. The door opened and Moira smiled to see Jenny from the café upstairs.

"Good morning Professor Ananke," Jenny said shyly.

"Hello, Jenny!" Moira pushed back her stool and waved Jenny in. She liked this young, hard-working woman. "What can I do for you?"

"I don't know if you remember, but last week I mentioned that I would be out for a few weeks." Jenny saw the blank expression on Professor Ananke's face. "Knee surgery? I have to have my knee operated on."

"Oh! Yes! I remember." Moira vaguely recalled the conversation but as usual, her mind was on something 500 years in the past and she wasn't paying much attention.

"You said you would recommend some books that I could read while I was laid up. I will be so bored having to stay housebound for several weeks."

"Yes, yes of course." Moira had indeed offered to put together some reading materials for Jenny. In fact, she remembered she had placed a pile of books on her desk for her. She walked around several boxes and stacks of papers on the floor to her desk. Reaching over the clutter, she grabbed the books and handed them to Jenny.

"I think you'll like these. Lots of Barbara Tuchman histories. She is easy to read and really makes history accessible to people."

"Thank you so much! I'll be sure to return them when I come back to work."

"No hurry. I hope all goes well." Moira smiled and closed the door behind Jenny as she left. She turned back to survey her office, sighed, and sat back down at the table.

Her thoughts still on Jenny she said, "I can imagine Eleanor must have gone stir crazy too, a virtual prisoner for 15 years. Especially given her ambitious and active personality. No doubt she requested a lot of books to keep her from being bored to death all those years. Is that all this is? A request for books to be sent to her while she was imprisoned by her own husband?" But it seemed to be more than that. There seemed to be an urgency to her words.

"Let's put them together with the other part of the manuscript. What did we figure out there?" She flipped back in her notes to where she and Simon had first worked on the palimpsest.

"It seems to have originally said something about killing an enemy. Those words are written with male endings. But then it has been changed to female endings, indicating it is a female, not a male involved." She silently re-read her notes from days before.

"*Caedere*. To kill, or murder or slaughter. It is crossed out and changed to *necare*. *Clades* meaning pest or bane---crossed out and above it written *inimicus*. What are the possible meanings of this?"

Moira wrote several Latin sentences in her journal, all versions of the same things, substituting different words each time. "Is this just too far fetched?" she quietly asked herself as she picked up her journal and stared at it.

"The original could have been something indicating a 'pest or problem that needs to be subdued or put down.' But if you change the words slightly, and substitute words that are similar but have a stronger meaning, you end up with a command to 'kill an enemy.' Someone took a rather mild message about getting rid of a pest, using male word endings, and changed it to mean, 'kill an enemy' using female word endings. And all of this is somehow connected with Eleanor." Moira stood up and walked in a small circle around jumbled towers of books on the floor. She needed to get the blood flowing again.

"There is really only one 'pest' I can think of that is tied to Eleanor and Henry. Only one 'enemy,' only one 'murder.' Thomas Becket."

Chapter Twenty Two

The quiet inside the library seemed as thick as a velvet cloak. They both stood still for a moment, unsure of what to do next. Then Bryn walked to the far side of the room where a large chest sat apart from all the others.

"I was waiting for Brother Felix once while one of the amarii asked him a question." Bryn noted Simon's blank look. "The amarii are the monks that supervise the scriptorium. They make all the assignments, who will do what. They give out materials and oversee all the work. Anyway, while they were talking I just wandered over here out of curiosity. When Brother Felix saw me he was furious! He yelled for me to come back immediately. I always wondered what was over here that I was not supposed to see."

They got down on their knees and examined the trunk. It was in a corner encased in shadows.

"Wait," Bryn whispered. "I have a candle stub." She took out a candle and a flint. Simon was impressed with how quickly she was able to strike a flame. He had traumatic memories of being the only boy at camp that couldn't get a fire striker to work. The small flame illuminated the ornate trunk.

"Try these." Bryn handed him several small bent pieces of metal.

"Don't tell me these are lock picks!" Simon looked at her in alarm.

"I saw Brother Felix use these on the other trunks. Edwin told me that a set like this can be used to open nearly any small lock like this."

Simon stared at her for a moment.

"Sometimes you really scare me, do you know that?"

She smiled and nodded toward the trunk, holding the candle near the lock. Simon spent several minutes trying the different sized picks until he heard a click and the heavy lock fell open. It worried him a little that he felt more satisfaction than guilt.

He slowly opened the heavy lid. For the size of the trunk, there were very few books inside. They looked like they hadn't been touched in many years. They were covered with a cloth that in turn seemed to be thickly covered with a greenish gray dust. Simon picked up the cloth and sneezed and coughed as the particles flew off the cloth into the air around him.

"Shhhh!" Bryn cautioned.

He gave her an annoyed look and picked up one of the books. He wasn't sure what he was expecting, but he felt very disappointed as he looked at the title. It appeared to be a book of poetry and stories of knightly chivalry. They looked at each other in bewilderment. Simon put the book down and picked up another one. This was a history of the Duchy of Aquitaine. Simon sneezed again. He felt his eyes and ears covered in the dust from the trunk. He rubbed his eyes but the dust on his hands only made it worse. Bryn nudged him to continue. There were four more books. All of them seemed quite normal and boring.

"It must not be the books themselves, there must be something inside them." Suddenly they heard the muffled sound of a church bell ringing. Bryn started, the candle sputtered as she quickly stood up.

"Vespers!" she said. "They'll all be coming back for prayers."

They both jumped up and shut the chest, quickly exiting through the door. Bryn carefully closed the door. The key seemed to turn more easily now, Simon guessed it had worn down to fit better. They tiptoed as quickly as possible across the scriptorium and down the stairs. As they reached the outside door they saw a line of monks carrying rakes and hoes coming across the courtyard. Simon grabbed for Bryn, forcing her to slow down and walk casually across the yard to the stables. There they mounted their horses and were let out by the porter.

Neither said anything until they were about a mile from the monastery. Bryn then looked sideways at Simon and both started to laugh in relief. Suddenly Simon pulled up, sitting up straight, his eyes round.

"What's the matter with you?" she said, stopping her horse alongside his. "You look like you've swallowed a frog."

Simon slowly turned toward her. "Bryn, do you have the lock picks?" he asked.

"No, you had them, remember?" Then her face turned white. "Simon, you're not telling me…"

"We left them in the trunk. They are still stuck in the lock of the trunk."

Neither of them felt like laughing anymore.

"We have to go back!" Bryn said, turning her horse.

"Don't be crazy!" Simon grabbed her reins. "We couldn't possibly go back now, who would let us into the library and what excuse would we use for returning?

Bryn said nothing for a moment, deep in thought.

"No one saw us go in, or come out. The porter knows we were with Brother Mark, far away from the library." She looked up at Simon. "It might be days or even weeks before anyone notices, and they might even fall out of the lock by then. Even if they do notice them, they won't think of us." She looked at Simon hopefully. "Right?"

"It doesn't really matter since we can't do anything about it," Simon said. "I think we just need to go on as if we know nothing." They turned their horses toward home and rode in silence for many miles, both deep in thought.

Simon felt a headache come on, a sharp pain in his right temple. He tried to take a deep breath and relax, despite his worries about the library. He realized they had not stopped to eat the lunches Agnes had prepared for them. This must be the cause of the pain he was beginning to feel in his stomach. But somehow the thought of food made him feel nauseous. He shook his head, sat up straighter on the horse and forced himself to think. Bryn was riding a few yards ahead of him and he could tell she too, was still worrying about the lock picks stuck in the chest. She turned her head and called back to him.

"Let's ride on until we come to the river. We can stop there to rest the horses and eat."

Simon didn't answer. He was beginning to worry now about his head and stomach. Both were getting worse. He could feel his pulse beating in his head and with each beat an increasing, searing pain. He put his hand up to his temple to press against his head. His stomach sharply cramped and he bent over in pain. He must have called out because Bryn suddenly stopped and turned.

"Simon!" she said, trotting up beside him. "What ever is wrong?"

Simon looked at her but could not seem to focus his eyes. The pains in his head and abdomen were increasing. His face felt hot and his heart seemed to pound against his chest. He could hear it beating loudly in his ears. He opened his mouth to say something to Bryn but couldn't seem to put any words together. As she stared at him, her eyes worried and scared, he slumped unconscious onto Alizay's arched neck.

It was dusk by the time the two horses plodded back into manor lands. Thankfully, Agnes' cottage was nearest the woods, the first one on the road leading into the village. Bryn nearly cried with relief when she saw it. The last four hours had been a nightmare. She had tried to revive Simon, calling to him, shaking him, but nothing would waken him. He was breathing shallowly and erratically and his face was pale. What worried her most was the blue tinge to his lips. Fortunately, Alizay had stood patiently

111

during this ordeal and Bryn took the long shawl she sometimes wore as a headscarf and tied it around Simon's waist to the saddle pommel. This kept him somewhat secured on the horse and she mounted her own palfrey, took Alizay's reins, and headed the horses home. They had to move slowly to keep Simon from falling off the horse and Bryn would look back every few minutes to make sure he was still breathing. Twice she heard him seem to gasp for breath and felt her own heart stop, but after a moment, he continued his ragged breathing.

Bryn tied the horses to the gates and ran up the path, banging on Agnes' door.

"Agnes!" She called, her voice shaking with fear and exhaustion. "Agnes, open the door."

The front door immediately opened and Agnes' face changed quickly from a welcoming smile to concern.

"Oh, my dear! What ever is wrong?" She looked over Bryn's shoulder and saw Simon slumped on Alizay's back. "God help us!" Agnes pushed past Bryn and trotted to the horse.

"Come now, help me get him inside," Agnes called to Bryn who came over. The two managed to pull Simon off the horse and together they carried him into the cottage. They laid him on the pallet on the floor. In the darkening room, Bryn could not see if he was breathing. She stepped back while Agnes immediately went to work, looking him over carefully, putting her hand on his chest, then bending her head to place her ear on his chest. She looked toward Bryn with a deep frown on her face.

"Where in heaven's name have you two been?" She asked Bryn. "What has happened?"

"I...I don't know. One minute he was fine, just riding behind me. The next he was slumped over and hardly breathing. Oh Agnes!" the tears had started to course down Bryn's face.

"Stop it, now! I'll need your help." Bryn was startled to hear this from Agnes, who usually seemed so muddle-headed and self-effacing. Now she took charge with a calm authority.

"I'm sorry. Of course. What do you need me to do?" Bryn asked, wiping her tears with the back of her hand.

"Run out to my garden. Along the back fence are some flowers growing, pink and white. They have thin, bristly stems..."

"Yes! I know. You mean the Devil's Weed." Bryn was already turning to go.

"Bring me a basket full, and hurry. I will start some water to boil on the fire." Agnes pushed herself up from the ground where she knelt next to Simon. Bryn was already out the door, a reed basket hanging off her arm. It was nearly too dark to see but she knew where Agnes grew the Devil's Weed, or thornapple as it was sometimes called. The white blossoms seemed to glow in the darkening garden.

Agnes poured water from the wooden bucket on the floor into a blackened iron cauldron and hung it on a hook over the small fire that glowed on the stone hearth. She was worried. She had seen this once before when a child from the village had accidentally eaten some Monk's Hood. It was a dangerous plant, both to humans and to animals. Used correctly, it could work to stimulate the heart, but in the wrong dosage, it would kill. Agnes had seen the bluish tinge to Simon's lips, a sure sign his heart was struggling. She didn't like his erratic breathing either. Somehow, she knew, Simon had ingested Monk's Hood. She hoped the thornapple would do its job, and set his heart aright.

Bryn came running back in, Agnes could see she had been crying again but she was in control and waiting for instructions.

"Put them on the table and use that knife to cut them up into small pieces. It's always better to make an elixir by steeping them whole in the water for several days, but we don't have time for that."

Bryn had already laid out the spindly stalks and was using the knife to cut them into pieces. Agnes swept them all from the table into her apron and dropped them into the now boiling water. She stirred the mixture every few minutes, taking out a spoonful of liquid and carrying it over to the candle on the table to check the color.

Suddenly they heard long, rasping gasp from the other room. Bryn looked in terror at Agnes and then toward the door of the room where Simon lay. Her feet were stone. She couldn't get them to move. Agnes put the spoon down and hurried into the room. Simon was deathly pale, his chest was heaving as he tried to get air, his eyelids, just barely opened, showed only the whites of his eyes.

"God save us." Agnes made the sign of the cross and quickly returned to the fire, pouring out some of the liquid into a wooden bowl.

"Is he…." Bryn couldn't finish the sentence.

"No, but he will be soon if we don't get this into him. Come, there is no time." She pushed past Bryn who followed behind her. Bryn knelt by the pallet, cradling Simon's head in her lap while Agnes dribbled the liquid between his lips. It was terribly hot but that couldn't be helped. Simon flinched but made no other movement.

"Turn his head a bit to the side, we don't want to choke him," Agnes instructed.

Bryn held Simon's head in her hands, tilting it just to the side so that the liquid could drain down his throat. After several minutes, the bowl was empty.

"We just have to wait now, dear. Let's cover him and let him rest. He's in God's hands now."

Agnes had to lift Bryn from the floor. They walked, arms around each other's shoulders, into the other room and sat at the table.

For several moments neither said anything. Then Agnes got up and brought some bread and cider and set it down in front of Bryn.

"Eat," she ordered. "You are exhausted and you will need your strength. This isn't over yet."

Bryn stared at the food in front of her, not seeing it.

"I just don't understand." She looked up at Agnes. "What happened? How did this happen?" she echoed Agnes' questions of before.

"I don't know how it happened but I know what happened," Agnes said. "He's been poisoned with Monk's Hood."

Bryn gasped and stared at Agnes unbelieving.

"That's impossible!" she said. "He's been with me the whole time. No one gave us anything to eat or drink, we didn't even have time to eat the lunches you made us. How is this possible?"

Agnes thought for a moment. "It could have been an accident. Did you stop anywhere to rest? Did you pick herbs or flowers along the way?"

"No, nothing like that at all!" Bryn answered.

"Tell me everything you did today."

Bryn looked at Agnes, trying to decide how much to tell her. She had always cared deeply for this woman who, when Bryn was young, had cared for her like a mother. As they both got older, Bryn had taken over the care of Agnes. But tonight she had seen a different side to Agnes. Perhaps she had underestimated her abilities. After all, it was Agnes to whom Bryn had run when she needed help for Simon. Agnes waited patiently for her reply. Bryn took a deep breath and began.

"Well, we rode out to the monastery this morning. I needed to see Brother Mark to get more parchment. When we got there, Brother Mark took Simon all around his shed, showing him how parchment was made."

"Wait," Agnes stopped her. "Did you see any tall, leafy plants with blue or purple flowers on top? Would he use something like that in making the parchment?"

Bryn closed her eyes and thought. "No, no I don't think so. He had barrels of lime but I don't remember seeing any kind of herb or plant at all."

Agnes indicated that Bryn should continue. Bryn looked down at her hands and then went on.

115

"We went into the library." She looked up at Agnes who was listening carefully, her face lined and worn, her eyes tired. Bryn knew she had to trust her.

"We weren't supposed to be there, Agnes. I, well, I managed to get some copies of the keys and Simon and I snuck inside and we looked through a chest trying to find...something." Agnes said nothing.

"We were trying to find some messages written in the margins of manuscripts or on scraps of parchment-----oh, why does any of this matter? There were no plants anywhere near us. We didn't eat or drink anything there was noth..." Bryn suddenly stopped and sat up straight.

"Yes?" Agnes asked anxiously.

"Agnes, when Simon was lifting the books out of the chest, he brushed away a lot of greenish gray dust. It was everywhere inside the trunk. It made him sneeze and cough and his eyes run. But, why would there be dust inside a locked trunk?"

Agnes looked at Bryn but said nothing. Then she got up and walked to a crude wooden cabinet against the wall. She opened the door and Bryn saw her push several pots and jars to one side and reach toward the back of the shelf. Agnes brought out a small clay jar with a cork in the lid. She walked over to the table and shook a small amount of a grey-green substance out onto the table.

"Did it look like that?" Agnes asked Bryn in a quiet voice.

"Yes!" Bryn leaned in for a closer look but Agnes stopped her, holding up a hand. "Don't get too close, you don't want to breath this in."

"What is it?" Bryn asked

"It's powdered Monk's Hood, but this is specially prepared, boiled with ginger, to take the poisons out. It works well for heart problems when it is prepared like this. But when it is not treated correctly, it kills."

"Agnes!" Bryn's face was white with horror. "Do you know what this means?" She sat back in silence for a moment as

116

she processed the thought. "Someone deliberately sprinkled powdered Monk's Hood in that chest, so that whoever opened it would be poisoned. What a horrible, evil thing to do!"

"Perhaps whatever it is that you and Simon are investigating is more than just a mystery. Perhaps it is something that someone will kill to keep hidden."

Bryn shivered. It had all been mostly exciting and fun to try to figure out the puzzle. Yet deep down she had to admit that she did feel there was something about it that was important, that drove her on. She had done this to Simon. It was her fault that he lay there now, fighting for his life. She felt her throat tighten and she fought tears once again.

"Agnes, will he be alright?

"I don't know dear. We've done all we can. We will take turns tonight watching."

"You sleep now, Agnes, I couldn't sleep if I tried. I will sit with him and wake you later."

Agnes nodded. She got up slowly and with a small grunt. She looked in to check on Simon. He was quiet, still unconscious, his breathing was ragged but regular and the blue tinge seemed to have left his lips. She nodded and went to her pallet to sleep. Bryn sat at the table staring at nothing for a long time. Finally she rubbed her eyes and walked in to sit on the floor beside Simon's pallet, her head resting against the wall. She fingered the silver figure hanging from the cord around her neck and closed her eyes.

Chapter Twenty Three

Professor Ananke stood just outside the classroom door. The hallway was quiet and dark even though it was midday. Dark oak woodwork and no windows kept the wide hallway dim even during the day. Most of the classroom doors along the wide hall were closed so only a suffused, opaque light came through the mottled glass in the doorways. She jumped as the bell just above her head rang discordantly, announcing the end of class. Immediately the doors in the hallway seemed to open simultaneously and children poured out. The hall was transformed into a noisy stream of young faces and voices. They surged around and past her, oblivious to her presence. She hugged her satchel to her chest as the wave of youth and energy passed, leaving her once again alone in the hall. Moira turned to go into the classroom behind her. As she stepped through the door she saw raised tiers of chairs along curved lines of wooden desks. Most of the desks had carved initials in them, reminding Moira of the cuneiform tablets she often worked with. She turned toward the front of the room and saw him standing behind his desk putting books into a brief case.

"Hello, Owen," she said.

He started and looked up and over his glasses that sat perched at the end of this nose.

"Moira!" he was obviously surprised. "Why, hello! Come in, come in!" He came around from behind the desk and offered his hand. She took it and felt his firm handshake.

"It's been ages it seems like. How have you been?" Owen Caddick seemed to really want to know.

"Oh, you know me, I've been busy with museum work as usual. What about you? How do you like it here?" Moira looked around the classroom.

Owen followed her gaze. "Well, it's different from the library certainly, but it leaves me the summers free to continue my own research and surprisingly, I actually enjoy teaching the little imps. Some of them even have promise," he smiled.

Moira had met Owen many years ago when they both worked in the rare documents division of York University. He was still handsome, she noted. Tall with dark, curly hair as was common among his Welch ancestors. There was some gray in the dark hair now, but then she had found a few gray hairs in her comb just the other day. They'd worked well together, both excited about the same subjects, both passionate about history. In fact, perhaps they had worked too well together. Moira remembered telling him she was leaving the University for a job at a museum in America. He'd been upset. He too, had felt they had a relationship that might develop into romance. He was hurt and upset when she wouldn't tell him why she was leaving. How could she possibly tell him that she kept away from developing romantic relationships? She'd found it too painful to outlive everyone who meant something to her. Keeping isolated was a survival technique. That was a long time ago. A few years ago he had taken a job at this prestigious preparatory school in the States. But this was the first time she had seen him since then. She brought her mind back to her task.

"I have some questions for you Owen. I need your help."

He smiled. "You always did get right to the point. OK, what can I do for you?"

Moira brought out her black journal and opened to a page where she had written several questions.

"I am working on a project for the museum. It has to do with Henry II and Eleanor of Aquitaine. That time period was one of your specialties wasn't it?"

119

"Yes, I did my PhD work on that era. What do you want to know?" he asked, intrigued.

"How much did Thomas Becket's death affect Henry? I mean, how important was it to his reign and authority?"

Owen took his glasses off and polished them on his woolen vest.

"Henry is actually considered one of the greatest kings of England. He was handsome and energetic and brought many needed reforms." He stood up. "Wait, I think I have something that might help." Owen walked over to his desk and poked through a set of books stacked on the corner.

"Ah, yes, here it is." He carried over a book bound with maroon leather and incised with gold lettering. "This is a very good history of England. I think it has a primary source document from Peter of Blois about Henry." He flipped quickly through the pages, finally stopping. He adjusted his glasses and began to read.

" '…the lord king has been red-haired so far, except that the coming of old age and gray hair has altered that color somewhat." Here Owen looked up with a grin. "I guess we all come to that, but let me continue, 'His height is medium, so that neither does he appear great among the small, nor yet does he seem small among the great…curved legs, a horseman's shins, broad chest, and a boxer's arms all announce him as a man strong, agile and bold…he never sits, unless riding a horse or eating…in a single day, if necessary, he can run through four or five day-marches and, thus foiling the plots of his enemies, frequently mocks their plots with surprise sudden arrivals… always are in his hands bow, sword, spear and arrow, unless he be in council or in books.' "

"Sounds rather intimidating," Moira commented.

"He was well liked among those who knew him well. But he also did many good things for England. Under Stephen, who had ruled before him, the nobles had taken upon themselves great power and often flouted the law. Henry brought back curbs to the nobles' powers and abuse of authority. He instated trials by jury and set up magistrate courts throughout England to lessen the load of the Royal courts. He put down rebellions in Scotland and tried, with only limited success, to control the power of the church."

"Yes, that's where Thomas Becket comes in."

"Exactly. Henry always swore that he had nothing to do with the death of Becket. His knights had acted on their own, misinterpreting Henry's anger over Becket's refusal to support his church reforms. There are conflicting reports about what actually was said to set the knights after Becket. Most record that Henry, in exasperation said something to the effect of 'Will no one rid me of this meddlesome priest?' and his knights assumed he wanted Becket killed."

Moira looked thoughtful. "Will no one subdue this pest?" she murmured to herself.

"I beg your pardon?" Owen asked.

"Oh, nothing!" Moira answered, grinning. "I was just thinking of something I'd read recently."

"Well," Owen continued. "Even though Thomas was not particularly liked when alive, he quickly became a saint when he was killed. Edward Grim, who was at Becket's side when he was attacked, told a harrowing and heroic story of Becket's death at the altar of the cathedral, giving his life up for God and the church. Later, when they dressed Becket for burial, they found he wore a hair shirt under his cassock. This of course, was a sign of a very holy man, willing to suffer daily to remind himself of Christ's suffering. That clinched it for Thomas. From then on, everyone considered him a saint."

"So Henry was blamed for his death?"

"Well, yes, at least at first. In fact, in 1174, Henry was faced with a Flemish army attacking by sea and a Scottish army, led by William the Lion, marching on him from the north. Many people, including Henry, saw this as God punishing him for the death of Becket. He made a pilgrimage to Canterbury Cathedral, where Thomas Becket was killed, and things seemed to improve."

"But for a time," Moira said, "it appeared that the murder of Thomas Becket could badly affect his authority as king—even threaten his rule?"

"Oh, yes. I am sure he was quite angry that Becket caused him as much trouble dead as he did alive," Owen smiled.

Moira sat in silence for minute then turned to thank Owen for his help.

"I hope I can return the favor sometime," she said with a smile and held out her hand.

"You can return the favor right now," Owen answered. "Come have lunch with me and we can catch up on each other's lives."

Moira hesitated, looking at Owen's smiling eyes.

"Yes," she decided, "that would be very nice."

Chapter Twenty Four

Simon was drowning. A small part of his brain wondered how he had gotten into this predicament. But by far the majority of his brain was screaming for oxygen. He tried to open his mouth to gasp for air but instead he gulped in great mouthfuls of cloudy-white water. He gasped again, his body convulsing with the desire for air. He must have fallen into Brother Mark's barrel of slaked lime. Heavy, sodden fleeces swirled around him, tangling his arms and legs as he struggled to free himself.

His strength finally failed him and a strong lethargy set in. He floated freely, giving himself up to this strange death. He knew what would happen next. Brother Mark would take him from the barrel and stretch him tightly on the wooden rack. There he would stay for days until the sun baked him and shrank him while the leather strips pulled his skin tighter and tighter. Brother Mark would appear holding his evil-looking curved knife and scrape all the hair from his body. His skin would be polished with pumice stone. He wondered what the monks in the scriptorium would use him for. He wondered what it would feel like to have their sharpened quills draw ink-black words all over his skin. He felt hot liquid in his mouth and it choked and gagged him. But it also seemed to calm his brain and he fell into blackness once more.

"Bryn!" A harsh whisper pulled Bryn back into consciousness. Agnes was bending over her, gently shaking her shoulder. Bryn focused her sleep-heavy eyes on Agnes' worried face. She sat up quickly.

"What? What's wrong?" she asked, fully awake. Agnes had relieved Bryn at Simon's side halfway through the night, and insisted that she lay down in Agnes' own bed to rest. Although Bryn thought she was too worried to sleep, in fact, she fell deeply asleep within minutes of lying down. Now Agnes was shaking her awake.

"Things are not good, dear." Agnes tried to keep her voice calm but the urgency couldn't be disguised. "He has been convulsing. I have tried to hold him still but when his breathing becomes labored, he has thrashed around in the bed, tangling himself in the covers. I have managed to give him some more Devils' Weed and it calms him for a while, but I fear what I have is not strong enough."

"Agnes, what are we to do?" Bryn felt completely helpless and horribly frightened.

"You need to go back to the monastery." Agnes was already handing Bryn her kirtle and shawl. "Brother Galen will have herbs that have been prepared correctly, to the right strength. Tell him we need whatever he has that can work against Monk's Hood. You must hurry."

"I will, Agnes. Eleanor will take me swiftly there and back." She started for the door but turned back. "Agnes, send a message up to the manor to Jasper. Tell him only that Simon is ill and I have gone to the monastery for medicines. Have him send someone to take Alizay home." Agnes nodded and shooed her out the door.

Both horses were content to spend the night in the field behind Agnes' cottage. Alizay looked lazily up at Bryn, new green grass hanging from his soft thick lips. She gave him a quick scratch on the nose as she walked past to saddle and mount Eleanor.

"Dear Eleanor." She leaned over the horse's neck to whisper in its ear. "Live up to your namesake. Be swift and strong and sure-footed." With a click of her tongue and a sharp dig of her heels into Eleanor's flanks, they jumped the low fence and set off at a gallop across the fields and into the still dark wood. The sun was only barely cresting the horizon and had not yet penetrated the thick trees of the forest. But Bryn trusted Eleanor to find her way.

Eleanor must have felt Bryn's tension and worry for she ran without stopping, jumping over fallen limbs and rounding corners in the road so sharply that several times Bryn's knees brushed against the trunks of trees. Bryn lay low against her neck, hanging onto to reins and mane until her fingers felt as if she would never be able to straighten them. She pulled the palfrey to a stop twice, for both of them to catch their breath and get water from the river that crossed over the road or sometimes ran parallel to it. The horse was covered with sweat and Bryn wiped a white froth from its mouth. But every minute that they were not moving forward increased her feeling of urgency. She kept the rest stops brief. Finally, the woods lightened, the trees grew more thinly and the land opened up around them. It was with great relief that Bryn saw the walls of the monastery in front of her. She heard the bells begin to ring and knew that Terce, prayers in the third hour of the day, had begun. She pulled Eleanor up in a skid at the front gate and hammered on the closed wooden window set in the door. For a full minute no one answered and Bryn panicked at the thought they all the monks were in the church for prayers, unable to hear her frantic pounding on the door. But then she heard the grating of an iron bar against wood and the small window opened. The porter's face, sour at this unannounced interruption, peered out.

"Porter, I must get to the infirmary immediately, it is a matter of grave necessity."

The window closed quickly and the door within the great gate swung open. Bryn urged her horse forward, ducking her head as she rode through the door. She quickly dismounted and handed the reins to a young novice who had come to take her mount.

"See that she is well cared for," Bryn commanded as she strode away toward the infirmary. She had never been in the infirmary but she knew it formed the short leg of a large "L" shaped building that also housed the dorter, where the monks slept. It was completely forbidden for her, a woman, to be in this part of the monastery but she took no thought about that. In fact, she pitied the monk who tried to stop her at this moment. Fortunately, most of the monks were already gathered in the chapel for Terce. She could hear their mono-tonal chanting of the morning prayers. The infirmarer, Brother Galen, would likely remain in the infirmary unless there was no one who needed tending. She prayed he would be there because she doubted that even with Sir Robert's protective authority, she would be able to break into the chapel and interrupt prayers.

She found the door to the infirmary at the far end of the long stone building that also housed the dorter. It was not locked but opened onto a narrow flight of stairs. She took the stairs two at a time, cursing her long skirts that twisted round her legs as she went. The stairs ended at a long narrow hall that contained several open doors. For the first time since arriving at the monastery, Bryn hesitated. She knew she was intruding on a very male, very regulated, very cloistered community. She felt uncomfortable walking down this hallway looking into doorways for Brother Galen. Then the thought of Simon's white face and pain-racked body came into her mind and she set off with determination. The first room on the left was the calefactory. This was the only room in the monastery where a fire for warming oneself on cold winter days was allowed. It was cold and empty on this spring morning. The next room seemed to be a storage room, full of clay pots and baskets and cloth bundles on shelves.

Finally she heard soft voices coming from the next room on the right. She quickly turned toward the sound. As she entered the door, she saw a monk standing at a door on the far side of the room. His hand was on the latch, as if ready to close the door, but he was talking softly to someone on the other side. Bryn could not hear or see the other person. The monk nodded and then gently closed and latched the door, and turned back into the room. As he did so he saw Bryn. He started and stopped short, so unused to seeing a female in the monastery. His face clouded over and he frowned at her fiercely.

"Who are you? You should not be here. I must ask you to leave immediately," he said sternly.

"Brother Galen, it is I, Mistress Berengar from Lord Montbury's Manor." Bryn hoped he would remember meeting her when she had accompanied Sir Robert on a visit to the abbot here several years ago.

For a moment Brother Galen stared at her, squinting his near-sighted eyes. Then the tension of his stance seemed to relax somewhat.

"Oh yes, of course Mistress Berengar. I do remember you. But I am afraid you cannot be here. It is against the rule to have females in this place." He made as if to usher her out the door.

"Please, Brother Galen. I know I am not supposed to be here but I come on a matter of grave importance." Galen stopped and allowed Bryn to continue.

"One of the young men at the manor is very ill. He has ingested Monk's Hood." Brother Galen's face changed from courteous curiosity to shocked concern. As Bryn continued to talk, he was already turning to a table against the wall where stood a small chest inset with many smaller drawers. He pulled several open.

"Agnes has given him Devil's Weed but she did not have any properly prepared. She fears it will not be effective."

"No, no, of course. I have several things for you." He had laid out four squares of rough cloth, likely pieces cut from a worn out monk's robe. He used a small wooden spoon to make several

127

piles of powders in the middle of each square of cloth. Bryn saw one small pyramid of powder that looked much like the thornapple or Devil's Weed that Agnes had, but the coloring was slightly different and it had something else mixed in with it. The other powders she didn't recognize. Galen said nothing but worked swiftly and efficiently. He soon had all four tidy packages tied with string. He handed them to Bryn who put them into the satchel that hung at her side.

"Here," Brother Galen was bending over a piece of parchment, quill in hand. "I have written down instructions. Is there anyone at the manor who can read these to Agnes, so that she will know what to do?"

"I can read," Bryn said and Galen looked at her in surprise.

"Good," he nodded. "Now you must go, and hurry—Monk's Hood does not take its time to kill."

Bryn went pale but nodded and ran out the door and down the stairs to the yard. She had left the infirmary so quickly, she did not notice the monk who had been silently listening at the door of the infirmary. Brother Felix, recently returned from his long trip to Durham, had just stopped by to get something to calm his persistent cough when Bryn had arrived. As Brother Galen had closed the door on him, he'd halted, hearing Bryn's voice behind the door. Someone at the manor was ill from Monk's Hood. That was very interesting information. He thought he could guess who that person was.

Chapter Twenty Five

Bryn knew she could not ride Eleanor as hard as they had run earlier that morning. The horse had had only a brief rest. Still, even Eleanor seemed to want to push to the limit to get back to Agnes' cottage. Except for a heart-stopping moment when the palfrey had stumbled on a log, they both made it back to the cottage by late afternoon. Agnes heard the pounding hoofs as Bryn emerged from the wood and came to the gate to meet her. Bryn looked anxiously for any sign of bad news reflected in Agnes' face. Though the old woman looked tired and grim, there was nothing to indicate that she was about to impart the worst news. Bryn swung her satchel off her shoulder and handed it to Agnes, then dismounted and, after setting Eleanor to graze in the back field, followed Agnes into the house.

Agnes was already at the table, untying the tiny knots on each small parcel from Brother Galen. She took a cautious sniff of each one, murmuring to herself. She looked up as Bryn came in and nodded toward the fire.

"Get some water on the fire please, dear. We should get these prepared as soon as possible."

"How has he been, Agnes? I came as fast as I could."

"The thornapple has kept him alive at least. The problem is, I had no dried weed, only what you had picked from the garden. The herb is much more potent when it has been dried and ground into powder." She pushed at the small pile of powdered herb on the table with her finger. "Yes, this should do much better. I see he has given us some hawthorn also, to help steady his heartbeat."

Together the women mixed the herbs with warm water in the wooden bowl and carried it into the room where Simon still lay on the pallet on the floor. Bryn was shocked at his pale face and clammy skin. His hair stuck in damp strands to his forehead. Although he was unconscious still, he did not look like he was asleep, his features seemed to reflect his struggles to breath and his erratic heartbeat. Bryn took a cloth from the pail of cool water on the floor and knelt by his head, wiping his brow and face. Agnes once again dribbled spoonfuls of the warm elixir between his lips. When she was done she stood and watched his face for several minutes. Bryn did notice some softening and relaxing of his features, she looked up at Agnes.

"Yes, we've done what we can. Let's leave him to rest and let the herbs do their work." Agnes picked up the empty bowl and held out her hand to help Bryn up.

"There is nothing you can do here, dear. You'd better take the horse home and care for her after her hard journey today. She deserves an extra scoop of oats I think," Agnes smiled.

Bryn wanted to argue that she could stay the night, but realized Agnes was right. There was nothing she could do here now but wait, and there were things that needed doing at the manor house. She thanked Agnes, cast a hesitant glance toward the door of Simon's room, and headed for the manor house.

Bryn waved Baldwin away as he came to take the horse from her. She wanted to tend to Eleanor herself. It gave her the chance to feel like she could do something to make someone better, even if it was only a horse. She wiped the horse down and brushed her coat until it shone. She made sure her water bucket was filled with fresh water and there were oats in her stall. This settled and calmed them both. Bryn gently kissed the soft nose of the horse and walked into the house.

It was hard to believe that she had only been gone a day. It seemed ages ago that she and Simon had set off for the monastery, excited about pursuing a puzzle. She would never forgive herself if Simon died. There. She had said it, if only in her mind. If Simon died. What would she do? Agnes was right that what they had thought was just an entertaining mystery was obviously of deadly seriousness for someone. If that someone ended up causing Simon's death, she didn't think she would be able to leave it alone. But she didn't want to think of that now.

Bryn found Jasper and his wife in the kitchen eating an informal meal. Jasper stood up when she came in.

" Mistress!" he bobbed his head. "I'm that sorry to hear about your friend bein' ill. Gladys has taken over Agnes' kitchen dooties to help out like." He nodded toward his plump wife.

"Thank you, both. We are hoping he will soon be better and Agnes can return to her duties here. Has all been well while I have been gone?"

Jasper sat back down and returned his attention to the bowl of steaming pottage in front of him. His wife had never let her attention wander from her bowl and now ripped a large hunk of dark brown bread from the loaf between them.

"We've had several new lambs and all but one look like they will survive. We've finished sowing the barley." While he spoke Bryn had turned to ladle some of the pottage into a bowl for herself.

"Oh, I nearly forgot. A messenger came today from Suffolk. Sir Robert hopes to return here as soon as his business with the king is over. He thinks he might be here by the end of the month, perhaps the 5th day before Kalends."

Bryn turned around quickly, sloshing some of the pottage on the floor.

"Jasper! Why didn't you tell me immediately! We have much to do to prepare if Sir Robert and Lady Montbury are coming. There are food stores and linens and…"

"No, Mistress! I don't think Sir Robert is bringing his household with him. And you know how Lady Montbury hates leaving their manor in Suffolk. His message seemed to indicate that he would be here just to check in on the manor and take care of some business."

Bryn breathed a sigh of relief and sat down heavily on the stool. She realized she had eaten nothing all day and the smell of the stew had awoken her stomach that was now growling for attention. Jasper managed to pry the loaf of bread away from his silent wife and rip off a large chunk that he passed to Bryn, who took it gratefully. They discussed manor business, made several plans for assigning tasks to the peasant farmers and the manor servants, talked about repairing the stable door and replacing several slates on the manor roof. Satisfied that all was in order, she left Jasper and headed for her room.

Bryn began to climb the steps to her room but stopped and turned back through the echoing, empty, dark great hall. She unlocked the door to the solar and, protecting her candle from guttering in the breezes that always flowed through the rooms, she walked over to the table where she and Simon had left the parchment with the puzzle. She had thought to spend some time over it tonight but was too exhausted. She picked up the parchment to take it up to her room and at least study it in her bed before she slept. She locked the solar, and climbed the cold, wide, stone stairs.

Bryn took several steps into her room and then paused. She put down her candle and the parchment and then pushed a heavy trunk in front of the door. Never in her life had she felt the need to lock herself in or barricade the door. But for some reason, she no longer felt confident that she could handle anything life had in store. Tonight, at least, she felt better with the door securely shut.

Chapter Twenty Six

Moira found herself humming as she sorted through the mail. It had been accumulating in a basket on the coffee table for a week. Most of it went into the recycle bin unopened. Bills got put into another basket that, with luck, she would remember to pay before the month was out.

Few people would recognize the music she hummed, Hildegard von Bingen's *O Ignis Spiritus*[3] Moira remembered meeting Hildegard when she was composing so many of her songs and in fact had encouraged Hildegard to write her music down.

"Strange, but interesting woman," Moira recalled. Hildegard, who was born in Germany in 1098, was the 10th child of her family. Being the 10th, she was "tithed" to the church and sent away by the age of eight years to live with an anchoress named Jutta. Moira remembered explaining all this to Jenny at the museum. They were setting up an exhibit on Hildegard von Bingen and Jenny, bringing a cup of tea over to Moira as she worked, had stayed and asked questions about her.

"The bible says that we are to pay a tithe of all our increase. That means 10% of everything we have. So, for instance, if my fields produce 10 bushels of grain, I need to give one bushel to the church."

"But a child! They gave their 10th child to the church? Was that also required?" Jenny asked appalled.

---

[3] Fire of the Spirit

Moira looked up at Jenny with a sardonic smile. She was bending over to take out a manuscript of Hildegard's *Scivias*, where she describes 26 spiritual visions.

"I imagine it benefited the family in several ways. First, they could be seen by others as supremely religious and second it was one less mouth to feed, wasn't it?"

Jenny had leaned over to peer into the glass display case. "This says she lived with a hermit in a single room. What a horrible life!"

Moira placed the manuscript in the display case and stood up, bending a bit backward to un-kink her spine.

"Some religious people in the Middle Ages became spiritual hermits. Males were called anchorites and females anchoresses. And frankly, it was a bit strange. These people decided to completely cut themselves off from the world and spend all their time in isolated religious study. They usually lived in a single cell or room, sometime with only a window whereby food could be passed to them. They even went through a sort of funeral service as they were to become 'dead to the world.' This sometimes included laying on a funeral bier." Jenny shivered but listened intently.

"Jutta," here Moira had pointed to a picture of a woman sitting with a book open on her lap, "was a famous anchoress who attracted many followers. Hildegard was sent to study with her. Hildegard was an amazing woman actually. She had many visions and heard heavenly music that she later wrote down to be sung in the convents she established. For a woman in the Middle Ages, she had a lot of authority and power, even the pope called upon her and sanctioned her writings."

Jenny had stayed a bit longer, looking over the partially completed exhibit. Moira always enjoyed talking with her, it was such a pleasant change to talk with someone who didn't argue every point or talk over you about their own research as so many of her colleagues did. Jenny was interested in everything Moira worked on.

Moira's stomach rumbled and her thoughts were brought back to the present. She reached for a can of condensed soup, dumping it into a dented pan on the stove. Her lunch with Owen Caddick had been very nice. Yes, very nice indeed. They had both talked about their work and what had happened in their lives over the past years. Moira was surprised to learn that Owen had married and divorced. He was not surprised to learn that she had never married. It had been so long since Moira had enjoyed the companionship of a male (other than Simon of course, that really wasn't the same thing at all) that she had forgotten how young and lighthearted it made one feel to have the attentions of a handsome man. Moira continued to sing under her breath as she took her soup into the study.

"Custodi eos qui carcerati sunt ab inimico, et solve legatos quos divina vis salvare vult."

"That's quite a catchy tune," Moira thought happily, her spirits high from her time with Owen. She translated it automatically in her head. *Caring for all those who are held down by enemies and break the chains, whom the divine will save and free.*

It didn't for a moment occur to her that most people humming a tune in high spirits, might choose something more appropriate. She sat down at her desk and sipped a spoonful of soup.

"Oh dear!" She swallowed with a grimace. "This tastes more like tomato paste than soup."

She put the cup down, making a mental note not to buy that brand of soup again. If Simon was there he would have pointed out to her that the directions on the can called for adding water to dilute the soup but Moira had never been good with reading directions, unless of course they were in Greek or Latin.

She pulled the palimpsest once more in front of her, adjusting the bright reading light over it. The song had reminded her of Queen Eleanor, '....*those who are held down by enemies and break the chains, whom the divine will save and free.*'

She once more opened her black journal and wrote down her scattered thoughts.

"Eleanor was being held a virtual prisoner by her husband, King Henry. It looks like she was in correspondence with someone who was trying to help her, at least this someone was sending her books." Moira hummed the tune again, *the divine will save and free.*"

"It makes perfect sense this person would be someone who had access to books, that limits the choices greatly. It would have to be a monk, a librarian or bibliothecarius." Moira looked despairingly at the computer on her desk. She preferred to rely on her own personal library or the museum's library, but she had the feeling this was going to take more than what she could literally lay her hands on. She pulled over a legal pad full of scribbled notes. She had taken many notes as Simon gave her tutorials on how to use the computer and search engines.

"Google, Cuil, Yahoo, Gigablast---Greek is easier to understand. Dogpile? That sounds disgusting," she muttered. "Yes, I made a note this one might work well for historic articles and journals—Ancient History Sourcebook. I'll start there." For the next hour, Moira read and wrote and clicked. She was beginning to feel quite accomplished and was also beginning to develop a picture—a rather alarming picture—of what this palimpsest might represent.

Chapter Twenty Seven

"*Mistress!*" Gunnora knocked loudly on Bryn's door. Her mistress had never before locked the door when Gunnora walked into the room each morning with water and clothing for the day. She knocked again. A muffled and somewhat irritated answer came from inside Bryn's room. Gunnora heard something heavy being slid away from the door. She stepped back when Bryn opened the door looking very disheveled and still half asleep.

"Come in, Gunnora." Bryn walked back to her bed and sat down heavily on it. She had slept poorly last night, starting at sounds that likely were there, unnoticed, every night. When she did fall asleep, her dreams were filled with images of riding quickly through a dangerous wood in pitch blackness. She was not ready to face the day.

Gunnora came in looking quite unsure. She glanced at the heavy chest that had obviously blocked the door and at her mistress's haggard face. Something was not right and this worried her. On top of that, Agnes sent Baldwin with a message for Bryn, Gunnora was to deliver it immediately Baldwin said.

"Mistress, I have a message from Agnes."

Bryn looked up quickly, her face changing from sleepy to tense. She really should have gone as soon as the sun rose to Agnes' cottage. But if she was truthful with herself, she was too cowardly to go. Somehow, she felt if she stayed here at the manor then life would be as it always was, with no bad news to reach her.

"Agnes says please come as soon as you can, and bring food if you please. I can help you dress…" But Bryn had already jumped up, splashing water on her face and struggling into her chemise. Gunnora quickly helped her pull her kirtle over her head and tie it at the waist. Bryn was out the door and down into the kitchen before another word was spoken.

"He is better. He must be better, she wouldn't have asked for food otherwise, certainly." Bryn spoke aloud to herself as she grabbed what was left of the brown bread and cheese and stuffed them into a cloth bag. She grabbed a small wooden bucket that held nuts on the table and dumped the nuts out, they clattered loudly as they skittered over the wooden surface. Into the now empty bucket she poured the leftover pottage from last night's supper. She ran out the door and across the cobbled courtyard, scattering chickens and geese that scuttered across the yard with loud and angry squawking. She saw Roger cutting wood by the wood shed and called him over. She spoke hurriedly to him and he nodded, putting down his axe and walking toward the shed that held the wagons and carts. Bryn watched him briefly and then turned and headed to the stable. She found Eleanor chewing contentedly on her breakfast oats

"Come on, girl. I promise we are only going down the hill today and I won't even saddle you," she said as she pulled the reins over the horse's head. Bryn swung the bag of food over the horse's neck and put the bucket of pottage on the shelf that held the grooming brushes. Then she pulled Eleanor's now empty grain bucket over and used it to boost herself up onto the horse's smooth bare back. Reaching over for the bucket, she gently nudged Eleanor out the stable door and down the hill toward Agnes' cottage.

Agnes was waiting at the door, just as she had been last night when Bryn had returned from the monastery with the medicines. But this morning Agnes' face was relaxed and she greeted Bryn with a comforting smile.

138

"Good morning, dear. And I have to say, thanks be to God, it is a good morning."

"He is well then?" Bryn hardly dared ask.

"I don't think I would call him well, but he is better and he will get well with time I am sure." Agnes took the food Bryn offered and they walked into the cottage to set it on the table. Bryn was bending over the table unpacking the food when she heard him.

"Hello, Bryn." A hoarse voice came from behind her. Startled, she turned around quickly and saw Simon leaning heavily against the doorway. She put her hand to her mouth and took a step toward him but then stopped and forced her face into a calm and reproachful look.

"Oh, I see you've decided to join us for breakfast? I was wondering just how long you were going to stay abed and ignore your responsibilities."

Simon smiled weakly and leaned his head against the door frame. He looked so weak and his face was still pale with sunken cheeks and dark circles under his eyes.

"If I had the energy and my brain was functioning, I am sure I would have a witty and appropriate remark to answer you with." He looked at the food on the table. "My stomach, however, is functioning properly and is demanding breakfast." He took a step forward but had to catch hold of the door frame to steady himself. Bryn and Agnes both quickly went to his side and helped him to a stool at the table.

"You shouldn't be up. You aren't ready," Agnes scolded.

"If I lay on that hard floor one more minute, I shall need more than your foul tasting herbs to cure me." Simon smelled the pottage that was warming on the fire. His mouth began to water and he reach over to take some bread. Bryn quickly tore off a large piece for him and cut several slices of creamy cheese. It looked like every movement he made was an effort and her heart wrenched in her chest.

"Simon," she said with a catch in her voice. He turned to look at her, resting his head on his hand, elbow on the table. "Simon, I am so sorry I brought this on you. It is all my fault."

Simon looked questioningly at her. She had not taken time to braid her hair and for the first time he noticed how beautifully gold it was as it flowed over her shoulders and down nearly to her waist. Her blue eyes, normally confident and amused, looked anxious and remorseful.

"First, before I decide to forgive you or not," he said with a weak smile, "I need to know what happened. The last thing I remember was riding through the woods on Alizay when I suddenly felt a tremendous pain in my head and chest. Then just blackness."

Bryn explained what had happened. She told him Agnes was sure he had been poisoned by Monk's Hood, and the theory that it had come from the powder in the trunk that had made him cough.

"Why would anyone do that? We saw what was in that trunk. There was nothing of great value or mystery. Just books on chivalric poetry and something about the duchy of Aquitaine."

Agnes was quietly listening, ladling hot pottage into three wooden bowls. She placed a bowl in front of each of them.

"Take care now, Simon. You don't want to overtax your stomach and I suppose it is my turn to apologize now, but your hoarse voice and sore throat come from me pouring too-hot liquid down your throat all night. So take care with this hot pottage." There was silence for several minutes while they all enjoyed the wonderful normalcy of being together on a beautiful spring morning eating good food. Then Agnes spoke.

"Books on chivalry and Aquitaine you said?" She looked thoughtful. "It sounds like you stumbled across the queen's own library doesn't it?"

Bryn and Simon in unison looked up at Agnes, spoons stopped in mid-air.

"What do you mean?" Bryn asked.

"Well, Eleanor is of course not just queen of England, she is in her own right Countess of Aquitaine. Also, Queen Eleanor and her daughter have promoted chivalry, or courtly love, by being the patrons of Cretien de Troyes who writes and sings chanson, love songs, all through her court." Agnes nodded her head at them both. "The library at Bridlethorpe Abbey holds her personal books and she is its patroness. Without Eleanor, you wouldn't have all those books you love so much," she told Bryn.

Bryn stared at Agnes. "How do you know all this, Agnes? You don't even read do you?"

"Oh no, dear. But my husband, God rest his soul, used to sing to me and recite poetry to me. He picked it up when he was with Sir Robert's household as they traveled to the King's court. He knew all about the queen and her efforts to encourage chivalry. If you ask me, it was her attempt to get better treatment for women," Agnes nodded sagely. "Now," she pushed herself up from the table, "we need to get Simon back to bed."

"Oh, I forgot to tell you both. I have arranged for Roger to bring a cart down here. He will bring Simon up to the manor house. Agnes, can you please come too? We will have more room, access to more of what he might need, and it is warmer at night than your little cottage."

As if to underline her words, they heard the squeak of a wheeled cart pull up to the gate. Agnes and Bryn helped steady Simon, one on each side, as he walked out to the cart. Both he and Agnes sat on the cart, she with a bundle of her medicines. Roger, with a grimace, began to pull them up the hill. Bryn walked Eleanor along side.

For the next several days Simon slowly recuperated. Agnes nursed him day and night, preparing food for him herself, heating water for him to wash, and to pass the long hours while he slept, she begun to sew a new set of clothing for him. In the chest in her house she kept all of her husband's clothing. He was a large man but that left lots of material that could be altered to fit

141

Simon's slim frame. Harald, Agnes' husband, had served Sir Robert as his ostler, caring for his horses. Because of this each year he was given rich fabrics to suitably outfit himself since he had to join Sir Robert as part of his household when he traveled. Agnes could not bear to part with her husband's clothes when he died. Now she felt she could put them to good use. She made new hosen, shirt and tunic for him from the Montbury colors of blue and gray. When Simon was up again, she would present them to him, she thought happily.

As Simon gained strength, Bryn caught up on all the work that needed doing around the manor. If Sir Roger would be coming to the manor, even for a brief visit, there were many things to prepare. She set Baldwin and Roger to whitewashing the walls of the outbuildings and pulling the grass from the cobbles in the courtyard. The food stores had to be seen to and linens washed and aired. The thresh on the floor of the great hall should be replaced and house servants needed to rid the manor of the dust that had accumulated from the long winter of continually blazing fires. Though she was busy, she frequently checked in on Agnes and Simon. He was often asleep but even in sleep she could see him improving. He was gaining weight back, his face was a healthy color, his breathing normal and his appetite good. Agnes had truly done well in nursing him back to health.

On the morning of the fourth day Simon, now dressed in his new tunic and hose, came down to find Bryn in the kitchen conferencing with Jasper. Both looked up as he came in. Jasper tipped his cap, looked at Bryn and left quickly. Bryn smiled brightly for the first time in many days.

"You look wonderful! Agnes told me she was making new clothing for you."

"Well, I feel a bit like a peacock but I have to say this cloth is much more comfortable than that heavy wool." He felt the smooth linen, a luxury for most people of that time. "I wondered if you had time to work on the manuscript today."

142

Bryn stared at him in disbelief. "You can't be serious, Simon. Our 'work on the manuscript' almost got you killed! How can you consider continuing to investigate?"

They both left the kitchen and by unspoken agreement walked through the great hall and toward the solar. They now stood outside the solar door.

"Bryn, the danger is real and is still there whether we investigate it or not. Isn't the safest thing for us to figure out what is really going on and put an end to this? We don't even know if whomever is behind this knows who we are and might still come after us. I would rather know who and what I am fighting than just wait in fear for something to happen."

Bryn thought of the chest she had pushed up against her door each night.

"You're right, of course. But we need to be more careful. This is no longer a game." Simon nodded and she took her ring of keys to open the solar door.

"Oh! I forgot that I took the manuscript up to my room. I'll go and get it now."

Simon waited in the solar while Bryn ran up the stairs to fetch the parchment with the puzzle. He looked around the room. It was his favorite in the house with the sun warming the space through the large windows, and the beautiful tapestries on the walls and floors. As he scanned the room, something caught his eye. He frowned and walked toward the large chest that contained Bryn's books from her tutor on the far side of the solar. The chest was closed but the lock hung open. Simon knelt down and examined the lock. It was broken, the metal latch twisted violently. He slowly and carefully opened the chest. The fabric, plate and even the books were still there, but obviously someone had ransacked them. All was in disorder, especially the books that were opened with pages creased and torn as if someone had hurriedly searched through them. He had one in his hand when Bryn returned.

"Here. I've got it," she said, and then saw Simon at the chest. "What are you doing? What's wrong?"

She hurried over and knelt beside him. He said nothing but handed her the book. Bryn slowly took it from him. She looked at the torn and wrinkled pages, her hands lovingly and softly trying to smooth the parchment. Suddenly she closed the book and began to cry. She put her hands over her face while she sobbed, bent over the books in her lap. Simon put his arms around her shaking shoulders. He guessed this was not only grief for the damage done to her beloved books, but also a release of all the fears and troubles she had gone through over the last week. She turned toward him and buried her face on his chest. He said nothing but just held her until her sobbing quieted.

Bryn reached for the handkerchief tucked into her kirtle. She wiped her eyes and nose and looked up at Simon.

"I'm sorry, I don't know what that was all about." She smiled awkwardly and blew her nose. "I must look a mess."

"Well," he said seriously, "yes, you do actually. Your eyes looked much better blue than red and your nose is glowing like a light bulb on a Christmas tree." He laughed.

"Light bulb? Christmas tree?" She sat back, brushing loose strands of hair from her face. "What are you talking about?"

"Never mind, it's a long story. Actually, it isn't even a story yet…" Simon helped her put the books back in the chest. Then he stood up and offered his hand to help her up. The two walked to the table and sat.

"What do you think this means? Do you think it is related to this?" Bryn picked up the parchment with the puzzle.

"It must be. It would be too much of a coincidence not to be. It looks to me like someone was looking for something in that chest. I just don't know what it could be, or if they found it."

Bryn glanced toward the chest. "Well, there is nothing missing, and even though the books are damaged," her voice caught, "they are still complete." She was unconsciously spinning the small piece of parchment around on the table. They both looked down at it.

"Could it be this they were looking for?" Simon took it from her.

"This has been in the solar since we found it, right?"

"Well, except for the night you got ill. I took it up to my room then and it has been there since."

"But anyone who knows you well, knows that you keep your books in that chest, and that you and I have been working on something in here together."

"In that case, they would come here thinking they would find the parchment, and of course they would look in the trunk, where I keep things that are important to me." Bryn shivered. The idea that whomever had done this was someone close to her, someone she knew, was not thinkable.

"We know it couldn't be Agnes, she has been glued to me since I fell ill," Simon said. "Not that we would ever consider her anyway."

"But that goes for everyone here in one way or another. Jasper could care less about such things, he doesn't even read so it would mean nothing even if he did find it. His wife is so lazy she wouldn't make the effort---unless I had a meat pie in there." Bryn nodded toward the chest and they both laughed.

"Well, someone made the effort." Simon pulled the parchment toward him. They both stared down at it in silence, re-reading the puzzle.

An enemy ended my life, deprived me of my physical strength; then he put me in water and drew me out again, and tied me in the sun where my skin hardened and my hair was lost. After that, the knife's sharp edge bit into me and my rough skin was scraped away; the bird's feather moved over my brown skin, making meaningful marks; ...leaving black tracks. Then a man bound me, covering me in a leather shroud, decorated with gold; ...wound about with shining metal...

Suddenly Simon stiffened and gasped. Bryn looked up quickly, for a moment in fear that he had somehow had a relapse of his illness. He was staring straight ahead with a frightful look on his face.

"Simon," Bryn grabbed his arm. "Simon, what's wrong?"
He shook his head as if to clear it and looked at her.

"I know what it means. I know what this is." He looked down again at the manuscript. "I had completely forgotten but seeing this brought it all back."

"What? What are you saying? Brought what back?" Bryn tugged at his arm.

"When I was ill, I had horrible dreams. One kept reoccurring. It must have been because we had just been to see Brother Mark and that was still on my mind. I had a dream that I was drowning, I couldn't breath."

"That's because you really <u>couldn't</u> breath, Simon. Your heart and lungs were closing down." Bryn felt her stomach lurch at the memory of that night.

"Yes, but in my dream it was because I had fallen into one of his slaked lime barrels. I dreamt that I was drowning in the barrel and the fleece was tangling my legs. Then Brother Mark took me out and stretched me tightly on one of those drying racks and used his knife to scrape my skin."

"Ugh! This is horrid! How awful for you—even if it was just a dream."

"It seemed very real at the time. But what I am trying to say is that is what this puzzle is. It is describing the process for making parchment. Look," Simon read following along with his finger.

...the bird's feather moved over my brown skin, making meaningful marks;...leaving black tracks.

"That's the quill writing on the parchment---meaningful marks are words made with ink."

Bryn looked again at the puzzle, reading from beginning to end. It seemed so obvious now, especially after being with Brother Mark.

"So the key to all this is a manuscript. Not just that clues are written in or on a manuscript, or even hidden in them, but the parchment itself is what we are looking for?"

"Yes, I think so. But that doesn't get us much further. I mean I guess now we know not to look for buried treasure or stolen artwork or some such thing. We know that what we want to find is a parchment or manuscript."

They sat for a moment in silence. Neither knew where to go from there. What parchment? Where? What could possibly be on it that was worth killing for?

"Maybe it's a map?" Simon suggested, thinking of all the adventure stories he had read.

"Of what? For what?" Bryn scoffed.

Simon had no answer to that so said nothing. As was his custom when trying to figure out a problem, he let his eyes wander around the room. (This habit had often gotten him in trouble during tests at school.) He noticed that Bryn had left the door to the solar open, and the key, with a blue tassel hanging from it, still hung in the lock. A thought occurred to him.

"Bryn," he said suddenly. "Who else has a key to this room?"

"No one. Well, no one but Sir Robert of course," Bryn answered firmly. "I am chatelaine of the manor when Sir Robert and Lady Montbury are not here—which is frankly most of the time." She jingled the ring of keys on her rope belt.

"OK. So who else has a key to that chest." Simon pointed toward the chest that had been broken into.

"There is only one key, and I have it here." She showed the delicate key to Simon.

"Well, someone had to break into the chest, since you have the key. But they did NOT have to break into the solar. The door was not damaged, none of the windows were broken or pried. Whoever got in here had a key."

"That's impossible. Only Sir Robert and I have keys and he is far away in Suffolk." Her words were firm but her voice was unsure.

Simon said nothing. He got up and removed the key from the solar door and handed it back to Bryn. He suddenly looked quite tired and Bryn worried that he was not yet fully recovered.

They walked back up to his room that had been the nursery of Sir Robert's children, and Simon lay down to rest. Bryn walked back to the kitchen to see to the evening meal, but her mind was not on her work.

Chapter Twenty Eight

It took four tries before Moira actually completed the phone call. She picked up the phone several times, and even managed to dial the number twice before quickly hanging up. Finally, angry with herself for acting like a teenage girl, she dialed the number and let it ring.

"Hello?" the voice on the other end said.

Moira's stomach flipped. How ridiculous! The next thing she knew she would be drawing hearts with intertwined initials in her journals.

"Hello, Owen. This is Moira."

"Moira! How good of you to call." She felt a wave of relief wash over her. She was not sure what she had expected. *"Moira who?"* or *"Not you again,"* perhaps? But Owen seemed genuinely glad to hear from her.

"I am still working on my little puzzle regarding Henry and Eleanor. I could really use someone with a background to give me some direction. I was hoping you might have some free time to let me ask some questions."

"Actually, you are catching me at a very good time. The long school holiday coming up gives me some extra time for grading so I would love to get together. What is a good time and place?"

They spent several minutes finding a time they could meet and finally agreed on the day after tomorrow, after Moira got home from work. It turned out that Owen loved to cook and he offered to bring ingredients to her apartment to cook for them both. Moira hung up. It was some time later she realized she still had an absurd smile on her face.

Moira frantically called Mrs. Joyce, her housekeeper and begged her to come an extra day that week. She wanted the apartment to look as nice as possible for Owen's visit. She determined that when she came home she would sit in one place and wait for him. Somehow she knew as soon as she started to move around in the apartment, it would fall into chaos as it always did.

Moira left the museum an hour early that day and stopped off at a department store on the way home. Although it had never bothered her before, she knew she was a terrible cook. That being the case she had never bothered to buy cooking utensils. Her few pots and pans were ancient and dented, having been left in the apartment by the previous owner.

The sales person was very helpful. Moira had no idea what to purchase. It would have been different if she were a young woman just moving into her first apartment. But one would think a woman of Moira's age would not only have accumulated cooking equipment, but know the difference between a skillet and a saucepan. However odd the salesperson thought her, she was polite and helpful and soon Moira's shopping cart held a Cook's Appeal 10-piece Cooking Set (30% off). She then asked the sales person to show her where the dinnerware could be found.

Moira generally ate out of the pan or the package. Peanut butter toast and hot chocolate required little more than a chipped mug and a paper towel. They moved down several aisles to find the dinnerware. Moira stopped, feeling an anxiety attack begin to form. She looked down what seemed to be an endless aisle that was stacked from floor to ceiling with colorful boxes of dinnerware. The sales person was about to leave when Moira grabbed her sleeve.

No!" she said with more force than was necessary. "I mean, perhaps you could choose something for me."

"Me?" the woman replied. "You want me to pick out some dinnerware for you?"

"Yes. Yes, that is what I want." Moira could think of nothing to explain this request so she didn't try.

"Well, ummm. Let's see." The woman started to slowly walk down the aisle. "What color is your kitchen, or perhaps you should coordinate with the color of your dining room."

Moira closed her eyes and thought. Was "clutter" a color? She had never bothered to decorate her apartment since most of her time was spent at the museum. As hard as she tried, she couldn't think of what color her dining room was.

"Oh! Wait! I don't have a dining room!" Moira was inordinately pleased with herself at remembering this.

The woman was no longer trying to hide her wonder at this strange customer. But the fact that she was buying a lot of quite expensive merchandise pushed her onward.

"Well then, maybe we should go with the kitchen colors. You do have a kitchen I take it?"

"Oh yes, I have a kitchen. I think of the color as 'landlord green.' You know that horrible sort of algae green that so many landlords paint everything?"

"Yes, well, perhaps we don't want to buy dinnerware to match that then. I know, how about a nice neutral cream or white?" She motioned Moira to follow her down the aisle. As they walked, Moira saw a box with a picture of off-white dishes with a pale green stripe.

"What about this one?" she stopped to point at the box.

"French Country 16-pc. Dinnerware Set – Green" the sales person read.

"Yes, I'll take that one. The color will match my kitchen." Moira pulled the box off the shelf.

"The color you hate you mean, the 'horrible landlord green?'"

"Yes, exactly. It matches perfectly." Moira grabbed her hand and shook it warmly. "Thank you so much, you've been a great help." She headed for the cashiers, one more happy customer.

The dinner was a success. Owen had brought ingredients for Linguine Alfredo with a tossed salad and garlic bread. He was very impressed with the shining cookware and didn't notice the sales sticker still stuck on the bottom of the dinner plates. He commented several times on Moira's apartment and the work she must put in keeping things 'looking brand new.' Moira had smiled and graciously accepted the compliment.

After dinner they settled down on the living room couch, each with a cup of tea. Moira had a drawing of the palimpsest (she certainly couldn't show him the photo Simon had taken) and all her notes. Heads together, they talked for hours, both very engaged in the mystery.

"I have come to a conclusion that fits all the facts, but seems impossible to believe."

Owen nodded and waited for her to continue.

"We have to remember that Henry was in a desperate circumstance. His people blamed him for the death of Thomas Becket, the Pope was threatening to excommunicate him, he was being attacked by Scots from the north and the Netherlands from the sea. His sons hated him and were spurred on by his wife to revolt against him. He must have desperately wanted a way out of all this."

"Yes, that makes sense so far." Owen leaned back against the couch and sipped his tea. Moira noticed one black curl that kept falling onto his forehead. She forced herself to focus.

"What if it turned out that it was Eleanor, not Henry who was behind the death of Thomas Becket?" Moira waited for Owen's response.

"I don't think I follow. What evidence is there that that might have been the case?"

"None. But just work with me on this. Henry and Eleanor probably hated each other at this point."

"Well, there is evidence to support that, surely," Owen agreed. "In fact, Henry had already fallen in love with another woman."

Moira stared. "What! He never told me that!"

"He never told you?" Owen looked strangely at Moira.

"I mean…I mean I have never read that anywhere. I guess I need to do some more research."

"Oh yes, her name was Rosamund Clifford. Henry was very much in love with her. She died in 1176 and was buried in Godstow Abbey. Henry later gave a great deal of money to abbey. There were rumors that Eleanor actually had her killed."

Moira continued to stare at Owen. Partly because of the astounding facts he was relating and partly because she liked to stare at him.

"Some say she was poisoned by the queen, some say she was stabbed, or beheaded, or bled to death in her own bath."

"You'd think if she was beheaded someone would notice that wouldn't you?" Moira spoke more to herself than to Owen.

He laughed. "You forget that historic accounts are often blurred over time."

That reminded Moira of the palimpsest. It too was blurred, both in meaning and in reality.

"Let's refocus here," Moira pointed to the drawing. "I have been digging in the digital archives of libraries all over England." Moira hoped he was impressed by her technological abilities, and at the same time, hoped he wouldn't ask too many questions that might show her for the technological novice she was.

"Here are all the notes I have taken." She opened her black journal to pages of spidery writing.

"So many things seem to point to a conspiracy between Henry and some of his top nobles to frame Eleanor for the crime."

Owen's eyebrows raised doubtfully.

"I know," she continued, "it doesn't make sense from what we both know about King Henry, but it would solve so many problems. First, he would be cleared of the archbishop's death. The woman he hates would be incriminated and he could legitimately rid himself of her. His sons would lose the one person who pushed them to revolt and supported them against their father. And now I find he would be free to be with Rosamund, also. It all fits so well." Moira was not happy with her conclusions. She had known Henry personally, and liked him. But there was no denying the mounting evidence supporting her theory.

Owen was thoughtful for a moment.

"It's true that he had been trying to get her to agree to an annulment of their marriage, and to appoint her abbess of Fontevraud. This would mean her inheritance, her lands in France, would go to him. Eleanor was too smart to agree to those terms," Owen added, beginning to see the possibilities of Moira's theory.

"And this," Moira pointed at the scrap of parchment. "this started it all I think."

Owen looked closely at the drawing of the parchment and then at Moira.

"Explain," he said.

Chapter Twenty Nine

A tentative knock at the kitchen door brought Bryn out of her thoughts. She frowned, wondering who would be knocking at the back entrance. Jasper would just walk in and a visitor would come to the front entrance. She opened the door in some surprise to see Edwin, the smith.

He bobbed his head once, looking very uncomfortable. He was, as usual, covered with a sticky dust. His job, hard physical labor in front of a blazing fire, always left him with a sheen of sweat. His open, dirt floored shed was often full of swirling dust that by midday covered him from head to foot.

Bryn could see that he had made some attempt to wash before coming up to the manor. He likely had stuck his upper body into the river that ran along the manor fields, as his hair was still dripping water, and while not actually clean, there were places on his face and neck where most of the dust was scrubbed off, making him look rather like he was moulting.

"Pardon me, mistress." Edwin looked down at his feet, every few seconds glancing quickly up at Bryn.

"Edwin!" Bryn opened the door wider. "Come in, please!"

"Oh no!" Edwin sounded horrified and took a step backward. "No, miss, I just heard that your friend was better and I thought…" Here he seemed to lose confidence and stumble into silence.

"Simon, you mean? Yes, he is in fact much better. Did you want to speak with him?" Bryn had heard that Simon had frequently visited Edwin, being fascinated by the craft of blacksmithing. She gathered they had become friends of a sort. She felt badly that she hadn't thought to send news to Edwin about Simon's condition but frankly she rarely saw the smith, usually sending Baldwin or Roger to speak to him when she wanted something done.

"Yes miss, Simon. I have something for him." Edwin brought his left hand from behind his back and handed a very strange object to Bryn.

Bryn looked at it in confusion and reached out to take it. "Heavens, Edwin. What is this thing?"

Edwin became animated. "It was Simon's idea miss. I guess he read about it in a book. He calls it a foil. He says it is a weapon, used like a sword."

Bryn wrapped her hand around the grip. The bell-guard, a bowl-like metal piece that wraps around the hand and protects it, seemed to fit her hand as if made for it. She raised the foil and brought it down with a swoop. Edwin took another step backward.

"What an extraordinary thing," she said, fascinated. "Did he say how it was used?"

"Unlike the broad sword, that hacks and cleaves at the opponent, this is mostly a thrusting weapon. The advantage is how light, flexible and agile it is. Simon said it is being developed in France."

Bryn again brought the foil up and back down in an elegant arch. She looked up and smiled at Edwin. "And you made this?"

"With directions from Simon. I just thought perhaps it would cheer him up to see it finished."

"He will be delighted, Edwin. I will take it to him directly. Thank you."

Edwin bobbed his head again and turned to go. Bryn closed the door and carried the foil upstairs to Simon's room. She knocked quickly on the door and entered. Simon was standing at the window overlooking the courtyard. He turned when he heard her enter. Immediately he saw the foil in her hand.

"Oh! My foil!" He ran across the room and took it from Bryn. She watched with a grin as he looked it over and tried its balance.

"Edwin's done very well with it hasn't he?" Simon said happily looking up at Bryn.

"Well, I wouldn't know since I've never seen one before, but if you say so." She sat down on the single chair in the room and watched Simon's continued antics. He stood with the foil in his right hand, held out straight in front of him at a slight upward angle. His body was positioned sideways, with knees slightly bent. His left hand was raised in an elegant arch behind him. Bryn watched in fascination as Simon went through what looked like a series of dance movements. He would bring his front foot forward, landing on his heel and then planting the foot firmly. The back foot would follow, always keeping his knees slightly bent. Bryn had seen men fighting before. She had been to several tournaments with Sir Robert's family and watched jousting and sword fighting competitions. This was very different from those. Men usually wore heavy, awkward armor and used two hands to hack at each other with large, flat broadswords.

She laughed. "I don't see how this is any match against someone with a broadsword. It would be like getting stung by a bee."

Simon stopped and faced her. "Not at all. Broadsword fighting is so much mindless, brute force. Fencing requires thought and strategy, the ability to out think your opponent, to make him think one thing while doing something else."

"How do you mean?" Bryn asked.

Simon looked around the room. He walked to a corner to pick up a walking stick that was leaning against the fireplace.

"Here," he said, handing the walking stick to Bryn. "Pretend you are going to attack me."

157

Bryn wrinkled her forehead questioningly but took the stick. She stood in front of Simon while he assumed his fencing posture.

"Now, just attack me as you would with a sword."

Bryn lunged forward to hit him in the chest. Simon moved only his wrist. With a flick of the foil, he deflected her. Bryn frowned and tried again, this time focusing on his left side. Again, with only a small movement of his elbow and wrist, the foil caught the stick and it slid away from him. Bryn stamped her foot, concentrating. She first tried again for his chest but then lunged for his right side. With two quick flicks Simon slapped the stick to the ground.

"You see," he said smiling. "You have to read your opponent's face and body language, watch their attack and then just use the foil to deflect it. You don't tire as easily because you don't have to heft a heavy sword, and if you are good at what you do, you don't even have to move much."

"OK," Bryn conceded. "But deflecting is one thing, what kind of offensive weapon is it?"

"Fencing relies on opportunism and set ups. I will make you think I am coming for your right shoulder." Here he lunged and Bryn quickly brought the walking stick up to protect her shoulder. Immediately Simon touched the foil on her left side. "Obviously, if we were really fighting, I would have inflicted a wound there. You try to get your opponent to leave open a vulnerable place by directing them elsewhere."

"It reminds me of when Eleanor is trying to catch a gadfly that is buzzing around her. One minute she throws her head back to her left flank to catch the fly, and it has already come around to bite her on her shoulder."

"Yes, that is a good analogy," Simon laughed. "I will have to do something for Edwin. He must have spent some time on this."

"I think he is very fond of you Simon," Bryn smiled. "I should have spoken to him when you were ill, he was likely anxious for news."

158

At that moment Agnes came into the room with a plate of food for Simon. The early peas had come out in the garden and there was a bowl full of them that looked very tempting. Simon never thought he would actually miss vegetables but realized how lucky the modern world was to have such things year round.

"Bryn, here you are. Baldwin is looking all over for you. He says he has a message for you from Brother Felix."

Bryn and Simon looked at each other, worried and wondering expressions on their faces. Without a word she quickly left the room to find Baldwin.

"Well, we might as well eat while we wait for her to return." There was little short of a catastrophe that would keep Agnes from feeding someone. She laid the tray on the table and pulled up a stool, patting the chair next to her for Simon.

A few minutes later Bryn returned with a paper in her hands. She sat on the stool next to Simon's chair and reached for a handful of pea pods. She looked at Simon and Agnes with worry.

"This is from Brother Felix at the monastery. He says he believes he has found the book I have been looking for connecting the Montbury family with William the Conqueror. He requests that we visit him so he can show it to us."

"Well, dear," Agnes said, biting a pea pod in half, "that's good news isn't it? You have been trying to find that information for months."

Bryn was staring at the window, a pensive look on her face.

"Hmmmm, yes."

She reached over to Simon's plate and stole a slice of cheese.

"Funny though. He never before took a real interest in my research. In fact, I always got the impression he very much resented having me there and was only putting up with me because of Sir Robert's support of the monastery."

"Well, maybe having Simon with you has made it more acceptable to him. He would have more respect for a learned young man wouldn't he? "

Bryn looked down at the note. "In fact, he made it a point of telling me to bring Simon with me when I come." Simon stopped in mid-crunch. "You seem to have made a friend, isn't that nice?" Bryn smiled broadly at him.

"So, when do we go?" Simon asked, very unsure of whether he was ready to return to that place.

"Tomorrow morning." Bryn stood up and brushed crumbs from her kirtle. She reached down to take the last slice of cheese from Simon's plate. Simon glared at her. She smiled and popped the cheese into her mouth. "Be ready bright and early."

Chapter Thirty

Moira sipped her tea, now gone cold. She grimaced and got up to dump it down the sink and put the kettle back on to heat up.

"Why don't you just nuke it?" Owen asked as he watched her from the living room.

"Nuke it?"

"Microwave? Why don't you just put it in the microwave and heat it up?"

Moira stared at him. She had never used or owned a microwave. She wasn't sure how 'uncool' that made her so she was debating her reply.

Owen laughed.

"Let me guess. You don't have a microwave and probably aren't really sure what one is. I've heard of 'out of touch' Moira, but this is ridiculous!"

He got up and came into the kitchen.

"I've gotten along just fine without one. Why train myself to need one now?" Moira said, as if not having a microwave was a conscious, ethical choice on her part. In fact, she just had no interest in the world around her and the newest gadgets. The last "newest gadget" she had any interest in was the invention of eyeglasses in 1284 by Salvino D'Armante of Pisa. He was kind enough to make a pair for her as she had left her own glasses in her apartment, 800 years in the future.

Owen nodded. "You have a point, I admit." The kettle was whistling and steaming. He removed it and refreshed both their teacups. They sat at the kitchen table.

"Now, tell me how this scrap of paper started a conspiracy to frame the queen of England for the murder of Thomas Becket."

"Look," she pointed to several areas of the parchment. "This is obviously not a professionally done manuscript. The parchment appears to have been a scrap to start with, you can tell by how the text fits the uneven boundaries of the parchment. If it was torn from a much larger piece, there would be congruity where each line of the text runs off the margins, right? So, as sometimes happened, this was a piece of parchment originally cut from a larger piece, and just re-used to make notes on. The writing is not the beautiful, professional script of a scribe. There is no illumination or artwork of any sort. We might just call this notes from a "brainstorming session.""

"Possible," Owen reluctantly agreed.

"The original text read something like; 'to subdue this pest.' And it has been subtly changed. See here we can see where words are crossed out and others written over the top. 'Subdue' has been changed to 'kill' and 'pest' has been changed to 'enemy.' We also see the Latin endings indicating a male has been changed to indicate a female."

"I'm not sure I see where this is leading." Owen took the drawing from her to look at it more closely.

"Well, this is where we have to make some guesses. Many historians believe that Henry really did not order Becket's death. That what he said was said only in frustration. Sort of like when you are really angry at someone and you say, 'I could just kill him'. We don't mean that at all."

"Yes," Owen smiled. "I have had that experience with some of my students."

"So what if Henry and a group of his supporters are sketching out a defense for him. They are trying to convince people he just thought of Thomas as a pest that needed to be

162

scolded. They might sketch out something like this," she pointed to the manuscript. "But then it occurs to them that maybe this could be turned around to their advantage. If they could plant information that Eleanor actually ordered Thomas' death, the anger of the kingdom would turn toward her. So many problems would be solved. Henry is exonerated, he can get rid of Eleanor, marry the woman he has fallen in love with, end his sons' revolt."

"So you think this parchment shows how the idea has occurred to them to change Henry's exclamation of 'who will rid me of this meddlesome priest,' to an order by Eleanor to kill Thomas? That's a big jump. Who would believe it?"

"Yes, I think that's what this is." Moira grew passionate as she explained. "Henry was already facing public outrage over the death of the archbishop. Canterbury Cathedral had become an instant place of pilgrimage. Even Henry went to place where Thomas was brutally murdered in a public display of grief and sorrow. He likely got together with his advisers to come up with some statement that proved he was only speaking in frustration about Thomas, not issuing a death threat, when it occurred to them that the blame could be placed on Eleanor. I think especially the change of male to female endings indicates that. Who else is a major player in this event that was female? No one but Eleanor."

Owen leaned back in the chair staring at the parchment. He'd taken off his reading glasses and was absentmindedly chewing on one end.

"It seems very far-fetched, and yet nothing else fits the facts so well. Henry was in a serious position. His kingship was already threatened by the Becket murder, and his own sons' rebellion. He may have felt he had no other choice." Owen looked up and smiled at Moira. "Pretty good piece of detective work, Professor Ananke. Too bad you already have your PhD, this would be a great thesis for a doctoral dissertation. What do you plan to do with the information?"

"Do with it?" Moira hadn't thought about that.

"Yes, I mean, you could write a book about it, it would change history wouldn't it?"

"Change history," Moira's thoughts went to Simon. Wherever and whenever he was right now, he was very likely in the thick of this, and perhaps in great danger, too.

Chapter Thirty One

They were nearly at the monastery. Bryn pulled her palfrey to a stop and laid her hand on Simon's arm. He reined in Alizay.

"Let's go over this again before we arrive," she said, absently patting Eleanor on the neck.

Simon sighed. "There isn't much to go over really, is there? I mean we don't know what to expect. We don't know if anyone, including Brother Felix, suspects us of anything. This could be exactly what it looks like—Brother Felix helping you with your research."

"It could be, yes. But after what happened to you, I don't want to take any chances. We stay together no matter what. We keep our eyes open."

"OK. We are looking for a book or manuscript in a library full of books and manuscripts. No problem." Simon said sarcastically as he urged Alizay forward and they continued on to the monastery gates.

"It was so kind of you, Brother Felix, to go through all this trouble. I am sure Sir Robert will be grateful," Bryn said in her sweetest voice. Brother Felix nodded and opened the library door. He stood aside to let them pass.

Felix locked the door behind them. Bryn and Simon expected to be seated at the lectern in the middle of the room as usual but instead Brother Felix walked across the room to a door on the far wall. Simon and Bryn looked questioningly at each other and followed. Another double lock opened the door and the three of them walked through.

They found themselves on a landing in the middle of a very narrow winding newel stair. Brother Felix once again locked the door behind them. They pressed themselves against the cold, damp, circular outer wall of the stairs to let him pass. He started up the stairs. Bryn and Simon followed single file. The stairs were very narrow and uneven. The stone steps worn in the center by years of leather-clad footsteps. It wound tightly to the right. Simon found himself getting dizzy, having to look down to keep his footing sure. The stairs were not only worn unevenly, but they were cut of varying widths. He kept his right hand on the newel, or central column, from which the stairs radiated. Then he tried hugging the outer wall where the triangular steps were the widest but found he felt more secure if he could brace himself against the newel column at his right They passed two more landings with iron-barred doors before stopping in front of a third arched door. His right knee ached from the seemingly endless upward movement.

Simon waited several steps below since there was not room on the landing for all three to stand. He noticed Bryn too, was winded from the steep climb. His chest hurt from strenuous breathing and head felt light. He wondered if he wasn't quite recovered from his illness.

"I can't imagine fainting," he thought as he looked behind him at the winding newel stair that spun down into darkness. "Beyond the embarrassment of making a fool of myself, it would be a nasty tumble down those stone stairs." He looked back up just as Bryn was following Brother Felix through the doorway.

The room they entered was dark and therefore it was hard to judge its dimensions. The newel stair at least had several long, narrow, cross-shaped window openings at regular intervals to let in light and air. At first Simon thought there were no windows at all in this room but as his eyes adjusted to the dimness, he saw very small slits of light high above their heads.

Brother Felix turned toward them, speaking for the first time.

"I have a very treasured copy of the Anglo Saxon Chronicles from Peterborough Abbey, written in 1116. It documents both King Harald's and King William's forces. I believe that you will find mention there of the Montbury family. If you will follow me, I will take you to it. It cannot be moved."

"Oh, of course." Bryn quickly followed Brother Felix, grabbing Simon by the sleeve and pulling him along. In the few minutes that he had stood in the room, Simon's eyes had adjusted somewhat to the dim light. The room was quite long, not narrow but rectangular shaped, more like a grand gallery. Simon felt more than saw that it was high, but the ceiling was still in darkness. He was starting to make out shelves that ran the whole length of the side walls. The shelves, he assumed, held books, or perhaps chests and boxes that contained books. He could make out oddly shaped objects piled on the shelves but it was still too dim to see them clearly.

"Bryn," Simon whispered in her ear. "I don't think…"

"Hush!" Bryn warned, indicating Brother Felix just in front of her.

"But Bryn, I really think…" Simon whispered again, this time grasping her sleeve.

She continued to ignore him. He squinted into the dimness, trying to better make out the objects on the shelves. They were definitely arranged in some kind of order. There seemed to be one shelf of rounded objects, and below that a shelf of long, thin objects. Scrolls perhaps?

He stepped a few feet to Bryn's side to get a bit closer to the wall. It was still easily 20 feet from him. Brother Felix had finally stopped at yet another door. The rattle of the keys was followed by a scraping as the door opened. Simon took advantage of this distraction to take a few steps toward the shelves. He gasped and turned to grab Bryn but she grabbed him first and pulled him through the door.

"For heaven's sake Simon, we said we would stay together. You are making Brother Felix suspicious." In the next moment both of them were in a small, stone room with a stone bench built into one wall and a long narrow table in the center of the room. The only other object in the room was a wooden box against the wall perpendicular to the door. They heard the door click shut and the scraping of the key in the lock. Bryn turned to ask Brother Felix about the book. He had disappeared. They were alone. Locked in this small, dark, damp, windowless, stone room. She saw Simon sit down, shoulders slumped, on the stone bench.

"Do you think he's gone to get the book?" Bryn asked in confusion.

"No. No, I don't think he has gone to get the book, if there even is a book," Simon said, staring at the floor.

"What do you mean? What are you saying?" Bryn came over and stood in front of Simon, hands on hips.

"I am saying that I think we have been tricked. Brother Felix had no intention of showing us a book. He has imprisoned us here."

Bryn stared angrily at Simon for a moment and then ran to the door and shook the handle. She pulled hard on it, one foot braced against the door frame for strength. She pounded on the door and yelled for Brother Felix. She went back to the center of room and turned around slowly, looking up at the ceiling high above, scanning the walls. Given the size of the room, this took only a matter of seconds.

"How can he think he can get away with this? People come to use the library all the time. They will hear us yelling, surely?"

"We are not in the library anymore, Bryn. I think those newel stairs took us high up into the tower, several stories above the library."

"Well then, what is all that out there?" Bryn pointed to the door. "Someone eventually will want access to those scrolls." Evidently she had noticed the scrolls on the shelves too.

"You mean the long, thin white objects? They're not scrolls." Simon finally looked up at Bryn. "That's what I thought at first too, but I got a better look when I stepped closer."

"Well? What are they?" Bryn asked impatiently.

"Leg bones. The shelves are filled with bones. Rows of skulls all piled together, then rows of ribs, then rows of arm and leg bones."

Bryn sunk down onto the hard bench next to Simon.

"An ossuary," she whispered.

"Of course." It was Simon's turn to get up and walk around the room. "Yes, of course. Many monasteries took the bones of the dead monks and kept them in ossuaries. In fact, some made elaborate decorations from them---huge chandeliers out of skulls and ribs and leg bones. The Sedlec Ossuary in the Czech Republic is incredible in its..." Simon stopped when he saw Bryn's face.

"Well, thank you for that enlightening lesson on burial customs," she said stingingly. "Do you have any idea why we are here, or what Brother Felix is planning for us? And by the way, Mr. Know Everything, where is 'here?'" Bryn waved her arm in an arch around the room.

Simon looked around. He focused on the table in the middle of the room. It was long and narrow but its most unusual feature was that it was slightly tilted toward one end. There was a narrow trough with a hole in the lower end. He looked up silently at Bryn.

" 'Here,' I would say, is where they take the dead bodies of the monks to prepare them for burial." He pointed to the table. "This table is slightly slanted to let the bodily fluids drain down into this trough. They would drip through the hole and be caught in a..."

"OK, OK, enough. I get the idea," Bryn paled. "So what you are saying is, no one is going to come up here unless someone dies."

"Yes, I would say so. And with these stone walls and floors, I think we could yell and scream until we are hoarse and no one would hear us. Brother Felix, I think, is planning on letting us die up here." They were both silent for a few moments, each thinking their own thoughts.

"I don't suppose, in your vast knowledge," Bryn finally said, "you know how long it takes to starve to death?"

Chapter Thirty Two

Brother Felix had calmly and quietly made his way back down the long, winding newel stair. His knees ached from the climb downward and he was winded by the time he reached the scriptorium door. He heard the amarius calling out to the scribes to put their quills down just as the bells began to ring for Nones, the fourth of the Little Hours of the divine office. The monks would soon be gathering in the church to recite prayers and chant the office. He nodded to the amarius as he walked through the scriptorium, hands concealed in his flowing brown sleeves. The other monks began to follow, out the door into the yard and through the cloisters to the church. Brother Felix slowed his steps, not unusual in a monk his age. The other brothers soon passed him by. When he saw the last monk go inside the church, he turned abruptly and quickened his pace heading for the stables. He would be alone now but he had to be quick. He walked into the stables and grabbed the reins of the two horses Bryn and Simon had rode to the monastery. He loosed the girths that held the saddles on, and led them from the stable yard, across the far side of the courtyard to the door in the wall that led to the orchard. Once through the door, he loosely looped the reins around each saddle pommel. He slapped each horse on the flank and waved his hands sending them galloping away from the monastery. Felix knew they would eventually find their way back to the manor riderless, and hopefully with saddles loose or fallen off. It would be assumed Bryn and Simon had had an accident or come upon brigands on the road. Whatever they thought, at least there would be no sign of them at the monastery.

"What time do you think it is?" Bryn asked Simon. It was her turn to sit on the bench, elbows on her knees, chin on hands.

"About 10 minutes later than the last time you asked me," Simon said, irritated. He had spent the last half hour fiddling with the large iron hinges on the door, hoping to find a way to loosen them. He kicked the door in frustration and walked over to sit next to Bryn.

"I'm hungry," Bryn said. "And I'm really thirsty." Simon glanced sideways at her but offered no comfort. "And worse, it smells in here."

"Well, it is a death room," Simon offered in explanation.

"It will smell a lot worse with our rotting corpses up here," Bryn added.

"That's a delightful thought. Thank you for sharing," Simon said crossly.

They sat next to each other in silence for some time. Finally Simon let out a long breath and stood up.

"Come on, we can't just sit here until we starve to death."

"I'll take any other option, if there are any," Bryn smiled.

"Let's at least talk through this. Let's go over everything we know," Simon suggested.

"OK, first, we know we are locked in a windowless room. The one door in or out is solid wood with iron strapping and it's double locked," Bryn began.

"We know it is unlikely anyone will come up here in the near future, and no one can possibly hear us yelling through several floors of stone," Simon added.

"We have no food, no water."

"No way to get help."

They were silent again, having run out of things to say.

"Well," said Bryn, getting up and brushing the wrinkles from her kirtle. "I certainly feel much better now that we clarified our situation. How about you?"

Simon glared at her, ignoring the sarcasm.

"Bryn, how well do you know the abbey? I mean can you mentally picture where we might be exactly?"

Bryn thought for a minute, staring up at the darkened ceiling.

"This place was originally a fortress built on the orders of William the Conqueror." She started to walk along the curved wall, one hand on the damp stone. "It was badly damaged in one of the battles between King Stephen and Queen Maud. When Sir Robert inherited it, he didn't think it was worth rebuilding as a fortress so he deeded it to the church to be rebuilt as an abbey instead."

"So this tower was probably really once a guard tower on the curtain wall before the monks turned it into a library— among other things." Simon thought of the ossuary beyond their door.

"Yes, most certainly. The monks did rebuild the stone curtain wall by taking down the other three towers and using the materials. If I remember, the wall has a wide battlement on top and connects the tower with the second floor of the dorter where the monks sleep."

Simon was thoughtful. "Theoretically then, we aren't just hanging in air." He looked at Bryn's questioning face.

"I mean, we know we are high up in the tower but if we could somehow get out we might be near enough to the top of the wall to be able to climb up to, or jump down to, the battlement. It's not like we would just be 200 feet up the air with no where to go."

"First off, how can we possibly get out of here? And second, how can we be sure we wouldn't be on the outer wall of the tower that drops down to the cliff edge?"

"Use your head! Let's figure it out," Simon said in frustration. "Isn't anything better than just sitting here waiting to die?"

Bryn looked about to argue but then shrugged her shoulders.

"Yes, I suppose you're right. Besides, I have to pee so we need to get out of here as soon as possible."

Simon stared at her in disbelief. She stared back, hands on hips. That always indicated her seriousness he had noticed. Suddenly they both laughed.

"Yes, that certainly gives us both motivation. Now, my thought is to find a place in the wall where the mortar looks weak. You said this place was built in William's time? That was over a hundred years ago. There must be places where the mortar joints have started to crumble, especially way up here where the monks wouldn't readily notice. What do we have for tools?" he looked around.

Bryn followed his gaze. "Nothing, I would say."

"We can at least use that box over there to stand on, or maybe even break it up into sharp sticks to dig at the mortar?" Simon suggested. Bryn nodded and walked over to the large wooden box against the wall.

"Ugh!" She covered her mouth and nose. "A rat must have died over here, the smell is much worse. Almost as bad as you the day we met." She smiled sweetly at Simon. As he came over to help, Bryn lifted the lid of the box.

Her scream echoed off the walls as she fell backwards, taking Simon to the floor with her. She was on her hands and knees in a flash, across the floor and pressing up against the far wall, trying to get as far away from the box as she could. Simon, the breath knocked out of him, raised himself from the floor and crept on hands and knees over to the box whose lid was askew. Inside was a hideous sight—the decaying corpse of a man. The eyes were gone, the hair like cobwebs, the skin on the face stretched tight over protruding cheekbones. The lips were pulled back into a gruesome smile but the lower jaw was slack and hung open. Simon gasped and rocked back on his heels.

He looked over at Bryn who still sat on the floor with her hands covering her face. She took her hands away and Simon saw terror in her eyes. Bryn jumped up and ran to the door. She banged and banged on it, frantically scratched at the hinges, pulled at the latch and kicked at the impervious wood. Simon quickly got up and ran to her. He grabbed both her hands, now bloodied, and pulled her away from the door. He took her over to the stone bench, as far from the thing in the box as possible and held her tightly. She was shaking, burying her head against his chest. Simon said nothing, holding her tightly until the shaking had calmed.

For several minutes neither moved. Bryn became quiet and Simon almost wondered if she had fainted or fallen asleep. But then he heard her voice, very muffled in the folds of his tunic.

"Simon," the muffled voice said.

"Hmmm?" Simon answered, stroking her hair with his hand. She kept her face turned into his shoulder.

"I don't have to pee anymore."

Chapter Thirty Three

Jasper came through the kitchen door. His face was grim. He looked around for Agnes and found her bent over a large barrel in the corner of the kitchen.

"Agnes!" he called sharply.

"Mpphgh!" Agnes bumped her head as she pulled herself out of the barrel. She was coated with flour from her elbows down. Loose strands of hair floated about her round face.

"God's bones you scared me!" she said crossly to Jasper.

"Well, I've got some news that will truly scare you," Jasper said grimly. "Eleanor and Alizay have just returned to the manor riderless. Eleanor's saddle is gone and Alizay's was loose, nearly falling off."

Agnes gasped, put her hand to her chest and sat down heavily on the stool.

"Blessed saints!" she whispered, then looked up at Jasper. "What can this mean?"

"I was hoping you could tell me," Jasper said sternly. "There have been strange goings-on here, ever since that boy arrived. If you know anything at all about this, Agnes…" he let the sentence hang in the air.

Agnes turned anguished eyes on him. "I only know very little. I know that Mistress Bryn and Simon were trying to discover some secret at the monastery. That's really where Simon got ill. He was poisoned while looking for something at the monastery. That's where they went this morning."

Jasper's face registered confusion. "The monastery? What in all the saint's names could be there?"

Agnes brought her apron up to cover her face and began to sob.

"Stop now, woman! This doesn't help either us or them. We don't even know if any harm has come to them. They might show up, tired and worn from walking, but fine. I will get some men from the village and we will ride through the forest to see if they have been thrown. Even if they were attacked by brigands," here Agnes began to sob again, "we should find some indication."

Jasper turned to go.

"S'blood!" he swore and hit the table with his fist. Agnes jumped. "Is there anyone else here that can write? We need to get a message to Sir Robert about all this."

Agnes shook her head. Bryn and Simon were the only two in the manor that she knew could read and write.

"Wait! The priest knows some Latin, perhaps he could write a letter for us?"

"See if you can manage to get him to do that," Jasper commanded. "That is if he knows anything other than the Lord's Prayer. A lot of good that would do. And Agnes, if they do return, they will need warm food and a warm fire. See to it."

Agnes nodded eagerly, glad for something useful to do, something to keep her mind and hands occupied. She wiped her nose on her apron, brushed the flour from her hands and set out to find the priest.

Chapter Thirty Four

"It's Brother Barnabas I'm certain," Bryn said, her voice still slightly shaky. "He had an odd scar on the left side of his face that you can still see on that…" she glanced at the box that held the corpse, "…on his face."

"The other librarian?" Simon asked. "But I thought no one knew what happened to him."

"No one did know." Bryn turned to face Simon. "I remember asking that young monk who helped me the day Brother Felix was ill. I wondered why they had assigned him to help me instead of Brother Barnabas."

"What did he say?" Simon asked.

"He said that Brother Felix told him that Brother Barnabas had been sent to Durham to pick up a manuscript and never returned. The monks at Durham said he'd never arrived. Everyone assumed he'd been killed by brigands or by a fall from his horse."

"But here he is." Simon looked with a grimace toward the box against the far wall. "Why would Brother Felix lie about it? He must be the one who brought the body up here since he is the only one with the keys."

"Because HE killed him of course," Bryn stated. "He killed Brother Barnabas and hid the body here, then made up a story about sending him to Durham."

"But why?" Simon queried.

"For the same reason he put powdered Monk's Hood in the chest of books? For the same reason he's locked us here to die?" Bryn asked.

"But what is that reason? We have to assume it is to keep us, or anyone else, from getting to the manuscript that the puzzle points to. Perhaps Brother Barnabas," Simon paused, it was hard to think of that disgusting thing in the box as Brother Barnabas, "perhaps he too was looking for the manuscript, or maybe even came across it accidentally. Brother Felix found out and had to kill him?"

"It makes sense. But what is worth killing three people over?" Bryn wondered. "It doesn't really matter right now though. We still need to find a way out of here." Bryn looked at Simon, fear growing in her eyes. "Simon, what if he decides not to wait for us to die of starvation? He could be back at any time to kill us."

"He's awfully old, do you think he could kill off two young people?" Simon asked.

"He killed Barnabas, didn't he?" They both looked again at the box on the floor across the room.

Simon stood up.

"We still need something to dig at the mortar with." He saw Bryn's panicked look. "I'll take some of the planks from the box, you stay here and try to imagine the position of the tower with regards to the wall. Where should we start to dig if we want to hit the battlement?" As Simon hoped, she looked relieved that he was not going to ask her to go back to that box and help retrieve some planks. He was far from happy about the task himself but knew there was no other way. He steeled himself, took a deep breath, hoping he would not have to breath in the foul odor and walked quickly over to the box.

Brother Barnabas still grinned hideously out from box. As much as the sight made his stomach queasy, he thought it might be important to see if there was any sign of how Barnabas had died. He didn't know if that would be important, but every piece of information seemed worth having. Perhaps, if Bryn was right and Brother Felix was coming back to kill them, knowing how Barnabas died would give them some idea of how they might protect themselves.

By now he had to let his breath out so he crooked his elbow over his mouth and nose trying to filter the smell as he took another breath. He knelt down next to the box. He would scan the body for obvious injuries but he drew the line at actually touching it. Simon could see nothing to indicate how the monk had been killed. He was about to turn his attention to retrieving some planks from the lid when something caught his eye. There was what looked like a roll or tube of leather tucked under the left arm of Brother Barnabas. It was tied with a leather strip and at the very end, where the leather flap fell loosely, he could see parchment. Simon looked over his shoulder at Bryn. She was standing up, hands on hips, staring at the tower wall. He guessed she was trying to draw a mental map of the monastery to determine where the wall met the tower. He decided not to bother her. She would not want to come over here anyway. With a grimace he used two fingers to gently lift the arm of the corpse and expose the leather roll. He was surprised at how light it felt, as if the sleeve was empty. With the other hand he slid the roll out and away from the body. It caught just as he was about to lift it out of the box.

Simon stopped, one hand pulling at the roll, the other holding up the dead arm of the monk. He bent his head to look under the arm and see what the roll had caught on. He saw a thin leather strap attached to the end of the leather case. The other end of the strap went under the shoulder of the monk. Evidently this was some kind of satchel made to carry parchment rolls and hang from one's shoulder.

Simon tugged again and the corpse's head lolled to one side with the movement. His stomach lurched. He carefully lowered the arm and used both hands to gently pull at the strap. It finally came loose and he snaked it out from under the arm and put the roll on the floor by his knees.

Simon looked at the wooden box lid. The long planks were still quite solid and he couldn't imagine using just his hands to break them apart and into useable pieces. But there were two short cross pieces that held the planks in place. He might be able to pry these off and they would work well to dig at the mortar of the tower stones.

"I'm going to have to drop this lid on the floor to see if I can break it up," he said over his shoulder.

"Fine," Bryn said, not turning around.

Simon stood up and held the lid high over his head. It was not terribly heavy but it was quite awkward. He slammed it to the stone floor. The noise seemed incredibly loud but it did little damage. Three more times he threw the lid to the floor and finally it bent and broke into three pieces.

"Yes!" Simon pulled at the two cross braces and used his feet to kick off the longer planks still attached. "Got it!" he turned toward Bryn, two pieces of wood held triumphantly in each hand.

"Here," Bryn pointed to the wall just above where they were sitting. "Given that the door to this room is in the same direction as the rooms of the library, then opposite the door must be the outer wall of the tower itself. So the curtain wall must be in this direction."

Simon slowly let his arms fall, miffed at Bryn for ignoring his moment of triumph. If she cared so little for his help, then maybe he wouldn't tell her about the parchment he had found. He tucked it inside his tunic.

"OK then, get to work." He threw a piece of wood toward Bryn who caught it with a scowl.

They both spent the next several minutes feeling around each stone in the wall for any sign of crumbling mortar. Bryn finally felt some loose beneath her fingers and called Simon over.

"Let's start here. We need to begin somewhere. It's strange though." She stood back and stared at the wall.

"What?" Simon asked.

"There is a narrow section of the wall right there that is not the same temperature as the wall on either side. Hardly noticeable unless you've been carefully running your hands along it as we have, but still, it is slightly warmer, slightly less damp."

181

"Maybe that is where the afternoon sun hits the tower?" Simon suggested.

"Hmmm." Bryn was thoughtful. "Well, it doesn't really matter does it, let's just get started."

For several hours the two scratched and dug and scraped at the mortar around several large stones in the wall. It was an exhausting process that seemed to be getting them nowhere. Several times one or the other stopped and sat, resting against the wall. They were covered with black dust and sweat. Lack of food and water, lack of sleep and the horrible experiences they had gone through were beginning to drain them of mental and physical energy.

"Simon," Bryn put her hand on Simon's arm. He stopped and turned to her. "Let's just sit for a minute and rest. I feel like we haven't even made a dent in the wall. Maybe if we just stop looking at it for a moment, and then go back to it, it will look better."

Simon nodded, too tired to speak. He wiped the sweat from his forehead with the sleeve of his tunic that was so dirty it merely left a darker streak of dirt on his face. They both sat on the floor, leaning back against the wall. Bryn leaned her head on Simon's shoulder and let the stick in her hand fall to the floor.

"I'm so sorry about all this, Simon. I got us into this and have endangered your life twice. If we don't get out of here..."

"We are getting out of here," Simon said with determination.

"Well if we don't, I just want to tell you that I'm truly sorry and I wouldn't want to die with anyone else but you."

There was silence for a moment.

"Thanks, I think," Simon said. "But we aren't dead yet." He got up and stared at the wall.

"Bryn, just move out of the way will you?" She looked at him oddly but slid several feet to the right. Simon walked over to the door and then ran toward the wall and jumped up and kicked at the stones. He fell to the floor but immediately picked himself up and repeated his running kick.

"Simon! I think I heard scraping. Yes, I am sure I did." Bryn quickly got up and looked at the stones. "Come over here and push with me."

Together they pushed and kicked at the stones, their energy and spirits renewed. Surely there was movement? Bits of crumbling mortar fell onto the ground. It took them both another half hour of kicking and scraping and pushing but then they felt the two large stones wobble and fall outward.

Bryn let out a sob and covered her face with her hands. Simon collapsed to his knees on the floor. They took several minutes to control their physical and emotional exhaustion, then Bryn reached down and offered Simon her hand. He shakily got to his feet and the two walked over to the hole in the tower wall. They said nothing for a moment, each staring at the black hole.

"Something isn't right," Bryn finally said.

"It's pitch black, could it be the middle of the night?" Simon took a step closer to the hole. "Oh! It smells worse out there than it does in here."

Bryn frowned and came closer. She started to put her head through hole, hoping to see the night sky and an outline of the wall. The black was complete. The smell was overwhelming.

"That's not a dead body smell. That's—that's the smell of a garderobe."

"Garderobe? What is that?" Simon asked covering his nose with his sleeve.

"Well," Bryn seemed uncertain how to answer. "It's where people go to…I mean in regular homes, we might use a chamber pot to—you know."

Simon's blank expression told her he did not know.

"Oh for heaven's sake. It's a room one uses to relieve oneself---to urinate or defecate." Bryn's cheeks reddened. This was not something a lady would discuss with a man. "In castle towers, they put garderobes up high in the towers and the…well, you know, the human waste, falls down a shoot to the bottom. That's why the temperature of the wall here was different. This

183

part of the tower is not exposed to the outside air, it abuts the garderobe shoot."

Simon looked at her disbelieving. "Do you mean to tell me we have spent all this time digging our way out only to have dug our way into a latrine?"

"Well, there must be a floor above us, where the toilet is, and this shoot goes from that toilet down the tower wall to the bottom. There would be a small opening at the bottom where the gong farmer would clean it out every once in a while."

"A gong farmer," Simon repeated, "well, that would be something to put on your resume I suppose." Bryn had learned to ignore these unintelligible statements he often made.

"Simon, this isn't really bad news. Think about it. If we had managed to open up a hole to the outside, we couldn't be sure we would be anywhere near the battlement to jump to safety. This way, we can crawl down this shoot to the bottom of the tower with no one seeing us."

Simon's face registered his shock and disgust.

"Do you seriously mean you want us to crawl into that?" he pointed to the black hole, where a warm and disgustingly pungent breeze now blew.

Bryn put her hands on her hips. "Do you have any other plan?"

They stared at each other for several seconds. Simon shook his head.

"OK, who's first?"

Chapter Thirty Five

Moira spent the next day in her office focused on the new museum exhibit. Her work had been badly neglected for days and she couldn't continue to ignore it. She also felt she had hit a wall with her work on the palimpsest. Worse, she felt a terrible guilt about being so giddily happy around Owen when she had no idea what kind of trouble Simon might be in.

"He isn't necessarily in any trouble." She had argued with herself after Owen had left that evening. But there were things that worried her deeply. Simon had some experience traveling through time. He had twice successfully gone and returned on separate journeys. So why hadn't he returned from this one then?

"Well, he could be really enjoying himself and he doesn't want to come back yet." But Moira knew Simon would not willingly leave her without any knowledge of where he was or what he was doing. She also knew he hadn't controlled this journey, something had pulled him there. "Something that needs doing, needs fixing." Moira thought. She had seriously considered trying to follow him. She did have a pretty good idea of the general time and place he might be. But 'general' time and place in time travel can be a huge target, she admitted to herself. "If I missed him by just one year, it would be completely useless, and I might even do more harm than good."

There were many uncontrollable factors in time travel. It wasn't a science. There were no formulas to guarantee where, when or how you traveled. With practice, you could get quite good, but there was no such thing as perfect control in this game. So she mostly had to wait and do what she could to figure out her end of the puzzle.

The phone on her office desk rang. As usual she ignored it and waited for the machine to pick it up. After four rings she heard a familiar voice that sent the butterflies in her stomach fluttering.

"Moira, it's Owen. I'm sorry to have missed you…"

Moira launched herself across the room and slid across her desk, grabbing the phone earpiece but sending everything else flying.

"Hello!" she said breathlessly. "I'm here!"

There were two seconds of confused silence followed by Owen's laugh. "You sound like you just ran a marathon."

"Oh, no." Moira tried to calm her breathing and automatically smoothed her disheveled hair. "No, I was just starting down the hall when I heard the phone ring, so I ran to pick it up," she lied.

"You must have changed then over the years," Owen said, with a smile in his voice. "You used to put the phone in the waste basket when it rang, or just let the answering machine get it. And I don't think I can ever remember you pressing the PLAY button on the machine to hear those messages."

Moira looked guiltily at the answering machine she had knocked to the floor in her dive for the phone. It had the number "56" blinking in red on it.

"What can I do for you?" she asked Owen and then grimaced. She sounded like she was taking his order at a fast food window.

"I spent a couple hours looking over the copies of all your materials on Henry and Eleanor. I have some thoughts about it. Can we have dinner together to talk about it?"

"Yes!" Moira said way too quickly. She coughed. "I mean, I might be able to cancel my dinner with," she looked desperately at her bookshelf and turned her head sideways to read the authors on the spine. A large book titled "The Medieval Age"

186

by Wilbur Haralfson caught her eye, "with Wilbur Haralfson." She closed her eyes and wondered what in heaven's name she was doing.

"Hmmm, that name is vaguely familiar—do I know him?"

"No, I'm sure you don't. Anyway, let's say 7:00 tonight?"

"That sounds great. To save time, why don't I bring Chinese take-out."

"Sure, sounds great. See you then." Moira hung up and looked at her watch. There was no time to call her housekeeper. If she left now, she could get most of the clutter of the apartment shoved under her bed before he came.

Chapter Thirty Six

Simon's hands were sore from hours of scraping at stone. Now they were slick with sweat and his fingers were tingling strangely. He knew that feeling. His uncle had taken him water skiing one summer. It was so frightening that his hands had felt weak and tingly as he held tightly to the rope that attached him to the boat. Now, as he braced himself against the garderobe tunnel, his back against one wall, his legs pushed stiff against the other wall and his fingers reaching for small holds on the rough inner stones, all he could think of was losing his grip and falling all the way down into…actually he didn't want to think about what was at the bottom of the shoot.

Bryn quietly called down to him. "Are you OK?"

He shook himself and craned his neck to look up. Not that either of them could see the other in the pitch dark.

"Yes, I'm OK. You can come down. It's narrow enough so that if you brace yourself with your feet on one wall, you can slide down with your back against the opposite wall. But you have to find niches with your hands to keep yourself from falling and kind of inch down. Can you do that?"

It was a moment before she answered.

"I guess I'll have to, won't I?"

Simon thought of how badly Bryn's hands were bruised from her hysterical pounding on the door, and then from hours of scraping at the tower stones.

"You'll be OK. If you think you are slipping, warn me and I'll brace myself to catch you."

"OK. OK, I'm starting down now."

It seemed an unending journey, inching very slowly, feeling in the dark for stones sticking out from the wall or holes in which to lodge fingers. Simon would move his legs, braced hard against the opposite wall, a few inches each time, then slide his back down to the same level holding on anywhere he could to keep some control. He was sure his back was rubbed raw from sliding down the rough wall and each movement hurt more than the last. The air was thick and humid and felt hotter as time went on although Simon thought that was probably just his own body heat in the enclosed space. He seemed to have gotten used to the smell or at least it hadn't gotten worse.

"Augh!" He heard Bryn call out and several small stones fell on him from above. He shoved his legs and back against the opposing walls to brace himself.

"It's OK, I'm OK," she said breathlessly. "A piece of rock I was holding onto broke off but I caught myself."

Simon let out his breath.

"Do you have any idea how much further to the bottom?" she asked, her voice quavering with exhaustion. Simon suddenly realized how hard this must be for her and stopped feeling badly for himself.

"Shhh!" he said. "Just listen for a second." He kicked out at the wall with one foot to loosen some stone. They listened as the stoned bounced briefly off the wall and then made a soft plop.

"Bryn," he said excitedly, "that sounded very close. I think we are really near the bottom. I think I can jump from here."

"Simon, please, please, are you sure? If you are wrong you will drop to your death."

"In a pile of dung," Simon thought. "That would be a heroic ending." He called up.

189

"Yes, I think it's fine. I'm going to try it."

He brought one leg down, braced himself upright in the shoot, pushed himself off the wall and dropped. He hit the bottom of the tunnel, landing up to his calves on the soft bottom.

"Bryn, come down just a few more feet and you'll be fine. You are only about 15 feet from the bottom."

The cool, fresh, night air was so delicious they both stood gulping in deep breaths. They had found the small wooden door at the bottom of the garderobe shoot and crawled out. It opened onto the very steep hillside outside the abbey wall.

"It makes sense really," Bryn explained. "The gong farmer, who is in charge of cleaning this out periodically, just opens the door at the bottom of the tower and shovels it all down the hill."

"Well, lucky for us we didn't walk out into the middle of the cloister where we could have been seen by anyone." Simon looked down the steep hillside where trees grew thickly. "But getting down this slope in one piece isn't going to be easy."

"We can't leave! We have to get the horses," Bryn insisted. Simon stared at her in disbelief.

"Are you raving mad?" Simon asked. "You can't seriously think we are going to just walk back into the monastery, looking like death by the way, and ride out on the horses."

Bryn glared him, trying to think of a way to get to the stables. Simon sighed, he knew how important Eleanor was to her.

"Think about it, Bryn. Brother Felix has likely sent them both back to the manor. How else would he explain our absence if the horses were still there?"

Bryn's face lightened. "Of course. They would have run back to the manor and that would have alerted Jasper and Agnes of trouble. Simon, they are probably out looking for us right now!"

"Well then," Simon said, relieved she had dropped her unreasonable request to retrieve the horses. "Let's give them something to find."

He took her hand and they carefully made their way down the steep slope away from the abbey. It was quite dark but some moonlight showed through a layer of scuttering clouds, allowing them to pick their way through trees and brush. They had both decided not to return to the road until they were some distance from the abbey, just in case Brother Felix had discovered their escape.

For the first hour the exhilaration of being out of the tower and breathing fresh, clean air gave them energy to go on. But soon they both felt a wave of exhaustion.

"Simon," Bryn stopped and sat down, her back against a large oak tree. "I just can't go on anymore. I feel sick with exhaustion."

Simon welcomed the chance to rest. He too was ready to collapse but didn't want to say so. He looked up at the moon.

"I think we are far enough away from the monastery for safety. And since we've stayed off the road, I don't know how they could find us even if someone were after us. Let's just get some rest for an hour and then we can try to find the road. It will be easier walking."

There was no shelter to be seen so they both lay down among the pine needles and decaying leaves. Simon could see Bryn was shivering in the cool night air. He lay down next to her and tried as best he could to cover her with folds of his tunic, thankful for once that Agnes had made it too large for him. Within minutes, both of them were deeply asleep.

Simon felt a sharp pain in his side. He groaned and rolled away from the stone that was making an indent in his ribs. Suddenly his eyes flew open and he quickly reached into his tunic. He had forgotten all about the roll of parchment he had hidden there. In the climb down the garderobe, it had become

191

flattened against his side. Yes, it was still there. He let out a sigh of relief. He looked around thinking to wake Bryn but realized she wasn't there. They had slept much longer than expected. In fact, the sun was up, sending weak, slanting rays of light through the forest. He was just starting to worry when he heard Bryn coming through the trees. She was humming quietly and combing her wet hair with her fingers.

"Good morning," she said brightly. "You look a fright! And you smell even worse. You do have a terrible habit of collecting nasty smells about you."

Simon looked down at himself. He was filthy. Covered with layers of thick black stone dust, broken twigs and leaves sticking to fabric and skin. He hair felt matted to his head and he guessed his face was as black as his arms.

"You seem awfully cheerful this morning given our situation. And I assume you looked and smelled as bad as I do when you woke up."

"Well yes, I did," she grinned, "but I knew the river couldn't be too far away so I took a bit of a walk and found it. There is a perfect place to bathe and wash your clothes. Come on, I'll show you."

Simon noticed her clothes were quite damp but at least somewhat cleaner. She must have rinsed them out in the river. In just a few minutes they were at the bank of the river. Bryn held out her hand.

"Give me your clothes, I'll wash them out for you while you bathe."

"I'm not taking off my clothes with you here!" Simon stepped back.

"Oh, for heaven's sake, Simon." She dropped her arm. "OK, I'll turn around. You just throw your clothes over there and then get into river. I promise I won't peek."

Simon hesitated, but the thought of getting at least some of the filth off of him was too enticing. He walked behind a tree and disrobed, throwing his tunic and hose over toward Bryn. He quietly placed the leather pouch with the parchment down beside the tree and then walked to the river bank, looking back over his shoulder several times to make sure Bryn was not looking.

"OH MY GOSH!" Simon yelled as he stepped into the river. It was ice cold. In seconds his feet were numb. "There is no WAY I am going in that river!"

"And there is no way I am going anywhere with you looking and smelling like that." Bryn called back over her shoulder.

"Bryn, this is crazy!" he protested.

"Simon, I am going to count to three and then I am turning around. Either you are in that river up to your neck, or I am going to see much more of you than either of us want. One, two …"

Bryn heard a splash and a loud yell. She smiled to herself, picked up the clothes and walked upstream to wash them whistling as she went.

Simon was standing behind the large tree waiting for Bryn to return with his clothes. His lips were blue and he couldn't stop himself from shaking violently. He felt terribly vulnerable standing frozen and naked behind a tree in the forest. Bryn came into view, still whistling loudly enough to warn Simon of her approach.

"I'm here!" Simon poked his head around the tree. He was shivering so much with the cold that his teeth were chattering. Bryn walked up to the tree and handed him his clothes. They were very damp but much cleaner. He grabbed them and put them on as quickly as his shaking hands would allow. For the first few seconds, they felt like sheets of ice but the damp quickly absorbed what little heat his body was producing and he felt some relief.

He tucked the parchment back under his tunic and stepped out.

"Feel better?" Bryn asked brightly.

"Ask me in an hour, when the sun has dried these clothes. I'm surprised I didn't hear you yell when you jumped in the river this morning," Simon said.

"Me?" Bryn stopped and looked at him in surprise. "Are you joking? That water is like ice. I just used my scarf as a wash cloth and stayed on the bank." She turned and began to walk toward the road. Simon stood, teeth still chattering, staring after her. Bryn looked back and smiled.

"Come on! We've a long way to go."

Chapter Thirty Seven

The kitchen table was covered with square white boxes and small clear packets of duck sauce and soy sauce. Moira had forgotten how much she liked Chinese food and after a few minutes of attempting to take tiny, feminine bites of her shrimp egg foo yong, decided to pay attention to her appetite instead of her vanity. She piled her plate high with sweet and sour chicken and pork fried rice. Now she chased the few remaining grains of rice around her plate with her fork and heaved a sigh of contentment. She looked up to see Owen smiling at her as he took his last bite of egg roll.

"That was wonderful!" Moira smiled. "I haven't had Chinese food since…"

"Probably since we had it together for dinner 8 years ago I would imagine," Owen said, wiping his mouth with a napkin.

Moira laughed. "I'm afraid you're right. Left to myself, I rarely think about food."

"Well, if either of us can move, let's go sit on the couch and I'll show you what I've been up to these past few days."

They both cleaned up the kitchen, putting the dishes in the sink and wiping down the kitchen table. Moira put the kettle on and got out mugs for tea. Owen brought his briefcase to the couch and pulled out a legal pad with hand written notes.

"It bothered me when I left last time, to think that Henry might have actually planned a conspiracy against Eleanor." He began. Moira opened her mouth to argue but he held up his hand to forestall her.

"I know. There is a lot of evidence that would support that. It would solve so many of his political and personal problems. But it somehow doesn't fit his character."

"I'm listening." Moira encouraged him to explain.

"Many historians do believe that Henry really didn't order his knights to kill Thomas. That it was in fact, a rash act by a few knights wanting to gain favor with the king and misinterpreting his statement of frustration with Thomas." Owen flipped through some pages on his legal pad. "People who were close to Henry spoke of him as being loyal to his friends and good-natured. He had a hot temper that is true, but his anger was usually quickly dispelled and forgotten."

Moira still looked doubtful.

"Think of the things he didn't do for instance. He could have had his sons killed for their rebellion. He could have done much worse to Eleanor than keep her locked up in castles. And lastly, Henry was a man of action. This," Owen shook the papers outlining the conspiracy in his hand. "this kind of secret planning and conspiracy is not at all like him."

"So what other explanation is there?" Moira asked as she got up to pour tea for them both.

"I've done some more research," Owen said. "Remember that Henry had done a lot to restrain the power of the nobles who had run wild during King Stephen's time. He made a lot of enemies because of that. There were many nobles who would like to see Henry's powers curtailed. Some supported the church and the pope hoping that would curb Henry's power. But there were others who might consider planning something like this to discredit him."

"How does our palimpsest fit in with that?" Moira brought over two steaming cups of Earl Grey tea. She folded one leg under her as she settled into the corner of the couch. Owen thanked her and blew gently on his tea to cool it before taking a sip.

"This conspiracy could be used two ways. It could be used to implicate Eleanor as the one who organized the murder of Thomas. But it could be used to show that Henry was trying to frame Eleanor. That would also point to his own guilt for the murder of Becket. If people thought that he was not only behind the murder of Becket, but also was intent on framing the queen, he would be seen as a liar and a coward. I am sure the environment of "chivalry" that Eleanor and her court had developed would find such behavior in a king despicable. It might go a long way toward swinging the pendulum of power back toward the nobles."

"I suppose really," Moira thought out loud, "that it is possible neither Henry nor Eleanor were responsible for Becket's death. She might have nothing to do with it. His knights might have done it on their own initiative and this could still be used to discredit either or both of them."

"Well, it's one possibility anyway. And it fits better with Henry's character from what I can see."

They both sat lost in their own thoughts for several minutes, sipping tea and reading over notes.

"I wonder what happened then," Moira finally said.

"What do you mean?" Owen asked.

"Well, apparently nothing ever came of this conspiracy. This palimpsest was not ever used either to frame Eleanor or to show Henry as a conspirator. I wonder why?"

"Hmmmm." Owen looked thoughtful. "We'll likely never know."

Moira hoped, if and when Simon returned, he might be able to tell her.

Chapter Thirty Eight

Their clothes had quickly dried in the strengthening sun. A night's rest and the chance to rid themselves of layers of dust and dirt had done much to renew their optimism and energy. It had done nothing to fill their empty stomachs however. The only thing that made it bearable was knowing they would reach the manor by evening if they kept going. The thought of a warm fire, Agnes' cooking and a real bed to sleep in was strong motivation. They decided to follow the road, but kept just off to the side, sheltered by trees and brush for safety's sake.

"Oh, look!" Bryn was down on her knees by the time Simon had caught up with her. "Early strawberries."

Simon saw the tiny, heart-shaped berries scattered amid low, white blossoms. For the next several minutes they picked handfuls, popping them into their mouths.

"I don't think I've ever tasted anything better," Bryn said, wiping red juice from her mouth.

"It is amazing how good food tastes when you haven't had any in a long time," Simon agreed. Both of them sat resting in the dappled sunlight that filtered through the leafy canopy above them. Simon had gotten over being miffed at Bryn about his cold morning bath in the river and he had to admit that it had greatly refreshed and energized him. That's not to say he hadn't briefly considered picking her up and tossing her into the icy water himself. Fortunately, the moment passed quickly as he had more important things to think about. He was, in fact, beginning to feel very guilty about not telling her about the parchment hidden under his tunic.

"Bryn," Simon looked sideways at Bryn, who was leaning against the tree trunk, face upturned to the sun, eyes closed.

"Hmmmm?" she asked, still soaking in the warm rays.

"In all that's happened since escaping from the tower, I'd forgotten to tell you about something I found on Brother Barnabas."

Bryn sat up and looked expectantly at Simon. He reached into his tunic and pulled out the now very flattened and damp leather pouch containing the parchment.

Bryn looked at it, looked up at Simon and then back down at the parchment roll.

"I suppose you decided I didn't deserve to know about this after tricking you into the river?" she asked.

"No. Yes. Not really, it's just been a rather odd 24 hours don't you think? I mean I kept forgetting about it and then things would happen and…"

"Don't worry about it, I guess I did deserve that. Anyway, let's have a look." She carefully untied the leather strap and rolled open the parchment. Simon leaned over to get a closer look. What he saw made him gasp and grab at the parchment.

"God's blood! What's wrong with you!" Bryn said, startled. Simon was intensely looking over the parchment, following the words with his finger, his mouth moving silently as he read. He looked up at Bryn, his face stark.

"Bryn, I've seen this before."

"How could you? Where? When?" Bryn asked dubiously.

"In Professor Ananke's office. This is what we were studying right before I was pulled here. I had just taken a picture of this manuscript when a moment later I found myself face down in a pile of leaves in these woods."

Bryn looked intently at Simon for several seconds before taking the parchment back and studying it. While she did so she unconsciously fingered the silver figure that hung from her neck.

"So," she finally spoke, "this is the thing that brought you here?"

"I guess so. I don't honestly know if that is possible but it must have something to do with it."

"Then this must be the key to everything." She rolled it carefully back up, along with several other pieces of parchment that were still in the leather pouch. They both jumped up suddenly as they heard horses hooves and men's voices approaching. Without a word they crept closer to the edge of road, keeping low and hiding behind the larger trees. They could see down the road for some distance until it curved sharply right. As they looked, three riders came into view. They seemed to be searching the forest on either side and calling out to each other at intervals.

"Jasper!" Bryn cried out and ran to the road. Simon quickly followed. "Jasper, we're here!"

The horses startled and the men quickly reined them in and rode up to the two young people standing at the edge of the road. Jasper and Edwin, the smith, quickly dismounted and handed their reins to a third man whom Simon did not recognize. Jasper walked up and grabbed Bryn by the shoulders.

"S'wounds girl! Where have you been? We've been out all night looking for you." Jasper was unsure whether to be angry or jubilant. He seemed to decide on something in between. Edwin however said nothing but his wide smile revealed his relief at finding them safe.

"It's a long story, Jasper. Can we talk about it when we get home?"

Jasper looked at Bryn and then at Simon. Evidently what he saw made him agree.

"Simon, up behind Edwin. Bryn, you climb up behind me." He called out to the third man who walked the two horses over to them. "Aelfric, you ride back as quickly as you can and tell Agnes they've been found safely. Tell her to try to send another message to Sir Robert as soon as she can."

Aelfric nodded, turned his horse and galloped off. The remaining four rode in pairs back to the manor. Simon found himself nodding off with the movement of the horse and the relief of finally feeling safe.

In the hours that followed their return home, neither Bryn nor Simon had a moment alone to talk about the parchment. Agnes had flown out of the manor house and taken control with an authority that even Jasper didn't dare challenge. The two took turns bathing in luxurious warm water in a large copper tub. Fresh bread, fish cooked on a spit, warm cider and even large slabs of mutton were put before them. Simon was surprised that although his eyes told him he could eat the whole table clean, his stomach in fact was not up to more than a plateful. Bryn seemed to feel the same but Agnes managed to fill them to bursting. They were then both sent up to their rooms where clean clothes were laid out and beds were turned down. As Simon lay down under his fleece covering, he felt his whole body immediately melt into a happy oblivion.

Agnes did not allow the two of them to be disturbed until they woke of their own accord late the next afternoon. As Bryn and Simon were sitting in the kitchen, somewhat muddled from such a long but healing sleep, Jasper walked in with a stern face. Agnes, feeling protective, sat between him and her charges bringing warmed hydromel for everyone. It was Agnes' firm belief that any problem could be solved if enough food and drink were applied to it.

Jasper took a long drink of the honeyed liquid and then put the mug down and looked at Bryn.

"Well?" he asked simply.

Bryn looked at Simon and then at Agnes before answering.

"Jasper, we're so sorry to have caused such an alarm. I don't know how much Agnes has told you," she looked at Agnes who shook her head slightly as if to let Bryn know she had said little to Jasper. "The fact is, we stumbled upon a mystery that we were trying to solve. At first it seemed like just a game really but then things started to happen that were worrisome."

"Agnes tells me you believe someone tried to poison Simon?" Jasper asked, his doubt clear in his voice.

"Not Simon specifically," Bryn corrected. "There was powdered Monk's Hood all over some books we'd found in a chest in the library. We think it was put there to harm anyone who was trying to gain access to the chest. It just happened to be Simon."

"So why would you return to the monastery if there was such danger there?" Jasper asked.

"We got a message from Brother Felix." Jasper looked up quickly at the mention of the monk's name. Bryn continued, "He said he had some information I needed for Sir Robert's genealogy and to meet him at the library. When we got there Brother Felix trapped us in a tower room and locked us there. It took us all day and into the night to get out."

For a moment Jasper said nothing. He stared down into the now empty mug he was holding with both hands. Then he looked up, his face serious and troubled.

"Last night, when we were looking for you, we rode first to the abbey, knowing you had gone there earlier. The prior met us to say he had not seen either of you but he was very upset for another reason." Bryn and Simon leaned forward, wondering what new trouble had occurred at the monastery.

"He said Brother Felix was missing," Jasper finished.

"Missing?" Simon spoke for the first time. "When? How? Did he tell you anything?"

Jasper was still not convinced that Simon was not behind all the recent trouble. Surely it had all started when he suddenly appeared out of nowhere. But he appreciated that Simon had helped Bryn to make it safely back to manor and he had no other choice but to trust him, as long as Bryn did.

"They said the last anyone had seen of Brother Felix was around Nones the day before. The amarius had noticed him coming from the library and crossing the scriptorium just as the bells for Nones were rung."

Bryn looked at Simon. "That must have been just after he left us locked in the tower."

"A few of the other monks remember him falling behind as they all walked to the church. No one can remember seeing him after that."

"Could he have run away, afraid someone would find out what he had done to Bryn and Simon?" Agnes offered.

They discussed possibilities a while longer but no one could offer anything that made sense. Finally, Jasper left to tend to his duties. Before leaving however, he sternly warned Bryn and Simon to end their investigation and stay away from the monastery. As the door closed behind him, Bryn signaled for Simon to follow her out of the kitchen.

"We can't stop now, we are so close," Bryn said in frustration to Simon. They were both in the solar sitting once again at the table. Bryn pulled out the parchment Simon had taken from the tower room and spread it out on the table. Heads together, they studied each word trying to fit them into some form that made sense.

"What did you and Moira decide about the piece you had?" Bryn asked, pulling the parchment that Simon had first seen in the museum over in front of them.

"We didn't get very far with it actually. She pointed out that it had been changed to show female instead of male endings."

"Simon," Bryn said suddenly. "I have to ask you this, it has been bothering me ever since we first met."

Simon looked inquiringly at her.

"Why did you have a rotting fish in your pocket when you first came here?"

Simon laughed. "At first, I wondered that myself. It's not something I make a habit of doing, keeping rotten fish in my pocket I mean. But then I figured it out. I was playing around with a fossil fish that Professor Ananke uses as a paper weight. I popped it into my pocket to pick up the camera so I could take a picture of the palimpsest." Bryn was looking more confused. "A camera is something that makes a picture of an object, without having to draw it. It's kind of complicated. Anyway, that was right before I got pulled here."

"I still don't get it. How did a fossil fish become a rotten fish in your pocket?" Bryn asked.

Simon took a deep breath. He wasn't sure he could explain it since he didn't completely understand it himself.

"Time travel is unpredictable. Time is sort of a living thing. It isn't just an idea or a concept. It's matter, and it flows like a river." Bryn listened intently, her forehead wrinkled in concentration. "For instance, sometimes you can be gone for weeks at a time and you return back and only hours have passed in your real life. Other times you think you've only traveled a day and you come back and weeks have gone by. It's because time doesn't flow evenly. Just like a river going over rocks or falls or widening and narrowing as it flows, the speed changes, and sometimes even the direction changes."

Simon realized from Bryn's expression that much of this wasn't making sense.

"Somehow this fish, that died millions of years ago and fossilized, was brought back to life because it traveled with me through time. Not just that, but it lived, died and was beginning to decay already just in the few seconds it took me to travel from my time to here."

"How come that didn't happen to you?" Bryn asked.

"Well, partly because I am a much more complex organism, partly because I have learned a little bit about controlling time travel, partly because my own life span is much,

204

much longer than a fish and partly because," he hesitated. Bryn raised her eyebrows, waiting for him to finish. "partly because I just don't know."

"You don't know?" Bryn asked in astonishment. "This seems to be a very dangerous business, this time travel thing, if you aren't even sure why you didn't arrive here as decayed as that fish."

"Well, apparently it's less dangerous than hanging around with you," Simon smiled.

Bryn was about to respond when she realized the truth of what Simon had said. She laughed as they went back to work on the parchment.

"This seems to be a collection of notes or plans of some sort." Simon pointed to one. "This one is the one from the museum and we can see it says something about a pest or a nuisance."

"It DID say something about a pest but the words have been changed to make it read more like an enemy." She pulled it closer. "It did say "rid me of this pest" and now it says "kill my enemy.""

"And these," Simon drew closer the other pieces of manuscript, "let's see, we've got 'culpa' fault or blame, and 'regina' queen."

Bryn grabbed the parchment from Simon and looked at it intently.

"Simon, this document outlines a plan to accuse the Queen of murder!"

"Murder of whom? Henry?" Simon asked.

"Possibly, it doesn't say. It's just so odd. It's not an accusation of murder, it's more like they are trying to create evidence to look like she…" There was a loud knock on the door. They both jumped. Bryn got up and walked to the door, speaking briefly with someone on the other side. She walked back to Simon with concerned look.

"What's wrong?" he asked.

"Jasper says Sir Robert has sent an urgent message. We are to travel to Carlisle Castle to meet with him. He is attending King Henry and can't leave. We are to leave tomorrow morning."

"Carlisle Castle?" asked Simon. "That's in Cumberland right? Close to the Scottish border. It must be 100 miles from here."

"A bit less but yes, I wonder what this can mean?" She looked at the papers on the table. "I think we'd better take these with us and guard them carefully. And now, we have much to do. I need to leave orders for the servants and tenants. You must tell Agnes to get things ready for us to leave in the morning." Bryn abruptly turned and walked out of the solar.

Simon gathered up the papers and rolled them all back into their leather case. He wasn't sure he was too anxious to meet Sir Robert and though he was sure they wouldn't actually meet King Henry, the thought of just seeing him from a distance was terribly exciting.

"I wish it was my digital camera I'd stuck in my pocket instead that paper weight," he thought with a smile. He blew out the candle and pulled the door shut behind him. He had some packing to do before tomorrow morning.

Chapter Thirty Nine

Brother Felix clutched at his chest. His heart pounded in his ears and his lungs were burning. For the last 20 years he had led a very sedentary life as the abbey librarian. For the last two days he had walked further than he ever had in his life, and he was no longer a young man. He sat down on a rock at the side of the road. Fortunately several people along the way, seeing his monk's robes, offered him food, drink and even rides in carts from one town to the next. Because of that he had made surprising progress toward Carlisle.

It had been foolish of him to rush off as he had with no preparation, but he had panicked. Just after Matins, the prayers at two o'clock in the morning, he snuck up into the tower to check on those pestilential youths. He hadn't thought through yet what he was going to do with them. They couldn't be allowed to go on. He quietly unlocked the door and peered in, candle in hand. What he saw made his heart stop—a hole in the tower wall and an empty cell. How was it possible? Somehow they had escaped. He lurched toward the wooden crate where he had hidden Brother Barnabas' body. Roughly he pushed aside the decaying robes and brittle bones. It was gone. Brother Felix collapsed onto the stone bench, where just a few hours before Bryn and Simon had sat, head in hands. They had found the parchment and escaped. It was over.

For several minutes Brother Felix sat in the dark, cold cell, his mind blank. Then an idea began to form. He couldn't possibly get to them while they were at the manor. But he could guess where they would be headed—to Carlisle. Felix had helped the Prior compose a letter just a few days ago to Sir Robert who was now attending the King at Castle Carlisle. He knew the king and the nobles would be at Carlisle several more days. At least there was a chance he could get to Bryn and Simon before they reached Sir Robert. A chance in that large castle, with the confusion and crowd of court, that he could stop them.

Brother Felix didn't dare return to the dorter, he might awaken the monks who would question his nighttime wanderings. He simply walked out the small door in the wall that led to the abbey orchards. The same door he had used to lead away Alizay and Eleanor yesterday. Refusing to recognize the fear and futility growing in his heart, he headed northwest, toward Carlisle.

Chapter Forty

"Sir Robert is sending two men to escort you," Jasper said to Bryn. They were standing at the far end of the courtyard, near the stables. Bryn and Jasper had spent the last hour discussing manor business. How the plantings were going, who was ill or in need in the village, what repairs needed doing on the manor house. Agnes had packed everything she thought they would need. That of course consisted of enough food for one of Caesar's legions. Now they were discussing the route they would take to Carlisle.

"If the weather holds and you don't run into any trouble, you should be there in four days," Jasper said. "You don't want to take much, no pack horses. That is just an invitation for thieves and brigands to attack. It's best if you travel light and fast."

Bryn nodded. "Jasper, did Sir Robert say why he wants us at Carlisle?"

"No." Jasper shook his head. "Perhaps he just wants to make sure you are truly well, having gotten a message that you'd been missing."

Bryn looked thoughtful. "Well, it hardly matters does it? If he wants us there, that's where we'll be."

Jasper looked over her shoulder at two riders coming across the courtyard.

"Looks like your escort is here." He nodded in their direction.

Bryn turned to look, squinting into the sun. As the men drew close, she gasped and ran across to them.

"John!" she said, grasping the hand of the young man mounted on a beautiful black stallion. He took her hand in his and kissed it lightly with a laugh.

"Mistress Berengar," he said as he jumped from his horse and gave her a mock bow. Simon came up beside them, having just come from Edwin's smithy. John glanced at him and threw Simon the reins of his horse.

"Take good care of him, he needs a brush down and a bucket of oats," he said dismissively.

Bryn looked quickly at Simon who stared at the reins in his hands as if they had appeared by magic.

"John, this is Simon. He's a nephew of Agnes' and he's been helping me with the Montbury history," she quickly explained.

John laughed, it had a familiar ring to it, Simon thought.

"Oh! I thought you were the stable boy. Well, you wouldn't mind tending to him would you?" John put his arm around Bryn and started walking toward the manor house. "Bryn and I have a lot to talk about."

He pulled Bryn along with him. She glanced back over her shoulder to see Simon still standing next to the stallion watching them go. She raised her eyebrows and grinned at him. Simon shrugged and walked John's horse into the stable. He knew one thing about John at least, he didn't like him.

"…so I was sent to escort you." John sat in Sir Robert's chair in the great hall. His booted feet were crossed on the table in front of him as he tilted back in the elaborately carved chair. "Bit of luck that I happened to be in Carlisle, but William and I were on an errand for Lord d'Ambray and since we know the way here, it made sense to send us."

Bryn had not met John's companion, William, before. He was rather quiet, at least compared to John, but then most people seemed quiet compared to John. She smiled at the thought. They both served Lord d'Ambray, who was a distant relative to Sir Robert, and a powerful lord in his own right.

Simon, finished with the horses, had come into the hall to ask Bryn about final plans for tomorrow's journey. He stopped by the door as he saw the two of them together at the table. John, goblet of wine in hand, was casually leaning back in Sir Robert's chair, muddied feet on the table. Bryn was listening intently to him, her hand covering his. Simon's stomach lurched.

"Must be because I haven't eaten," he thought with irritation. But he also felt as though he had no appetite. He turned around to leave the hall when Bryn caught sight of him.

"Simon!" she called across the echoing room. "Simon, come here and meet John properly."

Simon forced a smile onto his face and walked across the room. He felt he'd already had about all he wanted of John.

"And why," he thought angrily, "was John's arm around Bryn?"

"Simon Grant. John Berengar." Bryn presented them to each other.

"Berengar?" Simon asked stupidly. He looked at Bryn. She laughed and replied.

"Simon, this is my 'baby' brother, John."

Simon suddenly felt that perhaps he had misjudged the man. Perhaps he wasn't so bad after all. And that is why his laugh was so familiar. It was Bryn's laugh. In fact, he could see that a strong resemblance between the two now that he had a moment to look.

"Very nice to meet you," he said, holding out his hand. John grabbed Simon's outstretched hand and shook it painfully.

"And you," John slapped him roughly on the back. He frowned at Bryn. "Your insistence on calling me your 'baby brother' when you are only minutes older than me is rather irritating." He turned to Simon. "Bryn has been telling me about how helpful you've been with Sir Robert's family history. Never learned to read myself, I'm afraid. Didn't see much use for it."

211

Bryn rescued Simon's hand from her brother's grasp and suggested it was time to retire for the night. They would leave at dawn for Carlisle and needed to be rested. John gave his sister a huge hug, lifting her off the ground and spinning her around.

"It's good to see you again, Bryn. You've really become a beautiful woman, don't you think so?" he asked Simon. Simon made an inarticulate noise and felt his cheeks begin to redden. Fortunately, John and Bryn were already walking across the hall discussing final plans for the morning. As she bid her brother goodnight, she turned back to Simon.

"Come into the kitchen for a warm drink before bed," she invited.

They sat together near the fire staring at the red embers and sipping warmed hydromel.

"John is my twin brother, born a few minutes after me. Although he hates to admit that." She smiled but then became serious. "He barely survived. I think that is why my mother died shortly after we were born. She had never completely recovered from having twins."

Bryn's voice caught and Simon glanced up at her.

"I've always felt responsible for her death somehow, and for John even though we were raised apart from each other."

"How often do you see each other?" Simon asked.

"Well, I was sent to Sir Robert's household and John was raised with the d'Ambray household. We would see each other at Christmas and sometimes during the year if there was some business or event that brought the two households together."

"Now that I know he's your brother, I can see a lot of resemblance," Simon said. "He has the same laugh as you, and the same eyes. I would have thought he was older than you though."

"Well, I can't help that he is a lot taller than me," She laughed. "But it's true that boys are given many more opportunities than girls---he began training to be a knight when he was seven years old. He has traveled a lot. He has even accompanied Lord d'Ambray on some rather important diplomatic missions. It's made him grow up quickly I think." She glanced at Simon. "He's not as mature as he thinks he is though. He's always been a bit impulsive, and there have been a few times when he's shown some pretty poor judgment." She put her cup on the table and stood up, smoothing her skirts. "Do you know that beautiful stallion he has?" she asked Simon.

"Well, I just spent a good hour with it so yes, I do," Simon said sharply.

"Oh right, sorry about that. That's typical John actually," Bryn said with some chagrin. "He won that stallion from a horse trader in Suffolk on a bet. The man couldn't sell the beast because it wouldn't be broken. It had thrown everyone who tried to ride it, and the trader had even injured his leg trying to break the horse. John bet he could stay on it and the trader said if he could manage that he could have the horse."

Simon listened intently. He had to admit being quite intimidated by the huge, black horse as it had pawed at the floor of the stall while Simon brushed it.

"Well John had a brilliant idea," Bryn said with sarcasm. "He had a friend tie his wrists together and then several of them held the horse while John got on and slipped his tied arms around the neck of the horse. Then they let go and the horse took off with John essentially tied to it. It took about a half an hour of bucking and rearing and running wild but the horse finally tired out. John of course was nearly beaten to death by it all and couldn't have gotten off the horse if he wanted. It nearly killed him, but he won the horse and they've been together since."

Simon stared at Bryn in disbelief.

"You know," he finally said, "this explains an awful lot about you." Bryn hit him in the shoulder with her fist and took his cup from him.

"Well, we'd better say goodnight. We've got an early start."

That night before getting into bed, Simon checked the rolled blanket wherein he had packed his things. The few clothes

213

he owned were neatly packed inside. He felt around until he found the thin, bendable blade of his foil tucked in the very center.

Chapter Forty One

Moira took a few steps back to look at the brightly lit display case. The glass would definitely need fingerprints wiped off, but overall she was pleased with the effect. She was working on an exhibit of the history of writing. This display held early cuneiform tablets and signature seals. The small, carved, colorful seals looked like large beads from a gaudy necklace. She reached in and turned one slightly so that the carving was more visible. On the other side of the case was a copy of "The Gilgamesh Epic," the long story poem of an ancient hero written originally on clay tablets in Mesopotamia 4,000 years ago. Yes, it looked quite nice, she thought as she stepped back again. She slid the glass door shut and turned the small key in the silver lock.

It was difficult to keep her mind on her work. If she was honest with herself, the palimpsest was not the only problem distracting her. Owen was on her mind more frequently than she cared to admit. Years ago she had run from a relationship with him. She had been alone with her secret then. The thought of developing a close relationship with anyone, only to see herself outlive everyone in her life, continually saying goodbye to people she loved while she continued on through time, was more than she was willing to deal with. But somehow having Simon share her secret and perhaps even eventually take on her mantle of responsibility, gave her hope that she might live a normal life one day. She hoped she was not taking too great a risk by opening herself up to feelings for Owen again. Moira shook herself out of her thoughts and turned back to her work.

The next case over held several medieval manuscripts. There was an empty space where the palimpsest would be placed. She wasn't quite ready to let go of that. After several discussions with Owen, she felt she had gotten all the information she could out of it, but Moira somehow felt it was her only connection with Simon and she didn't want to let it out of her hands yet. When this exhibit was over, she knew she would have to return it to the cathedral archives in Durham, England.

Moira had another reason for holding onto the palimpsest. If it came down to it she would have to try to find Simon. That manuscript was her closest link to him. Fortunately, his uncle had left a message on her phone last night that he'd been delayed and would Moira mind keeping Simon a few more days. That was one less problem to deal with. But if Simon didn't return on his own very soon, she would have no choice but to try to travel back and find him. She knew it would be a nearly impossible task, finding the exact place and exact time where he was. But she had done everything she could here and...

Moira looked closer at one of the exhibits in the museum case. The curator in charge of maps for the museum had been asked to find a medieval map for the display case. The one he chose was a 12th century map of northwest England. The city of Carlisle featured prominently in its center. Moira had a vague recollection of reading a history of this area that mentioned an important conference of nobles called by Henry II at the castle of Carlisle. If Simon really was in the middle of some conspiracy regarding Henry II, perhaps this was the time and place to find him. Moira quickly locked the display case and hurried to the museum library to find the book where she had read this account. Perhaps, if she could find the details of this council of nobles, she might gain some hint as to where to find Simon, too.

Chapter Forty Two

They'd left the manor house before dawn, the sky still sprinkled with a few stars in the west while the eastern horizon showed a thin line of lighter gray. The horses were stamping impatiently on the ground, great puffs of steaming breath coming from their nostrils. Jasper, Baldwin and Roger helped them to secure their packs on the backs of the horses. William, John's companion, was ready before the rest and sat silently and easily on his brown rouncey, a horse Simon knew was bred for its swiftness. Simon, with little to bring but his blanket roll and the bundle of food Agnes had given him, was already atop Alizay.

Bryn and John were crossing the courtyard in animated discussion. Jasper approached them, shook hands with John and talked briefly with Bryn, getting last minute instructions and offering last minute advice. Finally everyone was ready and they rode out of the manor gates at a brisk trot, the sky already turning a pale pink and yellow. Bryn rode in front with John while Simon and William brought up the rear. For the first several miles, William's silence suited Simon as he had his own thoughts to work through. He had never undertaken so long a journey on horseback, and while his skills had greatly improved, he had a nagging fear of doing something that would show he was a novice.

As the sun rose and the air began to fill with birdsong, Simon relaxed enough to enjoy the journey. He glanced over at William who rode with an easy elegance. He looked a bit older than John and had thick, brown, wavy hair that fell to his shoulders. It suddenly occurred to Simon that he hadn't seen himself in a mirror for a very long time. He ran his hand through his hair and realized that it had also grown quite long. He wondered with a smile what his uncle would think of that when he returned.

"We will easily reach Middleham today."

Simon was startled out of his reverie by William's comment. "Robert Fitzrandolph has built a massive castle there. It will be comfortable lodging for tonight."

"I am sure I will welcome comfortable lodging by then," Simon smiled ruefully. "I'm afraid I'm not much of a horseman."

William nodded. "I understand you have been helping Mistress Berengar with her work on the Montbury family history." William waited for Simon to elaborate.

"Yes, I have some training in languages that proved useful for the documents she was using to trace Sir Robert's lineage." Simon preferred to steer the conversation away from himself. "Have you known John very long?" he asked.

William looked ahead to where John and Bryn where riding. He seemed to be thinking about how to answer Simon's simple question.

"John and I were both raised in the d'Ambray household. You probably know John's father was a valued vassal to Sir Robert. When John's mother died, Sir Robert arranged for John to be raised by Lord d'Ambray." William looked back at Simon and smiled. "But, while I've known him for a long time, we are very different in personality, as you've likely noticed. Because of that, we didn't always spend a lot of time together."

Simon nodded. The little he'd seen of Bryn's brother made him realize that he was a rather overwhelming character. Simon didn't wonder that quiet, calm William might not feel altogether comfortable with John.

"Yes, I can imagine. Bryn told him about how he won his horse."

"I could tell you many more stories about John just as harrowing," William laughed. "He was always the one who could run faster, climb higher and fight more fiercely than any of the other boys on the manor." William hesitated. "I will say that I did beat him in a sword fight once though. But I took advantage of a secret weakness."

"What is that?" Simon asked, intrigued.

"John fell out of a tree when we were both boys. He broke his arm rather badly. It never healed correctly. Because of that, he can't raise his right arm quite as high as his left." William smiled guiltily. "I used that knowledge to best him in a sword fight. I'd feel worse about it if he hadn't beaten me at everything else. As it is, I didn't mind taking the advantage."

The rest of the day was uneventful with a stop on a grassy slope by a river to eat the midday meal Agnes had packed for them. Simon had grown to like William and felt comfortable with the sporadic conversations they had as they traveled. Their journey was also broken up by the need to stop periodically and clear the road. It was narrow and not very well maintained. There were gullies where rain had washed away large sections of the road and once they had to dismount to drag a fallen tree from their path. Nonetheless, by evening, they were approaching Middleham Castle.

Simon stared in awe at Middleham Castle. They approached from the east, across a wooden drawbridge. The huge wooden gates and portcullis, open to allow them access, must have been impenetrable when closed. The keep, with its 12-foot thick walls, had three floors and made the Montbury manor house seem tiny in comparison. Stable boys immediately came to take their horses. Simon walked stiff-legged and sore behind the others as they were greeted by the castle steward. William and Simon carried their packs toward the entrance to the large, new keep recently built by Robert Fitzrandolph.

"Lord Robert has already left to join the other nobles at Carlisle. But the steward was told to welcome us and give us hospitality tonight." Bryn joined them after she and John had spoken with the steward. "They have a meal laid on in the great hall. You three will sleep there tonight and I have been given a room in the tower."

They ate with roughly fifteen other men in the great hall. The food was plentiful and Simon especially enjoyed a steaming meat pie with a thick crust that they called 'bake metis.' It contained chunks of meat with raisins, currents and nuts. He still had a hard time eating without a fork. He remembered from his history class that the fork was not used in England until around 1600. As he looked at the men around him, he saw they used their own short knives, taken from their belts, to eat everything. Flat pieces of stale bread, called trenchers, were used as plates. Simon had seen Agnes gather these after a meal and give them to the peasants in the village to eat.

Simon was seated at the very end of a long table. Bryn was eating in her own room away from this hall full of rough men. He missed being able to ask her questions and follow her lead but he felt comfortable enough if he just ate quietly and observed. John was not at the table and Simon assumed he was either with Bryn, or talking with the castle steward. The ale was flowing generously and many of the men at the long table were just a little bit drunk. Their talk got louder and louder as the meal wore on.

"Who does he think he is anyway?" One ruddy faced man leaned into the face of another, his cup sloshing brown ale on the table as it tilted in his hand. "He rode in on the skirts of his mother, didn't he?"

The other man nodded, staring into his own empty cup. "Empress Matilda had to wait until King Stephen died to make her own son king," he agreed.

"Henry first curtails the powers of the nobles, and now he's trying to steal the power of the church for himself." The ruddy faced man had gone from bluster to disgust. "If he thinks this 'conference of nobles' at Carlisle will smooth the ruffled feathers of his nobles, he'd better have something more to offer them than what he has given so far."

Simon glanced at William who sat quietly across from him. He too was listening to this conversation but kept his attention on the food in front of him. William glanced up at Simon, his face grave.

"Perhaps it is time to settle in for the night," he said and stood up. Simon quickly joined him. Several other men got up from the table but a small group of them ignored the rest and continued to drink and argue. There were hard benches along the walls of the great hall. The light from the candles on the table didn't reach far and as Simon laid down uncomfortably on one the benches, he was in darkness. But he could see the faces of the men still at the table, lit by a flickering candle. They were obviously intent on their conversation. The ruddy faced man would pound his fist on the table to emphasize a point. Just as Simon was about to close his eyes and pull his blanket over his head, he saw a shadowy figure approach from the door at the far end of the hall and walk over to the men. The figure, a young man, swung his leg over a chair and slapped the ruddy faced man on the back in friendly greeting. The men at the table looked up and greeted the young man and the conversation began again in earnest.

"Now what," thought Simon with some concern, "does John have to do with these quarrelsome men?"

He watched for a few more minutes as John seemed to take over the conversation and the other men listened with eagerness. Simon fell asleep, dreaming of being tied to a black stallion as it ran wildly along the road to Carlisle.

The rest of the trip to Carlisle went smoothly enough. Simon thought ruefully that his own time, he could have made the trip in two hours in a comfortable car with an MP3 player to

221

keep him from being bored. Instead, they rode for four days over rough and rutted roads, through several cold, soaking rains, stopping only to eat a simple meal of bread and cheese. John had arranged for them to stay at manors along the way. Bryn was usually given a place inside the manor and the others often slept in the hall or even in the stable lofts. Each night Simon felt a new sore spot somewhere on his body. His backside especially was sore from sitting for hours in the saddle. At one point, when Simon preferred to stand to eat the midday meal, William had taken pity on him.

"There are some tricks that can help ease sore muscles," he said with a laugh. "Use your stirrups every so often to lift yourself out of your saddle a few inches. And shift your weight by leaning forward or to one side. If it gets really bad, I fold my cloak underneath me." This advice did help to ease his sore muscles somewhat, although Alizay did not seem too happy with all his squirming in the saddle. But except for a tired back and a sore bottom, and the infrequent but drenching rain shower, the trip passed in relative ease. William would sometimes gallop on ahead of the group to make sure the road ahead was safe and open he said. But Simon guessed he just chafed at the leisurely pace and wanted a good run to release both his and his horse's energy. Bryn and John chatted together up front but Bryn would frequently rein in Eleanor and wait for Simon to come up beside her. Neither of them spoke about the manuscripts they carried with them but chatted about what they saw as they rode, or what to expect at Carlisle.

Chapter Forty Three

Brother Felix lay on a pallet on the floor of the small, dark cell. His feet, blistered, bleeding and swollen had been washed and bandaged. A bowl was on the small table near his pallet. The warm broth it held was a feast to his empty stomach. He thought it could only have been God that gave him the strength to walk without stopping for so long. Only God who put so many people in his way to offer him shelter, food and a ride on their carts from one market town to the next. Surely his mission was sanctioned by God or he never would have survived the journey. For a brief moment he felt a stab of guilt. He'd lied to the priest at Carlisle, telling him he was on an errand for the abbot of Bridlethorpe. He said he was bringing a message to Sir Robert here at the council of nobles. His horse had been stolen he told him, and so he'd walked for much of the journey. Surely such small lies were excusable in the eyes of God when his real mission to Carlisle was so important? He would go to confession when he returned to Bridlethorpe and do penance. For a moment Felix felt a pang of panic. How could he return to Bridlethorpe and his beloved library? Would they take him back? He refused to consider it. When this was all over they would understand why he did what he did. At least for the moment, the castle priest had taken him in, cared for his injuries and fed him. Tomorrow he would plan his next steps. He heard a commotion in the bailey. Men's voices called to each other and horses' hooves beat the cobblestones. Painfully Brother Felix pulled himself to his feet and looked out the tiny window of his room. Several men came to greet some new arrivals. Felix saw two men on horseback and behind them—he felt his throat constrict—behind them were Simon and Bryn.

Chapter Forty Four

From a distance Simon thought Carlisle Castle looked like something he might have made out of his building blocks when he was a child. A large, square, solid stone keep surrounded by tall battlements with a square stone gatehouse. The intimidating portcullis was drawn three-quarters up, allowing horsemen to come and go through the arched entry gate. The pointed metal ends of the portcullis looking like great shark's teeth in the gaping mouth of the gatehouse.

"There was originally a Roman fort on this hill," Bryn explained as the castle came in sight. "Then King William Rufus built an earth and timber castle in 1092. King Henry I, our king's grandfather, rebuilt the castle in stone. Henry II added the outer curtain wall and that southern gate." She pointed toward an enormous stone gate at one end of a bridge spanning a deep ditch. "I have asked John to find us rooms near to each other so that we can work on Sir Robert's history while we are here." She smiled at Simon, "Well, that and other things."

As they rode through the arched gate and into the bailey courtyard, they were met by several men who took their horses and led them into the keep. John and William separated from them to find Lord d'Ambray and report their return to Carlisle. Bryn and Simon were led to two adjoining rooms on the second floor of the keep. The furnishings were simple but more than adequate. Tapestries hung on the walls and each room contained the luxury of a bed and table and chairs.

"I want more than anything to wash and lay down for a bit," Bryn told Simon as they came to their rooms. "I will request that our evening meal be brought up here so we can have some time alone to plan our next step."

Simon agreed. He went into his own room and unpacked what little there was in his blanket roll. He had no idea why he had brought the foil Edwin had made him, but somehow he felt safer having it with him. He lay down on the bed, his saddle-sore body sinking into the mattress.

Brother Felix kept his head down, his rough, brown hood falling low over his face. His hands, hidden by the large folds of his robes, were clasped together around a small bottle. He was grateful that the castle's corridors were noisy and crowded as all the servants that accompanied so many noblemen were busy trying to gather the necessary food, linens and other comforts that their masters demanded. No one took any notice of him whatsoever. He came into the cavernous kitchens. Dozens of people swarmed in and out, cooking, tending the fires in the huge open fireplaces, carrying in buckets of water, carrying out buckets of peelings and garbage to be flung into the pig's trough. Felix stood for a moment, looking for someone who might be in charge. A very large woman in a white apron stood in the middle of the chaos, her face red from standing over boiling cauldrons and from yelling repeatedly at dull-witted servants who needed constant instruction. Felix approached her.

"I am with Sir Robert Montbury's retinue," he said. "His ward, Mistress Berengar, is not feeling well. He wishes me to bring her food and drink in her rooms."

The woman scowled at him and Felix felt sure he would suffer a tongue lashing for interrupting her while she oversaw the feeding of hundreds of people at the castle. But his monk's robes kept her tongue in check. She pointed to a large table at the far side of the kitchen that was laid fully with dozens of different dishes. Roast meats and meat pies, a whole pig with a large apple stuck in its mouth, steaming plates of vegetables, dozens of loaves of bread, plates of cheeses, a variety of different sized birds—stewed, roasted, put into pies. Felix's mouth began to water at the sight of all that food. The monastery did not serve such food as this. He nodded to the cook and took a platter whereon he placed some of the food from the table. He added to this a goblet filled with cider, balancing it carefully in the middle of the tray.

Felix had easily blended in with the other strangers gathered at Carlisle. Many nobles brought their spiritual advisers who were often priests or monks. During the day, head covered with his monk's hood, he had listened to conversations and asked casual questions to determine where Bryn and Simon were lodged. Now he carried his platter of food through long corridors and up two flights of stone steps to the section of the keep where he knew their rooms to be. He put the tray down on the floor just outside Bryn's door. Felix looked down the hall. It was very quiet and empty. Thin shafts of sunlight came through the slotted windows. He took out the small vial from his sleeve and emptied it into the goblet of cider. If all went as he had planned, in a very short time he would have the manuscripts in his hands. Felix walked away from the doorway and back down the stairs to wait in his room attached to the castle's chapel.

The message, written on a scrap of parchment was to the point. *"Meet me at Captain's Tower, must speak with you regarding important matter. John."* Simon didn't know who had delivered it. He hadn't meant to fall asleep but the comfort of this bed, compared to the last four nights he had spent on the road, had lulled him into a brief but deep sleep. A knock on the door awakened him. It took him a couple of minutes to force his brain back into consciousness. When he got out of bed he saw the scrap of paper on the floor by the door. Someone had obviously slid it under the door for him to find. Simon splashed water from the basin on his face to wake himself fully, tucked the note into his tunic and walked to the door. Suddenly he stopped and turned back. He walked to the bed and felt under the straw mattress. He pulled out the foil Edwin had made him and tucked it into his belt beneath the folds of his tunic. He had no clear thought as to why this gave him comfort but something in his gut was sending warning signals to his brain. Something—he couldn't point to what—something didn't feel right.

Simon knocked quietly on Bryn's door. When there was no answer he knocked again and called her name. Still no response. He assumed she too must have fallen asleep. Well, there was no need to bother her. He would talk to her about his meeting with John when he returned. He walked down the corridor, down two flights of stone steps, and across the great hall that was nearly empty now that the evening meal was over. He assumed the nobles were meeting with King Henry and their servants were unpacking, cleaning clothes soiled with the dust of travel and tending to tired horses. He exited through large wooden doors into the inner bailey.

The large keep was in the northeast corner of the inner bailey. Upon their arrival William had pointed out the inner gatehouse, called the Captain's Tower. It was an imposing square tower with heavy wooden doors, a huge portcullis that could be lowered to block entry to the bailey, and in the roof of the entrance Simon could see a row of murder holes. These he knew, were used in time of an attack to shower the enemy with arrows, boiling water or tar, or anything else on hand. He approached the Captain's Tower. There was one soldier inside a small room on the west side of the tower.

"I received a message to meet with John Berengar." Simon approached the guard. "He is with Lord d'Ambray's retinue. Do you know where I might find him?"

The guard glowered at Simon. "Haven't seen him. Check below, he might be in the guard's barracks." He pointed to a narrow, winding set of steps going up to the battlements on the wall and going down to the cramped, damp, dark barracks. Simon walked to the stairs. He looked back over his shoulder at the guard who was standing up and strapping on his sword, ready to begin his rounds. He hesitated for just a moment and then stepped into the blackness of the downward staircase.

Bryn tried one last time to rouse Simon. She knocked on the door and called his name loudly. Well, either he was deeply asleep or had gone off without saying anything to her. Either way it was his loss not hers. She was starving and the smells from the platter of food brought to her room were too enticing to wait. If he was lucky, she'd save him some, but she certainly wasn't going to wait any longer. Bryn picked up the tray from the floor near her door and placed it on the table in her room. She ate hungrily from the assortments of food, putting aside a plate for Simon when he returned. Bryn, noticing there was only one goblet of cider, saved half of that for him too.

"More than he deserves," she thought to herself. She spent the next few minutes unpacking her clothes while listening for Simon's return.

She was beginning to feel the exhaustion from their travels. Bryn fought off sleep, hoping to catch Simon before she went to bed. She knelt on the floor, folding the blanket used for the journey, pushing it under the bed. Suddenly she heard a sound outside her door.

It must be Simon. Bryn quickly jumped up. Immediately she felt sickly dizzy. She grabbed the edge of the bedpost and took a step forward. Just as she looked to see her door starting to open, she collapsed onto the floor.

Brother Felix quietly closed the door behind him. His timing was perfect. The poppy juice he had put into Bryn's drink had taken effect. She should sleep for several hours. Still he needed to hurry, especially as he didn't know how long Simon would be gone. He had slipped that note under Simon's door to get him out of the way long enough for him to search Bryn's room. But the two had frustrated his plans before so he was taking no chances.

Felix searched everywhere in the room for the manuscripts that he knew they had taken from the monastery tower. At first he was careful not to disturb anything. It would be much better if they never discovered he'd been there at all. But as he continued to search and find nothing, his anger and frustration grew. Soon he was tossing things about, even tearing apart the straw mattress, his panic growing. He sat in the chair, head in hands, shaking with frustration and anger. A low moan from the floor startled him. Bryn was beginning to wake up. She must not have drunk all of the poppy juice. Brother Felix nearly cried with despair. He MUST have those papers. He doubted that, given his age and weakened condition from his perilous journey here, he could subdue Bryn when she regained consciousness. He had no choice. He picked up the heavy candlestick on the table. Bryn moaned again and started to lift her head from the floor. Felix raised his arm and brought the candlestick down on her temple.

Chapter Forty Five

It was pitch black. Simon kept one hand on the damp, slimy stone wall as it curved downward to the small square room that housed the guards from the tower. He knew the larger soldiers' barracks were on the other side of the bailey. This room was used to provide temporary relief from winter cold or rain for soldiers on duty at the tower. The silence was as thick as the darkness, except for a periodic dripping of water on the stone steps. Simon knew he was below ground level and couldn't expect either light or air from a window. As he started around the last curve before the stairs ended in the underground room, he saw a small flicker of light ahead. John must already be there. Still not able to see the stairs, he carefully edged toward the door of the room. Now he could hear some hushed voices. The gnawing anxiety he had felt in his room grew. He stopped and listened.

"It has to be found!" one voice said in a harsh whisper. "Everything is for naught if we don't have it in our hands."

"We will find it," the other voice answered. "I know it is here in the castle somewhere and those two haven't had time to do anything with it yet. I am sure I can find it before tomorrow night."

"You do realize the importance of this?" the first voice said with frightening calm. "This is the one chance we have to discredit the king and return the balance of power to the nobles.

If we are successful, we will gut the king's authority and power for good."

There was a moment of tense silence. The second voice responded.

"Yes. And if we are not, it is we who will be gutted."

"Then we have no option, do we? And if anyone gets in your way you must get rid of them, do you understand?"

Simon didn't wait for an answer. He'd heard the scraping of chairs as the two stood up. He knew the only way out of the room was up the very stairs he was now standing on. He turned as quickly as he dared in the dark and started back up the stairs. Two pairs of footsteps were right behind him, just one turn of the stair away. He didn't dare run. He forced himself to breathe regularly, forced himself to see the uneven stone stairs in his mind as he hurried upward. One missed step and they would hear him—be on him in seconds. He was grateful for the soft leather boots that made no sound on the stone steps. He reached the top of the stairs. The guard room was empty. He raced across the room and out the door, turning sharply to duck behind the corner of the tower. It was already dusk and the shadow of the huge tower darkened the bailey. Simon cautiously looked around the corner and saw two men walking toward the outer bailey. He couldn't make out their faces but their tunics both bore an embroidered gold oak tree on a green background. He knew that symbol. It was the insignia of Lord d'Ambray. Perhaps that was what John wanted to talk to him about. Perhaps John had discovered a plot within the d'Ambray household. Simon waited until the men disappeared, then he dashed across the open bailey.

Felix used pieces of linen torn from the bedclothes to bind Bryn's ankles and wrists. There was blood running down the side of her face from the wound on her temple where he had hit her. It matted in her hair and flowed in a trickle down her neck. She was still breathing though, Felix thought with some relief. He really didn't want to harm anyone. If they had only just stayed away, stayed out of it. He spent several minutes trying to calm his mind and think rationally. The manuscripts weren't in this room. But Bryn must know where they are. It suddenly occurred to Felix that Simon would of course know where they were too. A plan was beginning to form. It would take all his strength but he had no choice. He needed something to bargain with. He looked out the door into the hall. It was dark and quiet. Felix, in his wanderings around the castle over the last two days, had discovered that the door at the end of the hallway opened onto a staircase that wound up to the very top of the keep. There was a storage room up there to be used only in case of an attack. If the castle wall was breached, each tower had its own stores of food to be able to hold out until help came. Felix went back inside and grabbed Bryn under the arms. He used all his strength to drag her to the stairway door. He sat and rested for a moment at the bottom. Then, with a prayer asking for strength, he slowly dragged her up to the top of the tower.

"Are you sure?" Simon asked. "He asked me to meet with him in the Captain's Tower, but he wasn't there."

"I'm sorry." William looked up from cleaning his sword. Simon had found him in the larger soldier's barracks. "I haven't seen John since we arrived. He said he had something he had to do for Lord d'Ambray."

"I've looked everywhere," Simon said more to himself than to William who had gone back to polishing his weapon. He unconsciously fingered the note that John had written to him asking to meet.

"He must have been here recently to have written…" Simon suddenly stopped. He felt sick to his stomach and his face had gone white.

"Are you unwell?" William looked up at the sudden silence.

For several seconds Simon stared into space, going over the possibilities.

"William, did John ask you to write a note for him?" Simon asked, although he thought he knew the answer already.

"Me?" William laughed. "I'm afraid I can't do much more than write my name, and that would be a challenge."

William shrugged his shoulders as Simon turned and ran out the door before he even finished his answer.

"John didn't write this note to me." Simon said to himself as he raced across the bailey and into the keep. "He said himself that he never learned to read or write. That's what was bothering me when I got the note. I knew something was wrong but I couldn't remember what." Simon ran across the great hall. Several men, milling around the hall looking for food and ale, glanced as he ran by. Simon took the double stair case two at a time and came finally, his chest heaving, to the door of Bryn's room. His mind was arguing with itself. There were innocent explanations, surely. No need to assume the worst. How silly would he look if he burst in on Bryn only to find her calmly eating her evening meal.

But his worst fears were realized when he found Bryn's door open. He called her name and pushed open the door further. Once again he felt his stomach lurch. The room was a mess. Things were tossed around, even the mattress was torn apart. As he walked slowly around the room, he stopped by the bed and felt his knees go weak. On the floor by the bed was a blood stain. Near it, a heavy candlestick also stained with blood—two, long golden strands of hair stuck to it. Simon sat down on the bed. His mind whirled but he could not get himself to think clearly. It seemed to him that he sat there for hours, his mind stuck in a thick haze.

"No!" he said aloud and stood up. His own angry voice seemed to stir him to action. He needed to find John for help. But he had spent the last hour looking for him and he might not even be on the castle grounds. He couldn't wait. Someone had written that note, pretending to be John, to get him away from Bryn. Now that someone had Bryn. He had to believe she was still alive, else why take her away? Simon closed the door behind him as he stepped out into the hall. He wasn't sure what to do or where to go. The only people he really knew at Carlisle were John and William. Perhaps he could go back to the barracks and enlist William's help. He turned to go when something at the far end of the hallway caught his eye. In the dim light it looked like a scrap of colored fabric on the floor by the doorway. Simon walked down the hall and reached down to pick it up. A delicate shoe with blue and green embroidery. The last time Simon had seen that shoe it was on Bryn's foot. He pushed open the door and looked up at a narrow staircase.

Chapter Forty Six

"So, I have a new one for you." Moira had her elbows on the counter, chin in hands.

Darrell's face was unwelcoming. "It's really not necessary for you to tell me a librarian joke every time you come, Professor Ananke."

"No, really it's my pleasure Darrell." Moira smiled coyly at him. "So how many librarians does it take to change a light bulb?"

Darrell said nothing. He refused to be a part of this irritating ritual of Professor Ananke's. There was something biting behind her jokes. She certainly had no respect for his job and for the fact that he did his job with exactitude. Yes, it was true that he always required her to show her employee ID when she borrowed a book. Yes, he knew who she was. Yes, he knew she had worked at the museum for many years but that was not the point. The rules were that everyone using the museum's library had to show identification. He couldn't help that this irritated her. She had a careless disregard for rules. She made it a point to always tell some silly joke about librarians that he felt was just to belittle him. He continued to stare without responding.

"Come on, Darrell, give it try. So, how many?" Moira still smiled as she leaned on the counter. "Do you want to have a committee meeting first to consider the answer? I can come back later if that's better."

"That's very funny, Professor Ananke. No, I don't need a committee meeting to consider the answer. I give up, how many librarians does it take to change a light bulb?"

Moira stood up, a shocked look on her face. "Change?!" she said. Darrell was silent. "Come on, Darrell, that's funny. Get it? Change? You know how difficult it is for librarians to consider change."

Darrell stood, unsmiling. "I'm afraid I don't understand, Professor."

"Darrell," Moira said as if speaking to a child. "Do you remember when this library had to change from a card catalog to a computer catalog?"

Darrell pursed his lips.

"It took two years to convince the librarians to throw out those thousands of small, square, white, neatly printed cards and learn how to use a computer terminal to look up books."

Darrell looked down at his keyboard.

"Librarians are creatures of habit and order and tradition, Darrell. Really, it's well-documented."

"Hmmm, yes. That's really quite funny Professor Ananke." Darrell answered, obviously not amused. "What exactly do you need today?"

"I need a book about Henry II, especially one that covers his council of nobles at Carlisle Castle." As she spoke Darrell was already typing into his station computer.

"We have 162 books on Henry II," he said, looking over his reading glasses at her. "Do you have an author?"

"No. I can't remember who wrote it. It was blue I think."

"Blue." Darrell looked at her, trying to keep the disgust off his face. "Well, by some oversight, Professor Ananke, the library system does not catalog books by color."

"Really?" Moira looked shocked. "That's too bad, because I'll bet most people would remember the color of a book they read before they remembered the author. Too bad you couldn't consider CHANGING the library system."

Darrell cleared his throat. "Might you remember a publisher? A genre even? Was it historical fiction? Was it a doctoral dissertation? Was it a biography?"

"Darrell," Moira leaned further across the counter, her voice deadly calm. "If I could remember all that I would probably remember exactly what I read the first time I had it and not need to check out the book again, would I?"

Darrell took a step backward. "Well yes, I suppose that might be true. If you will give me some time, I will try to track it down for you, perhaps cross-referencing it with the geographic location of Carlisle, England and the political reference to the council of nobles. That might narrow it down from just Henry II."

"You do that." Moira turned toward the door. "I'll be in my office late tonight, Darrell. If you can manage it, perhaps you could drop it by. I'll be sure to wear my staff ID just in case you don't recognize me." She walked out with a smile.

Chapter Forty Seven

For the second time that night, Simon quietly crept up a set of stairs. They turned at a landing, continuing up in the opposite direction. These stairs at least had narrow arrow loops in the outer wall that let in the cool night air and a bit of moonlight. He strained his ears but could hear nothing either above or below him. His eyes had grown accustomed to the darkness and the thin stream of moonlight helped to illuminate the stairs. He stopped when he saw that they ended at an arched door at the top of the tower. The door was open a crack and soft, yellow candlelight emanated from the room. There was still no sound. Simon leaned against the wall and reached under his tunic for his foil. The feel of the hard metal in his hand gave him courage. He stayed pressed against the wall for the last few steps. When he reached the door he held his breath as he listened for any sound. Nothing. He slowly pushed the door open with the toe of his leather boot. It swung inward with only the slightest sigh. He could make out wooden crates and burlap sacks stacked against the walls. Large wooden barrels too, were stacked in towers in one corner. Then he saw her. She lay on her side against the far wall, her eyes were closed and her face was deadly pale. Her arms appeared to be tied behind her back and her ankles also were bound with torn strips of linen. Dark red streaks of dried blood ran down the side of her face and her neck. Simon forgot his caution and flung open the door, running across the room to kneel down at Bryn's side. Thank God, she was breathing. He raised her onto his lap and used his foil to slice at the bindings on her wrists and ankles. He laid the foil down on the floor behind her so he could hold her up while brushing her hair from her face.

"Bryn." He called her name softly. There was no response. "Bryn, wake up." He called again.

"She's not dead." A voice from the far corner of the room said calmly. Simon jumped up. He saw a figure appear out of the shadows in the corner.

"Brother Felix!" Simon gasped. "You did this?"

"Regrettably, I had no choice," Felix answered. "Really, it was your fault, not mine."

"Are you insane?" Simon said, trying to control the anger and panic in his voice. "She needs help immediately, she could die."

Felix paused and looked at Bryn.

"Yes." He nodded sadly. "Yes, I'm afraid you are right. So let's end this as quickly as possible and get her the help she needs."

"End what? What in heaven's name are you talking about?" Simon asked in desperation.

"I think you know." Felix looked directly at Simon. "I need the manuscript that you took from Brother Barnabas that night in the tower. It is of no value to you but is very important to me."

Simon paused, he thought he'd heard a noise just outside the door. He remembered that Brother Felix was somewhat deaf. If he could stall, he might give time for help to arrive.

"You killed Brother Barnabas didn't you?" Simon asked. "You're a murderer."

A flash of pain and anger briefly crossed Brother Felix's face.

"You understand nothing," he yelled at Simon. "You don't have any idea of the need to make sacrifices for the greater good." Simon was now sure he had heard a sound just beyond the door. He didn't dare to look in that direction and draw attention to the door.

"Why?" Simon tried to get Felix to talk. "What did Barnabas do to you?"

"He was the one she was sending messages to. He was the one sending books to her. When she found out about the plot, she started to write coded messages in the books he sent so that he could help her."

Simon was truly confused. "Bryn? Bryn was writing coded messages to Barnabas?"

Felix closed his eyes briefly, as if the effort to explain was taking too much out of him.

"Queen Eleanor," he said, wiping his brow with the cuff of his robe. "It was the only way she could get messages out of the castle in her imprisonment."

Bryn moaned on the floor. Both Simon and Felix took a step nearer her. She had rolled over on her back but was still unconscious. Simon stood between her and Felix.

"Don't you go anywhere near her," he warned Felix.

"I don't want to harm her," Felix said reasonably. "Just give me the manuscript and we can end this all now."

Simon had not heard any more sounds from beyond the door, perhaps whoever was there had gone down to get help. He needed to keep Felix here longer.

"How did you get the manuscript?" he asked.

"Eleanor hid messages in her books to send them to Barnabas. She asked him to hide them. They were proof of King Henry's plot to blame the archbishop's death on her."

"All those puzzles and riddles," Simon thought out loud to himself "were a way for Eleanor and Barnabas to communicate without being found out?" Felix didn't bother to confirm Simon's surmise.

"But you found out? You found the messages?" Simon continued.

"Yes, and Barnabas saw me with them. He came after me. He tried to kill me. I was just defending myself. The fool didn't even realize I would have helped him, helped the queen." It seemed important to Felix that Simon believe him. "It was an

241

accident, I didn't mean to kill him. I hid his body in the tower room where you found him. At first, I hid the manuscript in the trunk of Eleanor's books and put powdered Monk's Hood all over them."

"Yes," Simon said grimly. "I know."

"When Bryn came into the infirmary to get help for you, I knew it was you two who had found it in the trunk. That's why I sent the message for you to come to the monastery. That's why I locked you in the tower." Felix seemed to be growing tired. "I had to move the manuscript and I couldn't think of any better place than to put it in the coffin with Brother Barnabas. No one would go into the tower room unless a monk died. It was a safe place."

"But why did you want the manuscript? What would you do with it?" As Simon asked, he heard the door behind him open. He quickly swung around. John stood casually in the doorway, leaning against the door jam.

"John!" Simon ran gratefully over to him. "It's Felix, he's behind all this. We need to get Bryn away."

John pushed himself off the door and slowly pulled his broad sword from its scabbard, the metallic 'slink' echoing off the stone walls.

"Brother Felix," he said smiling. "I was wondering if we'd ever meet face to face."

Felix blanched and began to shake. Suddenly he pulled a dagger from his robes and crouched down beside Bryn. In a quick movement he grabbed her hair and pulled her head back, holding his dagger against her throat. Bryn's eyes fluttered open. With a flash of pain she started to move but felt the dagger at her throat and froze.

"No!" Simon yelled and took a step toward Bryn. John grabbed him by his collar and roughly jerked him backward.

"Not yet!" he commanded. Simon stood, stunned and unsure.

"Simon asked you a question, Felix." John smiled down at the monk, whose hand was shaking dangerously near Bryn's neck. She closed her eyes for a moment and then opened them to look directly at Simon.

"What were you going to do with the manuscript?" John asked Felix with deceptive calm.

"I..." Felix stuttered. John raised his eyebrows. He still held his sword, pointed down at the floor. "It must be given to Queen Eleanor. She will use it to prove the king's treachery."

Felix looked back and forth between Simon and John. His eyes pleaded with them to understand.

"She is the patron of the abbey library, of my library. She has been ill-treated by the king for years." His hand, holding the dagger against Bryn's neck was shaking. "If this plot is successful, what would become of us? What would become of my library?" Felix didn't seem to realize that tears were streaming down his face.

John stared in disbelief at Felix. "Are you telling me you have done all this just to save your cursed books?" John took a step closer to Felix in his anger. "Do you have any idea how much trouble you have caused me? That manuscript must be used to bring down a king. To hell with your library!"

There was silence in the room. John looked around. Simon was staring at him, disbelief and confusion in his face. Felix gasped and stared at him, his grip on Bryn had loosened. She moved to sit upright and Felix pulled her toward him, his dagger now at her back.

"John," Bryn said, she seemed not to notice the dagger. "What are you saying? What have you become involved with?"

"Involved with?" John furiously spat. He took a step closer to Felix who instinctively pressed the dagger against Bryn. She flinched and closed her eyes. "The nobles have lost everything since Henry came to power. Under King Stephen we had power and authority. Henry has debased the nobility. He has changed laws, grabbed power and now he even tries to throttle the church in England."

Simon spoke up, he was beginning to understand.

"The council of nobles meeting here with King Henry would be the perfect time and place to disgrace the king."

John looked quickly in Simon's direction. He seemed to have forgotten he was there. Simon continued. Suddenly much of this made sense.

"It is not Eleanor that these papers are meant to incriminate, is it? It is King Henry. You already have many nobles angry at Henry, many ready to be swayed against him. What is to happen, John? Will you suddenly "find" the manuscript and read it out in front of the entire council and the King? Who would believe you?"

John scowled at Simon. "No one need believe me," he said with satisfaction, "but they would believe Lord d'Ambray."

"Yes," Bryn finally spoke. "I knew it would have to be someone you knew and trusted." She looked pleadingly at her brother.

"John, you were always hot headed. You don't think things through. You are too easily swayed and influenced by others. Don't do this, John, it will not end well."

John looked pained at his sister's words.

"Bryn, I do this for you and me. If Henry is allowed to continue, what do you think will come of the Montbury and the d'Ambray families? What will become of us?"

Felix knelt near Bryn during this discourse, a stunned look on his face. His thoughts were confused and disjointed. He was not sure what was happening, but he knew all he had worked for was falling apart. John would not allow him to have the manuscript, probably not allow him to leave Carlisle alive now that he knew of the plot. He would never be able to return to his beloved library. Suddenly anger and fear and despair exploded in him. With a wail he jumped up and ran for John, dagger in hand.

John, his attention distracted by Bryn, was caught off guard. He instinctively raised his sword and with one swift blow cut Felix down. The monk collapsed in a puddle of blood on the floor.

"NO!" Bryn screamed and covered her face. Simon ran toward her but John quickly swung around and used the hilt of his sword to hit Simon on the back of the neck. There was an explosion and a sudden brilliant white light in his head. He fell to his hands and knees.

"John, stop! Please!" Bryn cried out.

"Enough!" John yelled. He was shaking and sweating. None of this should be happening. His task was simple—to get the parchment and bring it to the council. He reached down and pulled Simon to his feet. The sudden movement made Simon feel sick. He stood unsteadily on his feet, his head pounding.

"Bryn, I must have the manuscript. The full council meets tomorrow. Lord d'Ambray must have that paper to bring forth at the council."

"John," Bryn had risen to her knees. "You are talking about overthrowing the lawful king of England. You will be put to death for this. Lord d'Ambray is just using you and your loyalty to him."

John hesitated, for a moment he looked uncertain and confused. Then he pushed Simon over toward Bryn.

"It's gone too far now. I must finish this. Take me to it now, Bryn. If not, he dies." John pointed his broad sword at Simon's neck. The candlelight flashed off the blade.

"Alright, alright," Bryn said hurriedly. "Simon hid them for me. He knows where they are."

While she was talking, Simon felt a movement behind him. The thin, stiff blade of his foil brushed his arm. Bryn had picked up the foil that was on the ground behind her and was handing it to Simon behind her back. Without any movement, he grasped the foil and held it close to his side.

"We'll take you there." Bryn purposely strode to the door. John quickly turned and followed. Simon took this chance to hide his foil under his tunic and he came behind John. He had to think, to plan. He had to use every possible advantage and right now, he couldn't think of a single advantage he had.

Chapter Forty Eight

William sat in the soldier's barracks. He polished the same spot on his weapon over and over as his mind was elsewhere, heedless of what his hands were doing. Simon had seemed upset, that was obvious. He was looking for John and seemed to think John had sent him a message to meet somewhere. William's gut feelings told him it didn't feel right. He stood up and sheathed his sword in its scabbard. This might be worth looking into. Time was short, whatever was going to happen would happen in the next 24 hours he was sure. He had a job to do and it was time to do it.

He walked out of the barracks into the bailey. It was night but there was a good moon and a scattering of stars. He looked up at the keep. The great hall was full of light and noise as men began to come in for a last drink before bedding down. There were few lights elsewhere except one flickering light in the top room of one of the towers. William stared at it for moment and then grimly set out.

Chapter Forty Nine

"*It's* in the stables," Simon said. "I put it under Alizay's saddle."

John grabbed Simon by the arm and dragged him down the long screen hallway that separated the great hall from the rest of the castle. Bryn, hurrying behind them, glanced through the carved wooden screen to the great hall. There were many men sitting at the table, others lying on benches or on pallets on the floor. Bryn thought how easy it would be to yell out, to attract their attention. But she saw the tip of John's sword stuck neatly in the small of Simon's back. She bit her tongue and remained silent.

The three of them walked across the bailey. It was mostly empty except for a few dogs scavenging for scraps and a serving girl just entering the kitchen doors with a bucket of water from the well. They crossed the bailey in silence toward the large, stone horse stables on the far side.

Simon was impressed with the stables when they first arrived. They were tremendous in size, newly built of stone with a thick thatch roof. A long, wide aisle ran down the center with dozens of wooden doors for separate horse stalls on each side. Against the stalls were wooden buckets for water and grain. Barrels and sheaves of straw and hay were piled high. John shoved Simon through the door of the stable. He stumbled and fell to one knee, keeping his right arm tight against his side to secure the hidden foil.

"Get it," John said sharply.

Simon slowly got up and walked down the center aisle to Alizay's stall. The horse nuzzled him as he opened the gate and walked to the back of the stall where a post held the saddle. The leather roll was still there, tucked under the saddle blanket. Simon pulled it free and shut the stall door behind him. He walked back toward Bryn and John but stopped twenty feet away.

"Bring it here!" John yelled angrily. He held out his hand. Simon threw the leather case to the ground between them.

"God's blood, you son of a goat," John snarled. "Bring that here to me." Simon stood still, he said nothing.

John swore and walked quickly to the case. He bent down to pick it up. As he did so, he heard a whistling swish of air. He jumped back startled. John jerked his arm away and looked disbelievingly at a bright red gash across the back of his hand. He looked up and saw Simon standing with his foil, stained with blood, in hand. Simon stood in his fencing stance. His right hand held his foil in front of him, his left hand arched over his head behind him. He balanced lightly on his feet, tense, his legs like springs.

John stepped back. He slowly raised his broad sword with two hands and brought it up and over his shoulder.

"You must want to die tonight," John said quietly. Simon didn't answer, he held John's gaze, unblinking. He was ever so slightly flexing his feet, rocking back and forth from heel to ball of foot, his legs positioned widely for balance and swiftness one in front of the other. John was calm but Simon could see he was unsure of what to expect. John had the advantage of size and experience fighting with a broad sword. But Simon was an unknown and John had never seen a weapon like the one Simon held. He would have laughed had he not already felt its swift bite. His hand stung and bled freely where Simon had slashed it, making it difficult to firmly hold his heavy sword. But John was not one to waste time on strategy. He acted. With a yell he charged at Simon, sword held high.

Simon spun around arching his back as the sword came down toward his shoulder. Before John had finished his attack,

Simon was behind him, carving a deep slash in John's tunic and slicing the skin on his back. Throughout their journey here Simon had noticed that both William and John wore chain mail under their surcoats. But that was to be prepared for the dangers of traveling. While at the castle, John saw no need for such protection.

John yelped in pain and staggered as he steadied his sword and swung around to face Simon. He was used to facing an opponent who, like him, charged straight at him with broad sword raised. This was like fighting a hummingbird with a deadly beak. Again, Simon took his fencing stance. He relied on natural instinct, on the same moves that had made him successful in his fencing matches at home. But he also needed to fight those instincts. Foil fencing was strictly regulated, only hits to the torso would count in a match. Simon knew he had to forget all the rules he was trained to obey in his competitive matches. The only rule in this match was to survive.

"You will pay for this," John said between clenched teeth. "I will make sure you pay for this mightily before I kill you."

Once again he rushed at Simon, both hands on his sword, this time swinging it in a wide arch from the side aiming for Simon's chest. Simon took three long steps toward him, always leading with his right foot, always keeping his balance with his back foot. He remembered William's story of fighting John as boys. He recalled John's right arm had been broken once, he couldn't raise it as high as his left. John, expecting Simon to turn and run, or at least to duck to the side, pulled up short and raised his sword over his head for a mighty blow. With one last leap Simon lunged forward, driving his foil deeply into John's right shoulder. John reeled backwards and looked with surprise as the blood began to flow down his chest.

In his pain and anger John rushed at Simon again, swinging his sword over his head with both hands. Simon ducked low this time and to the side. He jumped up on one of barrels stacked against a stall and leaped off it over John's back to his exposed left side. With a quick forward thrust his foil sunk deep into the flesh beneath John's raised arm.

John screamed in pain and dropped to his knees. His sword fell to the ground in front of him and he pressed his arm tight against the wound in his side to stop the flow of blood.

"John!" Bryn cried in anguish and rushed to his side. She had watched in horror as the fight progressed. For the first time in her life she could not act. She felt instinctive protection for her brother, but also terror for the danger Simon was in. An internal fight was happening in her mind and heart that kept her immobile. But when she saw her brother fall, badly wounded, she ran to him. She knelt at his side, arms around him. Simon, exhausted, sweat running down his face, walked over to them. Bryn looked up at him, her face a mixture of horror and pleading.

"Help him," she cried. "Please, Simon."

Simon came over and leaned down to help raise John to his feet. John shakily took his sword and used it to push himself up from the ground. Suddenly, with a great shout of effort, he grabbed the sword by the blade with both hands and swung the heavy hilt at Simon, hitting him hard on the side of the head. Simon collapsed with a groan and lay unconscious on the ground. Bryn stared at him in disbelief and then turned to her brother.

"What have you become?" she whispered. "Who are you?"

"I am a survivor." John smiled through bloodied lips. "You can't stop me, Bryn. Please don't try. I don't want to harm you." He staggered to his feet and stumbled over to where the leather pouch holding the manuscripts lay. He was still bleeding profusely and Bryn took a step toward him.

"I wouldn't, mistress." A voice from the stable doorway spoke harshly. Bryn looked up to see the ruddy-faced man they had seen at Middleham Castle on their journey here. He too, was wearing Lord d'Ambray's livery. He held a dagger that he kept pointed at Bryn while he ran to grab the leather pouch and help John up. Holding John and nearly dragging him out of the stable, the man looked over his shoulder to sneer at Bryn.

"It'll soon be over, mistress. You'd best tend to your friend there." He laughed and they disappeared into the bailey.

Bryn had stayed by Simon's side as he lay on the floor of stable after John and his companion had gone. She was afraid to move him, and doubted she could move him by herself. She was afraid to leave him to go get help. She sat holding his hand because she didn't know what else to do when she heard footsteps enter the stables. Bryn quickly stood up, shielding Simon, fearing they had come back to kill them both. But William walked in the door. He looked at her, glanced down to see Simon lying on floor and rushed over to kneel near him.

"I don't have time to explain," Bryn said, the relief in her voice clear. "Just please, please help me get him to the keep."

William looked up at her. "I know what happened," he said grimly. "At least I have a pretty good idea. It was John, wasn't it."

"How could you know?" Bryn asked in astonishment.

William looked searchingly at Bryn as if measuring what to say. He seemed to make a decision.

"King Henry was aware of a plot against him. He traced it to several nobles, but especially to Lord d'Ambray's household. I was recruited by the king to discover what I could about the plot —who was behind it, what plans were made."

"A spy?" Bryn asked in astonishment. "You have been spying for the king?"

"Yes, I guess you could call it that." William's face was sad. "What I found led me to suspect your brother, John, as a major player in this conspiracy. Lord d'Ambray has promised to make him an heir if he is successful. And filled his head with a lot of treasonous thoughts."

"How did you know to come here?" Bryn asked as William carefully felt Simon's skull to see how bad his injuries were.

"I was bothered by something Simon said earlier, about John sending him a note to meet at the Captain's Tower. Something didn't seem right about that but I wasn't sure what was going on. After he left, I decided to try to find John. I looked all over the castle grounds and even rode into the town to see if he was there. I finally decided to go to your rooms and confront Simon about it. When I got there, I saw the mess your room was in, the blood stains. I also saw the open door at the end of the hallway and followed the stairs up to the tower room." He looked grimly at Bryn. "I found the body of a monk in a pool of blood on the floor. I knew you were both in danger. I've been looking everywhere for you, until I found you here."

"Let's get Simon to safety. I'll fill you in on the rest," Bryn said solemnly.

Together they carried Simon up to his room. Bryn sent a serving girl rushing to find the castle infirmarer. He came with a basket of medicines and bandages and spent considerable time bandaging Simon's head and preparing herbal preparations to ease his pain and heal his wounds. William stayed with Bryn, listening with a stern expression as she told him her story from the beginning.

"He's more a fool than I thought," William said in disgust as he listened to Bryn tell of John's plan. He stood up, strapping his sword around his waist. "I must find him and get that manuscript back."

Bryn grabbed his arm. "Surely he wouldn't still have it?" she said reasonably, one part of her still wanting to protect her brother. "He would have given it to Lord d'Ambray by now."

William hesitated. "William, even if you confronted Lord d'Ambary, how could prove any of this? It would be his word, as a powerful noble, against yours."

"We can't just let this happen, Mistress Berengar," William said angrily.

"No," Bryn agreed. "But I can't think of anything we can do to stop it. Right now I have to make sure Simon will be OK. Then we can decide what to do."

"We have very little time to think. The full council of nobles meets tonight. Whatever will happen, will happen then." William walked angrily out of the room.

Simon stretched out his hands to feel his way through the pitch black. He could feel one rough wooden wall to his left that he ran his hand along as he walked. He could smell hay and very close by he could hear the heavy breathing and snorting of a horse. He must be in the stables, in one of the horse stalls. Why couldn't he see anything? Slowly, a pinpoint of light appeared and grew bigger. He made out the outlines of a huge, black stallion that turned in the stall to look at him with wild eyes. John's stallion. The horse reared and brought its hooves crashing down on Simon's skull. Simon yelled out in pain.

"It's all right. It's just a dream. You're safe." Bryn held Simon tightly as he woke with a cry of pain.

"It's just a dream, Simon. You're safe," she repeated soothingly. Simon, his head splitting with pain, kept his eyes closed. The sunlight coming in the arrow loop window felt like a knife in his eyes. He moaned and opened his eyes to a slit. Bryn's anxious face came into focus. He stared at her intently for a moment.

"You look awful," Simon mumbled.

"Well, thank you very much," she replied with a smile. "You don't look all that great yourself if you want me to be honest." Simon's right eye and cheek were swollen and badly bruised. He had a gash across his temple that still seeped blood.

"In fact," Bryn laughed and put her hand to her own temple. "We appear to have matching bruises."

Simon closed his eyes again at a stab of pain in his head. Suddenly he remembered the events of the last few hours and opened his eyes in alarm.

"Bryn," he grabbed at her arm. "Did he get it? Does he have the manuscript?"

Bryn's face reflected her sadness and defeat. "Yes, Simon. I'm sorry. There was nothing I could do."

"No," Simon whispered as he sank back onto the mattress. "Then it was all for nothing."

"It's not over yet," Bryn said grimly. "Simon, William is with us. He found us in the stable and helped me carry you here. I've told him everything."

Simon looked alarmed. "Bryn, we don't know who we can trust."

"We can trust William. He is working as a spy in the d'Ambray household for King Henry."

Simon looked thoughtful. "So what do we do?"

"I don't know yet," Bryn answered with determination, "but we'll think of something."

Chapter Fifty

Moira sat in a pool of yellow light in the broken recliner in her museum office. She could hear the custodian vacuuming down the hall. The museum was long closed for the evening and she was supposed to be out of her office hours ago. But Dave, the custodian who so bravely made the attempt to clean her office each night, knew Moira well enough to ignore the fact that she often stayed way beyond closing hours. She used to make him cookies and brownies as a way to thank him for allowing her to break museum rules. He finally got up the courage to ask her to stop cooking for him, as he generally got ill after eating something she'd made. They'd come to a mutual agreement that if he would allow her to stay as long as she liked after hours, she would settle for having him only empty her trash and recycling. It suited both of them well enough.

Now she sat in the sagging recliner intently reading the book that Darrell had brought her. He'd narrowed it down to an unpublished doctoral thesis on the legal reforms of Henry II, and a photocopy of a medieval manuscript found in Durham Cathedral written by a knight named William who had served King Henry.

"Yes!" said Moira, grabbing the book from Darrell's hands. "This is it! I remember it now!"

She looked up at Darrell, thanked him and shut the door in his face before he could ask her to show her staff ID badge. Now she sat intently reading the photocopied pages. It took her two hours to finish. It was essentially the memoirs of an aging knight, telling of his adventures as a young soldier under the reign of King Henry II. She had especially read and re-read the pages that detailed the knight's adventures at the council of nobles in Carlisle. Moira looked thoughtful as she shut the cover of the book. She tapped her pencil against her lip.

"I don't see any way around it," she said softly to herself.

Chapter Fifty One

"I insist you open this door immediately," Bryn yelled and banged on the heavy wooden door. Simon winced at the sound and put his hands to his head. Bryn ran over to his side.

"Oh Simon, I'm so sorry." She threw herself down on the edge of the bed. "I'm just so angry and frustrated!"

An hour before a young man had come with a message for Bryn from Sir Robert. The message was that Sir Robert had received word that both Bryn and Simon were in danger and until he put an end to this business, he insisted that they remain locked safely in Simon's room. Bryn refused to let the young man go until she had questioned him thoroughly.

"Who sent this message to Sir Robert?" she asked him.

"Why it was your brother, John, mistress," the messenger had answered. "He took Sir Robert aside and said he had uncovered a plot that put you in great danger. I believe they have arrested one of Lord d'Ambray's men, William, as part of the plot." Bryn gasped and looked at Simon.

"Sir Robert said he had gotten word from his steward a week ago that you were in danger at the Montbury manor, and he believed the danger had followed you here."

Bryn stamped her foot on the floor in frustration.

"Please, please take a message to Sir Robert that he has been misinformed. Tell him we must speak to him immediately."

"I will try, mistress," the young man responded, "but Sir Robert and the other nobles are meeting very shortly with the

King on important business. It cannot be interrupted. That is why he insisted that you be safely locked in your room until he can see to this business." With that the messenger left and they both heard the key turn in the lock.

Bryn turned frightened eyes to Simon. Over the last few hours he had greatly improved and was able to eat and drink. He still moved carefully but the pain in his head was now manageable.

"Simon," Bryn was close to tears. "He's done it. John has managed to get us locked up here and have William arrested. What can we do?"

Simon shakily stood up, holding onto the bedpost to steady himself. He lifted the corner of the mattress and brought out the cloth bag that Agnes had made him when he'd first arrived. He threw it to Bryn. She caught it and looked at him questioningly.

"Open it," he said and sat heavily down on the bed.

Bryn opened it and looked inside. She looked up at Simon in surprise and smiled. She reached in and took out the small set of lock picks like those she had used on the library door.

"Simon, you're brilliant! Another gift from Edwin I am guessing." She ran over and kissed him on the cheek making him wince in pain.

"Oh! Sorry!" she said, but kissed him again. "Come on." Bryn grabbed his hand and pulled him to the door. He grimaced with the dull pain in his head but was surprised that it wasn't as bad as he'd feared it would be.

"You're better at this than I am." Bryn handed the picks to him. "Which makes me wonder a little about you actually." She looked inquiringly at him.

Simon ignored her and carefully inserted the picks into the large iron lock on the door. In fact this one was much simpler than the one on the library door and within a few minutes he had the door open.

"Come on, let's get to Sir Robert now!" Bryn started down the hall.

"Bryn!" Simon called her back. She stopped and turned, hands on hips.

"Wait. We have to think this out." Bryn came back and waited for him to speak.

"There is no way they will let us into the council of nobles with the King. It is unlikely they will even allow us to send in a message to him. I think our best bet is to get down to the dungeon and find William. If we can get him out, he will know how best to get into the council."

Bryn reluctantly agreed. She was thoughtful for a moment and then seemed to make a decision. She pulled Simon into her room.

"We'll need a few things," she said. She grabbed her dark green riding cloak from a chest at foot of the bed. Then she walked over to the table and started to wash her face and undo her long braid.

"For heaven's sake Bryn!" Simon said in astonishment. "What do you think you are doing? You're not going to a party. We don't have time for this!"

"We need to make the time," Bryn spoke over her shoulder. "Turn around," she commanded Simon.

He looked at her in exasperation but shrugged his shoulders and turned away. He heard her taking something out of the trunk and for several minutes, as he waited impatiently, he heard various rustling noises.

"OK, you can turn around. I need help tying this up in the back."

Simon turned around. He opened his mouth in astonishment. Bryn had changed into a beautiful sky blue dress with fine lace and gold trim around a deep neckline. She had brushed out her long hair that now hung in a shining mass all around her shoulders. Simon thought she was stunningly beautiful. She turned her back to him.

"Tie up the laces in the back, will you?" She smiled at him over her shoulder. "I know you don't have much experience as a lady's maid but you're all I've got at the moment."

259

Simon shook himself out of his amazement. Without a word he walked over to Bryn and pulled the golden laces tight, tying them off the bottom.

"There," she said. "That should do it."

"Do what?" Simon finally was able to say.

"Do you think we are just going to walk casually into the dungeon, past the guard and politely ask if they would be so kind as to release William?"

Simon hadn't thought that far.

"I will go down first and cause a distraction," Bryn began. Simon mentally agreed that she was definitely a distraction at the moment. "While I am talking with the guard, you will sneak past and get William out."

She threw him the long, hooded cloak. "Give him this. It will hide him from anyone who knows him at the castle. Fortunately for us that is not many people. Come on," she grabbed his hand, "let's go."

They made two brief stops on the way. First, Simon ran back into his room to get his foil.

"Simon!" Bryn had looked at him in astonishment. "You are in no condition to be fighting with anyone."

"No, I'm not," he agreed. "But it may come down to that. We may not have any other choice." She watched him as he tucked his foil into his belt.

The next stop was at the kitchen. Bryn grabbed a large wooden bowl and filled it with breads and cheeses and cold meats. She motioned for Simon to grab a pitcher filled with ale.

"We need to come bearing gifts." She smiled at him.

The dungeon was in the very bottom of the east keep tower. They stayed as much to the back hallways and shadows as possible. They pushed open the tower door and followed the narrow steps down into the damp dungeon. Simon stopped just outside the room and leaned against the wall out of sight. Bryn marched with confidence up to the guard who sat at a small table in front of a barred door. He jumped up when he saw her approach. Simon, peaking around the door, saw the guard's face change from challenge to astonishment. It was unlikely he had seen any woman come down to this dreary place, never mind one as lovely as Bryn. Simon smiled as he heard Bryn begin her performance.

"Oh dear!" she said in surprise and looked all around her. "I'm afraid I'm lost."

She sat down heavily at the table. The guard still stood, unsure what to say to this young woman who was obviously of noble birth. Bryn looked up at him with her most charming smile. Simon almost felt sorry for him.

"I was supposed to bring some refreshment to my brothers who serve Lord d'Ambray. They said they would be in the Captain's Tower. Is that where I am?" she asked with concern.

"Oh no, mistress." The guard found his voice. "The Captain's Tower is across the bailey by the gatehouse. This is the dungeon."

Bryn jumped up in fright.

"The dungeon! Oh dear, how frightful! Do you mean there are criminals just behind that door?" Bryn put her hands up to cover her face. Simon rolled his eyes and shook his head.

"Oh, there's nothing to be afraid of mistress." The guard took a step toward her but then remembered himself and stepped back again. "They are all locked up tight."

Bryn put a delicate hand on her breast.

"And of course, you are here." Simon leaned his head back against the cold stone wall and closed his eyes. Was it possible the guard would fall for this?

"Yes, of course mistress. There's nothing to fear. Perhaps I could tell you how to get to your brothers in the Captain's Tower?" he suggested, feeling more confident in his role as protector.

261

"How wonderfully kind of you!" Bryn answered. She looked around. "Don't tell me they leave you here alone in this dreary place?"

The guard looked around as if noticing the dark, damp, windowless room for the first time. "Well, we rotate guard duty, mistress. But yes, we serve our shifts alone."

"How horribly lonely!" Bryn said with feeling. "Please, I insist that you take this." She put the bowl of food and the jug of ale down on the table. "They are making merry everywhere else in the castle tonight, how unjust that you should be stuck here in this damp hole with nothing to comfort you."

The guard's eyes widened as he looked at the feast of food and ale.

"Thank you, mistress, that is kind of you." He hesitated, looking over his shoulder at the locked door behind him. "Perhaps, if you like, I could take you up to the bailey and point out the Captain's Tower?"

Bryn laughed delightedly. "How thoughtful! I would so appreciate that. I really fear I would get lost again in this maze of hallways and towers. Of course, now I shall have to return to the kitchen for more food!" she smiled at the guard and put her hand on his arm.

Simon quickly squeezed behind the open door as they passed by him on their way up the stairs. As soon as their footsteps died away he ran into the room, knelt in front of the cell door and inserted the lock picks. His hands were wet with sweat and he dropped them twice.

"Idiot!" he said to himself as he picked them up from the floor the second time.

"You might try the ring of keys on the hook on the wall," a voice from the other side of the door casually said.

Simon jumped up and looked through the tiny barred window in the door.

"William!" he said with relief.

"I thoroughly enjoyed Mistress Berengar's performance. And while I appreciate your efforts with the lock picks, the guard left the keys hanging on the hook by the door. Look to your left."

Simon looked up and saw a large ring of keys hanging from a hook just above his head. With a snort of disgust he grabbed them and unlocked the door. William walked out smiling. Simon looked in and saw one other man in the cell asleep on the floor.

"He'll sleep for hours yet. He's in here for getting into a drunken brawl." He took the keys and relocked the door and hung them back on the hook. Simon handed him the long green cloak. William took it and swung it over his head and shoulders. The two of them ran up the stairs hugging the dark shadows of the inner curtain wall on their way to Simon's room. They found Bryn there waiting for them.

"They are all meeting in the great hall. Henry has the throne set up on the dais, all the lords and their retainers are seated on long tables that are set up in a "U" on the floor. Even that was argued over for hours. All the nobles fighting over who should sit where and how tables must be arranged to give everyone proper respect for their position." William shook his head in disgust.

They were seated in Simon's room. Simon sat on the edge of the bed. Bryn and William in the two chairs at the table against the wall.

"What is this conference for?" Bryn asked.

"Henry has instituted new laws and regulations for the court system. They are much needed changes. He is establishing royal courts in different counties to spread out the load and take some of the responsibility off the over-burdened high court. Unfortunately, many nobles had their own courts and made their own laws for their manors. They are not happy about what they see as a further restriction of their powers and further interference from Henry in their local rule."

"What do you suggest we do, William?" Simon asked.

William was silent for a moment as he thought.

"I don't think we have a lot of choice," he said. "I suggest we get into the minstrel's galley as the meeting begins. That will give us clear view of the whole proceedings. It is possible that they won't go through with this. They are taking a huge risk that other nobles will fall in behind them and support their treason against Henry. If they have called off the plan, then we won't have to do anything."

"But if they do go through with it?" Bryn asked.

William looked first at Bryn and then at Simon.

"If they go through with it, we will have to stand up and defy them. We will have to tell our story in front of the King and hope we will be believed."

William looked at Simon. "I suggest you take that weapon of yours with you. If it comes to it, we may have to fight our way out." Simon nodded.

Chapter Fifty Two

The three of them sat on the wood floor of the minstrel's gallery. This was a balcony high up on the wall of the great hall. Two long banners bearing Carlisle Castle insignia hung on either side of the gallery, reaching almost to the floor. During festivities musicians would play from this balcony while everyone feasted below. But there were no musicians for this somber conference and Bryn, Simon and William sat on the floor of the gallery, backs against the cool stone wall.

They could see the crowded hall below them through the carved wooden balcony. It was very noisy as everyone ate and drank and waited for the King to arrive. Bryn grabbed Simon and pointed out Sir Robert, standing by a doorway drink in hand talking to another lord.

Suddenly a trumpet sounded and a voice announced the arrival of the king. The talking immediately stopped and everyone turned toward the dais. Simon crawled forward to peer through the carved balustrade of the minstrel's gallery. He saw a man of medium height, with a broad chest and muscled arms march confidently to the throne. His legs were bowed probably Simon thought, from too much living on a horse. He sat down and there was a murmur of hushed voices and rustling as the crowd of nobles also took their seats.

Henry had short, red hair and a freckled face. He looked over the assembled nobles and began to speak. Simon was shocked to hear him. His voice was harsh and cracked. It sounded as though he was hoarse from too many nights sleeping out of doors. But he commanded authority and everyone listened in silence. Bryn had crawled up to lay on her stomach next to Simon. She too peered out from the gallery at the crowded floor of the great hall. Henry was speaking from his throne on the raised platform at the head of the hall. There was silence as the nobles listened intently. Bryn scanned the crowd looking for her brother.

"Simon," she whispered sharply. "There in the far corner, standing against the wall."

Simon looked in the direction she pointed. He saw John leaning against a large tapestry on the broad back wall. Simon saw with some satisfaction that he kept one hand pressed against his side. He looked pale and in pain from the wounds he had received in his duel with Simon. John leaned over to listen to the ruddy-faced man who whispered something in his ear. John nodded grimly and leaned his head back against the wall, closing his eyes.

"Bryn, look at the man next to him. The one we saw at Middleham Castle." Simon pointed. "He's got the manuscript hanging from his shoulder."

"I see," Bryn said grimly. "So it looks like they are planning on going through with it after all."

They continued to watch and listen from their perch high on the wall. Henry had gotten up from his throne and was walking back and forth across the raised dais, sometimes gesticulating with his arms as he spoke passionately to his nobles. Simon scanned the crowded hall. Some of the nobles nodded in agreement with much of what Henry said. Others remained stone-faced and silent as they listened to their king speak of moving the kingdom forward, of modernizing the court system and unifying the fiefdoms. He concluded his speech asking for their cooperation to make England strong.

As Henry finished speaking and turned to sit on his throne, a nobleman at the front of the room stood.

"Are these reforms to make England strong?" he called out and turned to face the crowd. "Or are they to make the king strong, and his nobles weak?"

Simon saw William sitting against the back wall of the gallery tense and move forward to look down at the speaker.

"That's Lord Barrow. He's a vassal of d'Ambray's," William spoke softly. "It looks like the show is about to begin."

There was a nervous movement among the crowd below and a low murmuring of agreement from some of the other nobles. Henry slowly turned to the crowd and spoke.

"If England is to be strong, its king must be strong." Henry paused and looked out over the crowd. "If our nobles are squabbling amongst themselves, if they set up their own little kingdoms, if there is no unity of law or government, we cannot hope to stand together against our enemies."

A voice from the crowd called out. "And is the church our enemy too?"

There was a gasp from the assembled nobles. They all knew this was a direct reference to the murder of the archbishop. Henry stood silently in front of them, his face stern.

"Is there anyone here dare accuse me of being an enemy to the church?" he said, his voice frighteningly calm. No one spoke. "Is there anyone here dare to say I have been anything but fierce in my stand for what is right and just?" He stood, feet firmly on the dais and muscled fists planted on his hips.

Suddenly a voice from the back of the room called out.

"I do!" John stepped forward. Simon heard Bryn draw in a quick breath.

"John," She whispered to herself, "no, please no."

Simon saw the nobles part as John walked forward, the leather pouch in his hand. Simon thought he looked like he was forcing himself to walk steadily to the middle of the room. His confidence seemed strained. He definitely favored his left side, no doubt still in pain from his fight with Simon.

John stepped up onto the table and held up the leather pouch. He slowly turned as he spoke so that the whole hall could clearly hear him. Henry silently watched and listened.

"I have here documents that prove the perfidy of the king."

Several nobles jumped up, swords in hand, ready to defend their king. Others jumped up to support John. The king held up his hand and called out loudly.

"Stop!" All eyes turned toward Henry. "Let us hear what he has to say. I have nothing to fear if he speaks only the truth." Henry turned to John. "Are you prepared to swear that what you speak is the truth? Will you swear that before God?"

John faltered and lowered his arm. He looked around nervously at the crowd and then found the face of Lord d'Ambray. Simon saw d'Ambray give the slightest nod to John. John took a deep breath and faced the king.

"I do so swear," he said loudly. The murmuring in the crowd grew louder and more tense.

"Then proceed." Henry turned and sat comfortably on his throne. "Perhaps you might first tell us, brave knight, who you are?"

John faltered again, he glanced quickly at d'Ambray who made no sign.

"I am John Berengar. I am a knight with the household of Lord d'Ambray." A wave of whispering swept the crowd as faces turned toward d'Ambray. He stood unmoving and stone-faced.

"He's going to wait to see how it goes before he decides whether or not to let John hang himself," William whispered to Bryn and Simon. "If the crowd falls for it, he will step forward to claim it was all done at his bidding. If John fails, he will let the crowd have him."

Bryn turned to look aghast at William. "How can he do this?" She quickly looked back as John began to speak.

"The king says he has honor and integrity. He says he supports the church and stands for what is right and just." John was beginning to gain confidence as the crowd silently listened to his every word.

"I have here proof that the king, King Henry himself, not only was behind the murder of Archbishop Thomas Becket…" several nobles once again jumped up, but were held back by those near them. "But also that he had detailed plans to put the blame for the murder on our beloved Queen Eleanor so that he could freely return to his mistress, Rosamund Clifford."

At this there was an eruption in the crowd. Swords were drawn and the sides were clearly parted. A small but significant group of nobles gathered around John defying the larger group that had risen up in anger at John's accusations. Henry stood and roared for the crowd's attention. There was immediate silence as they turned to face the king.

"These are serious accusations John Berengar," Henry said calmly. "Perhaps before we pursue this further, you could show us your evidence?"

For a brief moment John hesitated. Then he regained his usual bravado and jumped off the table, walking confidently up to the king. Henry motioned for a monk who was standing at the far end of the dais to come forward.

"Let us have an unbiased observer tell us what these documents hold." He waved for one of his guards to take the documents from John. The guard handed the documents to the monk who brought them over to a table near Henry's throne. There was tense silence as the monk slowly unrolled a piece of parchment. Bending over the table, finger following the script, he silently read the manuscript.

Bryn turned to William. "What should we do? He will read out to this fractious crowd all the evidence they have created to bring Henry down. Should we speak up now, before everything erupts?"

Simon answered. "I think we should wait until the document has been read. There is something going on here I don't understand. If Henry had some idea of this conspiracy, why would he calmly allow this to happen now?"

"I don't know but I think we'd both better get ready for whatever happens in the next few minutes." William stood up and very quietly unsheathed his sword. Simon stood at the other corner of the gallery and pulled his foil out of his belt.

"Well?" Henry's voice split the silence. "What damning evidence does this document contain?"

The monk stood up and cleared his throat. He looked at the tense crowd awaiting his answer and then he looked at Henry.

"My lord, I fear I cannot make sense of it," the monk said.

There was a confused murmur among the crowd.

"Is it in a language unknown to you?" Henry asked the monk.

"Oh no, sire. It is written in excellent Latin."

"Perhaps the handwriting is poor?" Henry inquired.

"Certainly not sire. It is a beautiful script."

"Perhaps you should read it aloud for us. If I am to answer these accusations, I must know of what I stand accused," Henry replied.

The monk swallowed and picked up the manuscript with both hands. He took one step toward the edge of the dais and began to read with a clear voice.

"Mary had a little lamb. Its fleece was white as snow." He nervously looked toward Henry who raised an eyebrow. Simon gasped. Bryn and William turned quickly to look at him.

"What do you know of this?" Bryn hissed. Simon opened his mouth to answer but the monk had begun to read again.

"And everywhere that Mary went. The lamb was sure to go." The monk stopped.

No one seemed to know what to say or do. Before the crowd could react, Henry again questioned the monk.

"Is there nothing else on this document?" he asked the monk.

The monk looked down at the manuscript in his hands.

"Yes, sire, there is more." He wiped perspiration from his forehead. "I am afraid it appears to be a recipe for soup."

Someone in the audience laughed. Several others started to yell and call for John Berengar to be held. John, who had stood as if paralyzed during this whole ordeal, swiftly realized his situation. He spun around sword in hand. The crowd that had started to close in on him quickly pulled back. John, holding his sword in front of him, searched above their heads for Lord d'Ambray. His face hardened with anger and hatred when he realized d'Ambray was gone, leaving him to be devoured by the crowd.

John jumped up on the table and began to run down its length heading for escape through the double doors of the great hall. William nodded to Simon and then jumped from the minstrel's gallery onto the table below. Simon leaped up onto the gallery balustrade and then jumped into the air grabbing onto the flowing banner that ran down the side of the minstrel's gallery flanking the hall doors. Firmly gripping the heavy cloth with one hand, he kicked out from the wall and swung in an arch over John's head and onto the table behind him.

"John!" he yelled.

John looked over his shoulder but continued to run. William landed at the far end of the table, blocking John's exit through the hall doors. John skidded to a stop halfway between Simon and William. The crowd, closing in, stopped and waited. These were men who respected armed combat between equal foes. They pulled back to watch what would develop.

John was sweating and he gripped his heavy sword with both hands, slowly moving it from one side to other.

"John, it's over," William calmly said. "If you give up now, you can be sure those who pushed you to do this will be punished."

"Oh?" John's laugh was harsh and cracked. "Do you really think these nobles will allow one of their own to be punished when they have me to tear apart instead?" He looked toward Simon who stood to his left, foil raised and ready. With a great yell John charged William, hoping to cut him down and make it through to the doorway. William raised his sword and the

271

two came together with a loud clash of metal on metal. Simon watched in fascination as the heavy broad swords swung through the air almost in slow motion. William blocked a downward swing toward his left shoulder, first holding and then throwing off John's sword with his own. John spun around with the momentum of William's parry and landed on his knees. William lifted his sword to attack.

"No!" came a scream from the gallery. William, startled, looked up and stumbled. Bryn was leaning over the gallery, her long hair hanging down over the gallery balustrade. Tears streamed down her face as she looked at her brother. John, still on his knees, glanced up at Bryn and smiled. Then, before William could recover, he brought his sword swiftly across William's legs. With a yell of anguish William folded onto the table, grabbing his bleeding legs. John was on his feet but his way was blocked by William.

He remembered just in time that Simon was behind him and quickly turned around to face him. Simon stood in position, foil raised, right leg out in front of him, left leg stretched behind, knees slightly bent. John, now familiar with the speed and agility of Simon's attack, threw his heavy broad sword down and reached under his tunic. He drew out a dagger. Lighter and easier to handle, he felt he stood a better chance against Simon with this weapon. For several seconds they both stood, tense and ready to spring.

Simon slowly drew a circle in the air with his foil, his stance wide for balance and agility. He knew his enemy. He knew John was impatient and would make the first move. John lunged with a yell straight toward Simon's chest. Without even moving his feet, Simon made a small movement with his wrist and the dagger slid along the foil and off to the side. John staggered, off balance. There was a gasp from the crowd who had never seen such a weapon or such a strategy before.

Simon returned to his position, knees slightly bent, left hand arched over his head, right hand with foil outstretched. John wiped his sleeve across his face and then lunged again, this time trying for Simon's left side. Simon took a small step forward, and with slight twist of his wrist, angled the foil downward and outward. Again the foil neatly deflected the dagger thrust. There was the sound of metal sliding on metal and John was once again thrown off balance. This time Simon took the advantage. John, his right hand holding the dagger and his left hand grabbing at the air felt the foil tear open his tunic and stab into his side. He jerked backward and flailed his arms for balance. Simon took two fast forward steps and thrust the foil first into John's left shoulder and then with a quick curve of the blade, across his chest and into his right thigh. John, still in pain from his previous duel with Simon, collapsed onto his knees on the table and then fell onto the floor. Simon stood in position for a few brief seconds and then lowered his foil.

The crowd rushed in to help William and two of Henry's guards dragged John out of the hall. Simon wiped the sweat from his eyes and looked up to the minstrel's gallery. It was empty.

Chapter Fifty Three

The crowd in the great hall quickly dispersed. Some to try to hide any connection they might have had to the conspiracy to dethrone Henry, others to spread word of this upset and discuss how they might gain from the fallout. Simon had jumped down from the long table and sat on the bench, watching in silence as small circles of men talked in anxious whispers. He realized that he was not entirely recovered from his beating in the stable. His head ached and he felt vaguely sick. He closed his eyes and let his head fall forward on his chest. Just a moment's rest would be welcome.

Suddenly two strong hands grabbed Simon by the arms and jerked him to his feet. Startled, he opened his eyes to see two of Henry's guards on either side of him. His automatic reaction was to resist and for a brief moment he struggled against their iron grip. He soon realized that beyond making his head hurt worse, his efforts were futile.

"Where are you taking me?" he asked the guard on his right. There was no response. They stared straight ahead as they roughly walked him down a long hallway and up a flight of stairs. At the top of the stairs was a large, arched door. Two more guards stood on either side of the door, broadswords at their side. They moved aside to allow them to pass. The door opened into a room very much like the solar at Montbury manor house. There was a large fireplace, lit on this cool spring evening. The honey-colored stone walls were hung with colorful tapestries. A table covered with papers stood in the middle of the room. Around it were several high-backed carved chairs. Simon looked at the person seated in the biggest chair in the center of the table. Henry II, king of England, looked back with interest at Simon as he was brought to stand in front of him by the guards.

"Welcome." Henry nodded to Simon and indicated for him to be seated in the chair across from him. "I believe I owe you thanks for your service in thwarting a conspiracy to overthrow the rightful king of England."

Simon was unsure how to answer this, or even if it was appropriate for him to answer. He swallowed with some difficulty.

"I was glad to be of service, your highness." Simon was encouraged by Henry's informal and welcoming manner. "I wondered..." he stopped as Henry raised his eyebrow.

"Yes," he said. "You wondered?" Simon wondered how he had the nerve to ask what he was about to ask, but it was too late now to back out.

"I wonder, your highness, if I might be allowed to speak in John Berengar's defense, sir." Simon swallowed again, trying to get the lump out of his throat. "I believe he has been used and manipulated..."

Henry held up his hand. Simon stopped in mid-sentence.

"Good job, Simon." He thought to himself, "you meet the king of England and in the first minute you tell him how to do his job." He guessed his next stop would be the castle dungeons, probably sitting right next to John.

"There is no need to defend John Berengar," Henry said sternly. "He is a young fool and he will have to pay for his misjudgments. However," Henry turned his head to look over Simon's shoulder toward a corner of the room, "you are not alone in your defense of him. I have heard much about this plan and believe I can make a fair judgment on all involved."

Simon turned in his chair to look behind him. He saw Bryn, eyes and nose red from crying, sitting silently against the wall. She was leaning against a woman who sat next to her with a comforting arm around Bryn's shoulder. Bryn gave Simon a wan smile just as the woman turned her head to look directly at him. Simon jumped up.

"Professor Ananke!" he cried and ran over to them. Before he could think of what he was doing he had thrown his arms around both of them. They returned the gesture with warmth. The opening of the door interrupted their reunion. Sir Robert Montbury walked swiftly in followed by William who limped behind him, using a hickory cane to support his wounded legs. Montbury walked directly to Henry and spoke quietly in his ear. Henry nodded and smiled wryly. Bryn jumped up quickly and helped William to a chair at the table. He looked at her gratefully.

"I had invited Lord d'Ambray to join us," Henry said. "Apparently he has urgent business in France and won't be able to make it." Henry laughed. "Sir Robert, I believe you haven't yet met our young hero, Simon Grant?"

Simon nervously stood up. Lord Montbury walked over to him, his face grave.

"I believe I owe you great thanks, young man," Sir Robert held out his hand. "I have been told you have done much to keep Bryn safe from harm."

Simon wasn't sure what to say. He returned the handshake.

"Thank you, Sir Robert, but I think Bryn does a pretty good job of taking care of herself mostly." Simon heard a stifled laugh from William who kept his head down to hide his smile. Lord Montbury also seemed to be trying hard to keep his face stern as he stole a look at Bryn over Simon's shoulder.

"I regret that we will not have time to speak more of this," he said. "The king has requested that I leave immediately for France and bring Lord d'Ambray back to face justice."

He turned to bow to Henry, who dismissed him with a nod. In a moment he was gone to carry out his mission to bring back d'Ambray in disgrace.

Bryn, William, Simon and Professor Ananke all sat together at the table with the king. He had dismissed his guards and Simon began to understand why his close friends were fiercely loyal to him. Although he carried himself with authority when necessary, he could also be open and accessible. Simon had many questions he wanted to ask. The king ordered food and drink and soon they were sitting very comfortably discussing the evening's events.

"Bryn has told me, Simon, that she knows how you got here," Moira began the conversation. "You can speak freely. Henry and I are good friends and I have visited him before. He is rather open-minded about such things." Moira smiled at Henry.

"How did you know how to find me?" Simon asked.

"I am sorry, actually, that it took so long," she said. "I had to find the exact time and place I thought you would be in order to have our paths cross. If I was off even by a month, or a mile, I might never have found you. It took a lot of research to finally pull the facts together. After puzzling over the mystery of the palimpsest and finally finding a document that detailed the conspiracy that was brought against Henry on this day in Carlisle, I guessed coming here would be my best chance of finding you."

Henry interrupted. "Moira found me late this afternoon. She explained what she knew, or at least what she guessed, about d'Ambray's plot to use falsified documents to condemn me. When John was brought to the infirmary to have his wounds tended to after his fight with you in the stables," here Henry looked at Simon, "she took the opportunity to exchange the documents that were in the leather case for the ones you heard read out tonight."

Moira blushed. "Yes. Well, I apologize for that bit of theater. I was in a terrible hurry at home and I guessed I might need a decoy. So I grabbed the first thing I could find that might look like medieval text. Of course it was the nursery rhyme Simon had written in Latin that was pinned to my study wall and a soup recipe from a 5th century cookbook that was laying on my kitchen counter." She paused. "I wouldn't recommend it by the way, tastes horrendous."

Simon hid a smile. He was very familiar with Moira's ability to destroy anything she tried to cook.

"But didn't you take quite a chance that he would notice the switch?" Simon asked.

"It wasn't much of a chance really. He couldn't read, remember. One Latin document would look much like another to him," Moira explained.

"There's still one thing left unanswered." Bryn spoke for the first time. Her voice was hoarse from crying and she paused to clear her throat. "Who broke into the manor house and damaged my books?"

"I think I can answer that." They all turned to William who had been silent up to this point. One of his legs was heavily bandaged and he rested it on a carved wood stool. "You remember Sir Robert had sent a message to your steward, Jasper, that he needed to return briefly to the manor?"

"Yes," Bryn confirmed. "Jasper told me he would be coming in a few weeks."

Sir Robert had some documents outlining leases for his lands that needed to be delivered to Bridlethorpe Abbey. John heard about his plans. He told Sir Robert that he was going through Yorkshire and would be happy to deliver them and save Sir Robert the journey. Robert readily agreed, giving John keys to the manor house so that he could return the signed documents there after the abbot had finished with them."

Simon cut in. "Yes, we thought it odd that whoever broke into the manor had keys to everything except the chest the books were kept in."

William nodded. "For months John has been trying to find out what happened to the papers that Queen Eleanor had sent to Brother Barnabas. He tried to break into the monastery library without luck. When he found out Bryn was regularly visiting the library, he thought it possible that she had found them. He broke

278

into the chest knowing only that was where she kept papers and books most important to her."

Bryn lowered her head. Simon put his arm around her. She looked up, anger in her eyes.

"He has betrayed everyone who meant anything to him," she said. She looked at Henry. "What will happen to him?" Even now, she couldn't help feeling protective of her twin brother.

"It depends on how cooperative he will be," Henry said. "If he will testify against d'Ambray, we will show some leniency." Henry looked at William. "Which brings me to another point."

"William," Henry said seriously. "You have served me well these past months. I know you owed fealty to Lord d'Ambray. Asking you to spy for me was difficult. But I think I might say I owe you much for your service. Of course d'Ambray will forfeit his holdings because of his treachery against our person. In recognition of your service to us, William, I am investing you with his titles and lands."

William was speechless. Bryn smiled and put her hand on his arm. Moira leaned over to Simon and whispered in his ear.

"I hope he enjoys them for a long time. It was his memoirs that led me here tonight." Simon looked up at her in surprise. What strange twists this story had, he thought.

Chapter Fifty Four

Moira, Bryn and Simon sat together on the large bed in Simon's room. The servants had cleaned and put in order Bryn's room, but there was still a red bloodstain on the floor that could not be scrubbed from the rough stone. Simon's room felt more welcoming.

"Moira," Bryn looked questioningly at the woman she had not seen for so many years, "how did John get involved in all this?"

Moira gave a deep sigh. "I'm not sure exactly, but I have pieced most of it together." She ate the last strawberry, wiped red juice from her mouth and began. "You probably know that history records King Henry as saying, in his frustration about Thomas Becket, 'Who will rid me of this meddlesome priest?'"

Bryn and Simon nodded.

"Apparently d'Ambray and Henry were working together on a document setting the record straight about the event. Henry wanted to reaffirm that this statement, said only in frustration, was misinterpreted by his knights who then attacked and killed Becket."

Simon joined in. "Henry didn't then know that d'Ambray was already disillusioned with the king and looking for some way to depose him."

Moira nodded. "When several nobles gathered at d'Ambray's home to discuss how to curb the king's powers, this document gave them the idea. They could use this document, written by Henry himself, and make some minor changes to make it look like it was a plot to blame Eleanor for Becket's death. Change a few word endings to make the statement appear as if spoken by a female instead of a male, change a few words to make it sound more potent and angry that it really was. The papers were found by Eleanor, who believed they really were a plot by Henry to get rid of her. When it was discovered the papers were gone, the conspirators were desperate to get them back."

"They had a measure of safety for themselves by enlisting John to find the papers and to make the accusations," Simon added. "As William told us, Lord d'Ambray promised John that he would make him his heir if he went along with it."

"I am sure it was more than that," Bryn said sadly. "John always had this need to be a hero. I am sure d'Ambray made it seem like Henry was the bad guy, stealing lands and power from them. For John it would have been the noble thing to do." She reached over and took Moira's hand. "You will talk to King Henry for me, won't you? You might be able to influence him to be merciful to John."

Moira squeezed her hand and nodded. "I'll do what I can." She stood up and stretched. "Well, we'd best get some sleep. Simon, you and I need to return to our own time tomorrow before your uncle begins to notice how long you've been gone." She picked up her cloak and walked to the door. "I'll be sure to talk with Henry before I leave, Bryn." She smiled and closed the door behind her.

There was silence in the room for several minutes. Simon had not thought about returning to his own time since he had come. There was always too much else to consider and to do. Professor Ananke's words had hit him like a hammer. He looked over at Bryn. She was sitting silently on the bed beside him, looking down at her hands that were folded in her lap.

"Come back with me," Simon whispered. He was not even sure he had said it aloud. He reached out to touch her cheek and turned her face toward him. "I wish you could come back with me, Bryn," he said aloud.

Tears began to run down her cheeks. Simon brushed them away.

"I can't," she cried. "I can't leave John. There is no one here for him but me. Simon, surely you see that?"

He said nothing for several seconds. Then he pulled her toward him and softly kissed her. It was not a passionate kiss, but the sweet goodbye neither wanted to put into words. She cried, her face buried on his chest. After a moment she stopped and pulled away.

"I have done nothing but cry today. And you have frequently told me how unattractive I look when I cry."

Simon laughed. "Well, it is the truth." Simon used his sleeve to wipe her face. "So, we have 24 hours left together then. What shall we do with it?"

"We have had enough excitement to last a lifetime. I want calm and peace and quiet, just you and me," Bryn smiled. "I know! The ocean is just west of here. Let's leave now. We'll take some food and blankets. Just you and me, and of course Eleanor and Alizay." Simon laughed as Bryn continued. "We'll ride to the sea where there are no plotting nobles, no schemes or kings or bishops or monks. Just you and I and the sea for the whole day." Bryn jumped up and grabbed his hand.

Twenty minutes later they were riding out of the castle gates, Eleanor and Alizay happy to be once more on the road. The night was calm and cool but the horizon was already showing a thin line of light, the stars already beginning to fade. Simon felt alive, the exhaustion of the past days swept away with the cool, salty sea breeze. Earlier as he had waited in the courtyard for Bryn to join him, he pondered something Moira had said. He knew in his heart that Bryn could not return with him.

He knew he could never be sure he would find her again in a time and place that would allow them to be together. Such thoughts were an unfair and unlikely hope for both of them. But Moira had said she read an account of these past days written by William in his old age. Simon knew William couldn't write. Who would have been with him, a companion through his life, who would have been able to write his memoirs for him so many years from now? Who else but Bryn? He had seen William's glance of admiration toward Bryn. And as much as it hurt to admit it, he knew she would be well cared for and loved by him. The thought helped to heal some of the pain he felt at not being a part of her continuing story.

"Simon," Bryn rode up beside him, breaking into his thoughts. She wrapped the reins around the saddle pommel and reached behind her neck. She took off the necklace given to her so many years ago by Professor Ananke. "I don't think I need this anymore." She handed it to him. "But if I give it to you, will you promise never to forget me?"

Simon reached out and took the necklace. With one hand he put it around his own neck. Then he reached over and took her hand in his.

"Never in a thousand years," he said with certainty.

They rode together, the sun just beginning to rise behind them, toward the sound of the sea.

Afterword

Despite the many tumultuous events that occurred in King Henry's time, his reign from 1154-1189 established the beginning of the Plantagenet kings in England. This family tree included Henry and Eleanor's sons, the famous crusader King Richard the Lionheart and his brother, King John of England, who signed the Magna Carta in 1215. Both kings might be better known from their appearances in the stories of Robin Hood.

Henry II is known as one of the greatest kings of England. He reformed England's legal system, setting up Magistrate Courts and essentially doing away with the brutal "trial by ordeal," replacing it with an early form of trial by jury. During the reign of the previous king, Stephen, English nobles had become very powerful, undermining royal authority. Henry had most of their "renegade" castles torn down and forced the nobles to either provide him with military service, or pay a "scutage" tax that allowed him to hire mercenaries. In this way he took back control of the kingdom and subdued his rebellious nobles.

Henry's wife, Eleanor of Aquitaine, was powerful and impressive in her own right. First married to a French king, she ruled many rich lands in France as part of her inheritance. After divorcing her first husband, she married Henry and became Queen of England. She had five sons and three daughters with him. But Henry and Eleanor were both strong willed with powerful personalities and there was often strife between them. When Eleanor supported her sons in an unsuccessful uprising against their father, Henry imprisoned her in several different castles for 16 years. Upon Henry's death, she was freed by her son, Richard the Lionheart, and was known to be active in helping him rule England.

Our fictional characters continue their lives beyond the pages of this book too. Bryn and William eventually fall in love and marry. William, who becomes a baron under Henry II, devotes his life to the service of his king and the running of his own feudal manors. Bryn, as a learned noblewoman of high rank, becomes patroness of her own abbey with a library to rival that of Bridlethorpe and, in a move that would make Queen Eleanor proud, a place to provide an education for females.

Moira and Simon continue their own adventures and explorations of history. Moira is slowly building a relationship with Owen and trying to figure out what it means to have a normal life. Simon, between his studies at school, his youth bureau fencing lessons and keeping his room clean, has stumbled upon a very interesting piece of Roman pottery in the museum storerooms. . .

Read a sample of

The Time Traveler's Apprentice, Book Two

below.

The Time Traveler's Apprentice
Book Two

Chapter One

Blackness. Thick, absolute darkness. It was the kind of darkness that confuses your eyes. They start to create their own flashes of light, floating spots of brightness just to reassure your brain that they are still functioning. Simon held one hand up in front of his face. Nothing. It occurred to him to wonder if his eyes really were still functioning. Surely, he would know if he had suddenly gone blind, wouldn't he? He pushed himself up to a sitting position and waited one more minute for his eyes to adjust to the darkness. They began to ache with the strain of trying to distinguish at least shadow from shadow. The darkness refused to cooperate. It remained a solid, thick, musty, warm mass around him. He decided to accept the darkness and move onto another problem. There were plenty to consider.

First, where was he? Second, how did he get there? Third, how was he going to get out? Simon shook his head, moved his arms and stretched out his legs. At least everything was working, although he could feel bruises on his shoulder, and his head ached. He must have fallen down here, landing on his back from the feel of it. He couldn't remember.

What he did remember was that just a little while before he had been carrying a bright red Roman Samianware bowl down to the museum storage rooms. Professor Ananke had finished with it, giving Simon her keys to the security doors that led down to the maze of corridors in the basement of the museum in order to return the bowl to storage. After a few false turns in the maze of hallways, he had eventually found the room for the storage of ancient Roman artifacts. He'd unlocked the door and walked up and down the tall, metal shelving units until he found the spot where the bowl belonged. He'd gently placed the bowl inside the low wooden frame layered with cotton batting to protect the ancient pottery from damage. The bowl tilted to the left. He'd centered it in the frame again, again it slid to the left. Simon remembered setting the bowl aside to take out the cotton batting. He'd reached into the bottom of the frame and found the culprit. Someone had dropped a set of keys in the bottom which had caused the bowl to tilt in its protective base.

Simon was just lifting the keys out of the frame when the lights flickered.

"Oh, great," his voice echoed in this large storage space full of metal shelves and cataloged bits of history. He thought of the miles of winding corridors he would have to feel his way through should the electricity go out while he was in this vast windowless basement. He quickly shoved the keys into his pocket and put the Samianware bowl safely into its frame. Simon was about halfway to the metal safety door of the storage room, jiggling the keys in his pocket and wondering to whom they belonged, when the lights again flickered briefly, and went out. He immediately stopped and reached out in the darkness to touch the cold metal shelving on either side of him. If he just kept walking slowly he could reach the door to the main corridor. The metal frames seemed to go on forever. He had to be careful not to jostle any of the hundreds of artifacts as he slowly moved down the rows of shelving. Twice his hands felt the end of the set of shelves and he tried to remember which direction he'd taken when he'd come into the room. Once, he lightly brushed some small bottle off the shelf. He winced as he heard it fall to the floor and break into pieces.

"I really hope that wasn't some irreplaceable artifact," he thought. But there wasn't much he could do about it in the pitch black. He must have taken a wrong turn at some point because after what seemed like hours, he was totally and completely lost. Simon considered yelling to get someone's attention. Perhaps a security guard with a flashlight would hear and find him. There were two problems with that solution however. First, he was not supposed to be down here since he was not an employee of the museum. Professor Ananke would likely get into trouble for allowing him her keys to the secure storage area. Secondly, it was after hours in the museum when the guards did their rounds primarily in the upstairs public galleries. It was highly unlikely they would be down here in the bowels of the building.

"Just think, will you?" Simon chastised himself. "The worst case scenario is I will be stuck down here until the lights come back on, and how long could that be?" He could not count on Professor Ananke noticing that he had been gone longer than needed to return a bowl to storage. Given her absent-mindedness, she would likely finish her work, lock up and go home before it occurred to her that he hadn't ever come back from his errand. As he thought over the possibilities, he kept walking, carefully and slowly, keeping one hand lightly brushing the shelving units on either side. Suddenly his foot hit a wall.

"Yes!" Simon let out a breath of relief. He could at least follow the wall until he came to the door. In only a few minutes his hand encountered the hinges of a door.

"This is not the door I came in, obviously," he said to himself. "This one is wooden, the other was a metal fire-safe do

or. I really hope this doesn't just lead to a custodian's closet." He took out Professor Ananke's key ring and blindly fumbled to insert first one, and then another key, feeling for the keyhole with his fingertips. None of the four keys on the ring fit the lock. Simon swore in frustration. He made a mental apology to Professor Ananke. He could just hear her say, "Profanity is the weapon of the witless."

"Well, it was pretty witless of me to get stuck down here, so I'm excused," Simon responded to himself. In a flash of inspiration, he remembered the keys he had found in the bottom of the wooden frame for the Samianware bowl. "If it was a custodian, or a guard who dropped them, they might open this door."

Simon reached into his other pocket and pulled out the keys. They felt heavier and larger than Professor Ananke's keys. There were three on this ring. The first one he tried slid easily into the lock and turned. Feeling like he'd accomplished something at least, Simon pushed open the door. A warm, musty breath of air hit his face.

"Well, at least it's not a closet," he thought as he took a step through the door. And then he was falling into the darkness.

CPSIA information can be obtained at www.ICGtesting.com
Printed in the USA
LVOW132325300613

340916LV00002B/418/P